P.L. Ripley wrote about gay men in trouble, and how they changed their trouble for something a bit more to their liking. These aren't tales where love heals all, but you can be certain that sex changes things.

In Breaking and Entering, ForbiddenFiction.com presents all the stories P.L. Ripley published with us, collected in one volume as a testament to his life and work. Here you will find tales of thieves who found an unusual—and erotic—way to escape the law, of how one man gave his life for love, of how another learned to let loose and live, and even one story where pursuit of the man of his dreams leads out of fear and into love.

Rest well, P.L. Ripley. You will be missed.

Also recommended...

If you enjoyed this work, you may also like these other ForbiddenFiction works:

Bring the Love

There is something about the love of men for men that speaks to the heart. There is something about these stories that show men opening–sometimes eagerly, sometimes reluctantly–to love. In all, eleven stories of love and romance between men from ForbiddenFiction's top authors, including award-winners Julian Keys and Lynn Kelling. To you, our readers, we bring the love.

My Brother's Lover by Lynn Kelling

Growing up gay in a small town with no mother, Evan Savage learned the hard way to cherish his secrets above all else. Now he's 18, not even his father can hurt him anymore. When his long-lost twin brother Brennan shows up out of nowhere looking for a new home, Evan's world, and his very identity, comes crashing down around him all over again. (M/M+)

Breaking and Entering

P.L. Ripley

ForbiddenFiction
www.forbiddenfiction.com

an imprint of

Fantastic Fiction Publishing
www.fantasticfictionpublishing.com

BREAKING AND ENTERING

A ForbiddenFiction book

Fantastic Fiction Publishing Hayward, California

CREDITS
Editor: James L. Wolf and Lon Sarver
Cover Design: Siolnatine
Inside Cover Designs: D.M. Atkins and Siolnatine
Cover Art: Adapted from photo by S Photos at Shutterstock.
Inside Cover Art: Photos from Roman Sinichkin at Shutterstock and Timhesterphotography at Dreamstime. Photo by Naypong at Shutterstock. Adatped from photos © Julenochek at Dreamstime.com and © NeonShot at Shutterstock.com. Elena Rostunova and Naypong at Shutterstock. Photo by Lentolo at Dreamstime.
Production Editor: Kaye O'Malley
Proofreading: JhP323, Kailin Morgan, and Todd Michaels

SKU: PLR-1.100026-01 FFP
ISBN: 978-1-62234-338-6

Published in the United States of America

DISCLAIMER

This book is a work of fiction which contains explicit erotic content; it is intended for mature readers. Do not read this if it's not legal for you. However, all characters depicted in this work of fiction are 18 years of age or older.

All the characters, locations and events herein are fictional. While elements of existing locations or historical characters or events may be used fictitiously, any resemblance to actual people, places or events is coincidental.

This story is not intended to be used as an instruction manual. It may contain descriptions of erotic acts that are immoral, illegal, or unsafe. Do not take the events in this story as proof of the plausibility or safety of any particular practice.

Dedication

To Philip Williams

Contents

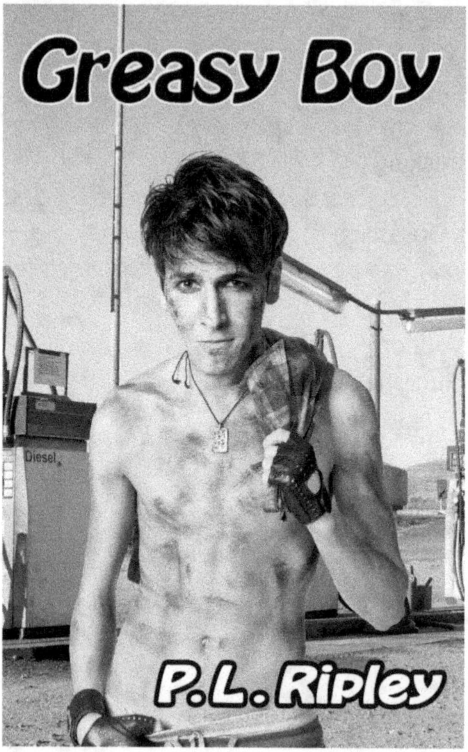
Greasy Boy
Diesel
P.L. Ripley

Greasy Boy

Chapter 1: Clean Getaway

The conference was supposed to go all day but Simon bolted at one o'clock. He had a three-hour drive back home and didn't relish the idea of spending his evening on the road. He wanted to get home before dark. To be home in case Peter came back.

He jogged out to his car, threw his briefcase in the backseat, pulled off his jacket and tossed that on top of the case. "Where the hell are you going?" a voice said from behind him. Simon turned to see Danny Weisman, one of his old college friends that now worked for the D.A.'s office, leaning against a BMW with a menthol cigarette jammed between his lips. "Cutting out kind of early, aren't you?" Danny said, the menthol bouncing up and down like a metronome, keeping time with his words.

"I'm going home," Simon snapped, the irritation obvious in his voice. Danny had a bad habit of telling the truth exactly as he saw it, which was an admirable quality most of the time, just not when it was directed at Simon himself. Simon could see what was coming. It was the same 'conversation' they had been having for months. The conversation about Peter.

He slid behind the wheel of his Lexus, rolled down the driver's side window with the push of a button and lit a Camel.

Simon had quit smoking a year ago, after months of Peter badgering him about it, then Peter turned around and quit him just a few months later. It hurt just thinking about it. The cigarettes came back not long after.

"He's not coming back, you know," Danny said as he pushed himself from the BMW and knelt next to Simon's open window. "No matter how much you hide in that apartment, he isn't coming back to you."

"What am I supposed to do? Just forget about him? We were together for five years."

"Yeah, forget about him. I'm sure he has forgotten you."

"Fuck you, Danny. I miss him," Simon said, and felt his throat tighten. He choked the ball of emotions back down, burying it in his chest where it would ferment and come back as heartburn. Like a zombie in a George Romero horror movie, the pain of losing Peter just wouldn't stay dead.

"I know you do. But, the only way to get over him is to start living again. Trust old Danny, I know what I'm talking about."

"Yeah, live like you do?" Simon scoffed. For all the years Simon knew Danny, his friend had never had a full time lover. There had been boyfriends, guys he dated now and again, but never a real, honest partnership. When he wasn't dating, he supplemented his sexual needs with trips to the back room of the leather bar or, when he was away from home, like now, he cruised well-traveled parks or highway rest areas.

"Maybe," Danny replied, smiling. "A back alley blowjob might just be what you need." He grinned when he said this and wiggled his eyebrows. They looked like two caterpillars squaring off for the fight of the century. Simon laughed, feeling the tension moving out of his shoulders. This was why they were friends; Danny told him what he didn't want to hear, but needed to, then made him laugh afterward. Danny was right and Simon knew it. He had to let go. He had to start living again. Now, if only he could figure out how to do that.

"What I need," Simon said, "is to get home. I need Peter to come back to me."

"No," Danny replied, grinding his cigarette out on the pavement between his feet. "That's what you want. Sometimes, what we want and what we need are two different things. What you need is to get your shit together. I love you, man, and that's why I'm telling you this. You need to move on. Go get laid. You'll feel better, or maybe you'll just feel less. Either way is good."

Simon sighed. Again, Danny was right. He did need to get laid. His balls had ached for days now; no matter how much he jerked off, it didn't relieve the pressure. In fact, it seemed to make it worse. But, he didn't think he could live like Danny. Anonymous sex scared the hell out of him. Sex should not be casual, Simon felt. It should mean something to the participants more than just the inevitable orgasm. There had to be a connection there, a history that each could use to enhance the experience for the other. It should be tender and gentle and loving.

But, that was not what Peter had wanted. He'd wanted to "explore" his sexual limits, to "test his boundaries," was the way he had phrased it the last night they were together. Essentially, he'd wanted Simon to tie him up and flog the shit out of him with the assortment of leather toys he had brought home.

Simon couldn't do it, though. He couldn't inflict pain on Peter, even when Peter wanted him to. He couldn't allow himself to consent to this new kink that his lover had so recently become enamored with, this deviance of rough sex. And he couldn't live his life like Danny. He couldn't risk his reputation with public sex or fucking someone without even knowing their name, or as Danny often bragged, care. In Danny's world, names could be dangerous. Many of his partners were married or had high profile jobs that could be destroyed if others discovered what they did in their free time. So, the men were reduced to physical attributes. They became Mr. Curved Dick or Ol' Fuzzy Bottom.

A car pulled into the lot, parked. The engine ticked as it settled and began to cool. The driver opened the door and got out, a briefcase tucked under his arm. The driver was tall, handsome with a dark beard that was cut so close to his skin it seemed painted on. Simon and Danny watched the man, watched him confidently stride into the building, his head held high, shoulders back, firm chest lying just under the hard starched white shirt and conservative dark tie.

"Ooh, that's what I need," Danny said once the man was safely inside the building. "A little afternoon pick-me-up."

Simon started up the engine. "Go get him, Tiger." Simon laughed and shot Danny a quick wave then pulled the Lexus out of the parking lot.

When he got on I-95 South, Simon slipped his tie from around his neck, nearly fumbling his glasses off in the process, and dropped it in the passenger seat, where the tie coiled around itself like a snake, ready to pounce. He flipped through the radio stations, found nothing good, then shook another Camel from the pack in the passenger seat and lit it.

Simon pulled on the cigarette, feeling the warm smoke fill his lungs. The best taste in the world, except for maybe cock, he thought and felt a moan rise up in his throat.

Sex. It nearly drove him mad thinking about it. He hadn't been with anyone since Peter left and the many months of sexual prohibition were now starting to affect his mind, he feared. He no longer thought about Peter when he masturbated. He no longer saw Peter's smooth, tight little body writhing under his imagined tongue, squirming as daydream Simon licked him from his nipples to his hard ridged belly, then further down. He could no longer taste Peters cock in his mind as he caressed himself, one hand pulling the thick fold of foreskin over his own cock, warm, sweet precome oozing from the head, slickening his curled fingers and running down the long shaft to mire itself in the forest of blond pubic hair, while his other hand dipped down under his balls. The thick fingers dancing in and out of his ass, manipulating his prostate until he came with the force of a volcano.

Peter never entered his mind while he came. Instead, he saw himself in one of Danny's midnight trick tales or of a new cruising spot he had recently discovered. He saw himself, in the woods, on his knees, with a stranger before him. He imagined himself hungrily pulling the strangers pants down and feasting on the cock before him. He could almost smell the raw, sweaty funk of the man, taste the coppery tang of the engorged cock as it was thrust down his throat. He could hear the hard, happy grunts of the man as the stranger rushed on to orgasm. The threat of literally getting caught with his pants down, forcing the stranger to come far sooner than either wanted, yet adding to the excitement of what they were doing.

He thought of Peter afterward, while he lay in the bed, his arms wrapped around the otherwise unused pillow, the come drying on his belly. He thought about what Peter might be doing now. Then he remembered the hairy backed gorilla Peter had run off with. An investment banker from Boston who wore leather on the weekends. He could see them in his mind. Peter was so small and perfect. *They are always perfect when they are no longer around*, Simon thought, with that hulking monstrosity he had run off with, slithering up next to him. He saw Peter's beautiful body lying prone on a thick bed of feathers and satin sheets while the gorilla, lustfully panting, hot steam shooting from his nostrils, dipping his arm in a tub of Crisco, preparing his fist to enter Peter.

Of course, this was all in his mind. Peter probably was not into fisting, but he had wanted Simon to abuse him. He had wanted to be tied down and beaten and Simon couldn't do it. He couldn't do it then, and perhaps still couldn't. The thought of what Peter might be doing now, of Peter exploring his masochistic tendencies, was beginning to excite Simon. Public sex and sadism was finding its way into Simon's fantasies. He wondered, *Is this just because I am so god-damned horny, or is something else going on? Am I in fact, becoming like Peter? Or like Danny? Do I really want dangerous sex?*

In frustration he grit his teeth, forgetting about the Camel stuck between them and nearly severed the filter off. He pulled it from his mouth and mashed the stub out in the ashtray. He ran his fingers through his hair, platinum blond with just the tinniest hint of gray, and felt the grime of the road. He'd spent the morning sitting in an overheated conference room sipping cold coffee and eating heavily sugared pastries. The graying hair bothered him. He was only twenty-six and he wondered, what would it be when he was forty? Completely white, probably. Just like his father was at that age. His skin was still young though, smooth, blemish free and the pale color of ivory. He rarely went out in the sun, he couldn't tan anyway, but the sun aged skin. So did smoking, but it was easier to stay indoors than it was to give up nicotine. Especially when there was no one there to insist you quit the habit.

Another Camel found its way into his mouth and as he smoked, that sticky, tacky dry feeling smoking always did to his mouth and throat urged him to find something to wash the taste out.

A single empty water bottle rolled around in the passenger seat. A sign up ahead indicated the upcoming exit as having gas, food and lodging. It was a rural exit and the tall grass lining the exit seemed to wave at Simon as he pulled the Lexus off the highway, down into this tiny community. A single two-lane road met him. To the right, the Big Pine Motel, a dilapidated rest stop for the weary and not-very-choosy traveler. Several of the letters in its sign had long since disappeared so it now read, Bi Pin otel. On the left, a small service station with a single island of gas pumps.

He sat for a moment at the stop sign, checking both ways for traffic before pulling onto the narrow road. But there was no traffic. He could see a good distance beyond the motel on the right and the gas station on the left and there was not even the faintest hint of another body out there. It was as though he had come to the end of the Universe and he was the only visitor. The great pine trees that gave the motel its name reached up from both sides of the road, shading it so just tiny dapples of sunlight flickered on the pavement. He took the left and turned into the gas station.

Simon pulled up to the super-unleaded pump and jumped out of the Lexus, unscrewed the gas cap and slid the pump nozzle in the hole. He had more than half a tank of gas, but since he was here he might as well fill up. "Help ya?" a voice called, startling him into looking up at the source.

A young man walked out of the service bay, wiping his hands on a greasy towel. He looked to be about twenty with oily black hair and a matted goatee on his face. His shirt was open down to the navel and the wife beater undershirt covering his thin frame was covered in spots of oil, grease and sweat. He wore blue Dickies pants that hung from his thin hips as though they were defying gravity. How they stayed up was anyone's guess. Maybe he stapled them to his bones, Simon thought.

"I'll take it," the young man said, sliding his hand over Simon's to relieve him of the pump handle. His hands were blackened with oil and dirt stains. Simon pulled his own hand away. "Full service. You want me to fill it?" The tag on his shirt informed Simon that his name was Rick.

"Sure," Simon replied. "Can you check the oil too?"

"Yup." Rick smiled, revealing a mouth full of even white teeth with the exception of one front tooth that was chipped. Simon felt a stirring in him at that imperfection. It made the young man seem... vulnerable was the only word he could come up with, but that wasn't quite right. Vulnerable often meant weak and he appeared anything but that. He had a strength to him, a raw toughness to him that men in Simon's world of the overeducated and well-paid often lacked or kept well hidden.

No, he was not vulnerable but the chipped tooth did give him the appearance of a wounded man. A man who might have seen bad things and been hurt by them. It stirred in Simon that protective spirit that had, so long ago, urged him into a career in law. It was the big brother in him, the Florence Nightingale. The boy didn't need Simon's protection, but it was hot to think he might.

The gas station was small, two mechanics' bays and a small glass-fronted office. On the curb before the office door was a soda machine with one of its fluorescent bulbs flickering behind the plastic panel advertising the ice cold drinks inside. Simon threw a fistful of quarters in and a can of soda dropped into his hand. He pulled the tab and guzzled half of it down. The cold soda burned a sweet trail down his throat. Draining the can, Simon tossed the empty in a rusted oil drum that had been transformed into a garbage can. It clanged against the sides.

The soda had quenched his thirst but now he had to piss. Simon asked Rick, "You got a restroom here?"

The young man read the oil dipstick, then slid it back in its hole. He looked up and smiled at Simon, his hands still working the dipstick. He licked his bottom lip, his tongue rasping against the stubble on his chin. "Yup. Around the back." He pointed toward the left of the office. "Here's the key." He shoved his fist in his pants pocket, pushing the Dickies down slightly to reveal a heavy bush of dark pubic hair. Simon looked, then quickly pulled his eyes away before Rick noticed. He tossed the keys to Simon, then slammed the Lexus' hood shut. "Oil's fine."

Simon nodded, thought about pulling out his keys and hitting the little red security button to lock the doors before going off to the bathroom, then thought against it. He didn't want to look like an untrusting asshole in front of the guy. Men like Rick were tough, thick-skinned yet easy to offend. How a man was perceived by his fellow man was as important as he perceived himself. If a man was seen as untrustworthy by his neighbors then he might as well have moved to another town or lived up to his nefarious reputation because no matter what he did, how he was seen was what he was.

Simon didn't lock his car not only because he didn't want to offend the guy by inadvertently suggesting he might do something to the vehicle, but also because he realized he was attracted to the mechanic. Rick was a nice looking man and when he had smiled at Simon, that chipped tooth flashing like a beacon, Simon felt something going on in his belly. Butterflies, or just the slightest quiver of excitement. He had been horny as hell since Peter left and the six month dry spell was making him near insane and this greasy mechanic, Rick, was sending his lust meter into the red. He would rather risk losing some meaningless object from the glove compartment or the handful of coins in the center console than offend Rick.

It's not like I have a chance with him, Simon thought. Rick was probably, likely, straight, but the probability of something happening between them was not the motivation of his concern for Rick's feelings. It was the possibility.

"Thank you," Simon said. He caught the key ring in his hands and watched as Rick pulled the loose Dickies up onto his hips again. He noticed the slight swell of his crotch, the lump that shifted down his left leg as he dropped the Lexus' hood back into place and moved back to the pump. Simon turned and walked around the back of the building to the bathroom. He unlocked the door and went in. It was small. There were two dirt-stained sinks ahead of him, with smoky mirrors above each. Oily fingerprints marred the glass surface. To the right were two toilet stalls. He chose one and felt his bowels churn, which meant he had to sit. He hated sitting on public toilets, especially one this dirty, but he was two hours from home and it wouldn't wait. Simon lined the seat with toilet paper, then pulled his pants and underwear down and gently sat on the paper.

The wall separating the stalls was filled with graffiti.

Suck my cock!

For a good time call....

Jane M. takes it up the ass and Jeffrey Dahmer burns in hell were some of the witticisms left by previous shithouse poets.

There was something else in the wall as well: a hole about waist-high that could easily swallow Simon's fist. He glanced through the portal and saw the toilet on the other side.

It was a glory hole. Simon chuckled under his breath. Danny would be thrilled to find this, he thought.

The hand carved addition in the wall slightly disturbed him, the thought of what went on here, and yet, he felt a rush of excitement in his belly as well. Scenarios from the Falcon videos he and Peter had rented came back to him. Hard muscled men engaging in anonymous sex that would be risky in the real world, but exciting in the make believe world of porn. He realized that rarely did a porn movie show a committed couple making love; most were strangers meeting for the first time by swallowing each other's cocks. Was porn programming gay men to act out these scenes, he often wondered, or were men naturally promiscuous and only restricted to relationships because society directed people in that direction?

He finished, flushed. Just then the restroom door opened and someone walked in. The newcomer entered the stall next to Simon's and he could hear the rustling of clothing, the familiar rasp of a zipper being undone. He glanced through the hole and saw blue Dickies hanging from thin hips slide down a pair of pale, hairy legs. A set of white briefs that had become gray with age and large dark yellow piss stains on the front, blushed dully in the dim light of the other stall. A large bulge slowly rose from the dirty cloth like a time-elapsed film of a volcano forming on a small island. It was Rick on the other side and he didn't seem to be in a hurry to do anything but massage himself. He didn't free himself to urinate and if there was ever an instance when the real world could resemble a cruising scene in a porn video, it was now. Simon's throat became as dry as the Sahara. His heart banged in his chest like it was trying to get out.

He watched as Rick slid a greasy hand over his basket and massaged it, toying with his balls until the bulge began to grow too large for his briefs to hold it in.

Rick slid a finger in his briefs and slowly pulled them down. He exposed the patch of wiry pubic hair Simon had seen earlier, then the stem of his cock. More and more, until his entire erection sprang out and slammed against the dirty wife beater undershirt with a muffled slap. He pushed his underwear to his ankles along with his pants, then wrapped a dirty hand around his dick and began tugging on it. It was about seven inches long, circumcised and weighted down with enormous hairy balls.

Simon pushed his face closer to the hole and felt revulsion at himself for doing so. He wasn't supposed to do something like that, he wasn't supposed to want to do something like that, but he did want it just the same.

Rick turned and lined up the thick cockhead with the hole in the wall and pushed it through.

Simon leaned back as the hard cock came through to his side. He could smell the hot sweaty sex of the erect cock, the heavy cloud of pheromones with just the lightest hint of piss. It smelled heavenly. An aroma he had missed in the last six months of sexual isolation.

"Suck it!" Rick called from the other side of the wall.

Going down on a dirty dick is insane, he thought and ignored Rick. He wanted to suck it, though. Man, how he wanted to pull it down into his throat. The raw stench filled his nostrils, enveloping him in hot, wet lust. He wanted it, he wanted the sweaty, pissy cock in his mouth but still, his vanilla mind kept screaming at him, "NO!"

But another voice rose up beneath his own, a voice that

demanded him to try it, just this once, let go and do something he wanted, instead of what he should. It was Danny's voice and he could almost see him, here in the stall, a menthol jammed between his lips, bouncing up and down as he egged him on.

"Do it," Danny said. "Who gives a fuck what other people think? Do it because you want to do it. Do it, because this opportunity won't come again."

"Suck it," Rick called again his voice deeper, gruffer than before, forceful even. "Do it!"

Chapter 2: Getting Dirty

Simon slid from the toilet seat to the cement floor, his pants still around his ankles, his heart hammering in his chest as he nervously reached out to the mechanic's cock. He could feel the heat rising off the pulsating head as his fingers came dangerously close to making contact. Simon's breath came out in jagged gasps. He wanted it, he needed it but.... *Don't do this*, the rational voice in his head begged. *Don't cross that line.*

His fingers hovered just a breath away from this object of his lust. Hovered and waited and resisting the urge to back away, Simon ran his fingertips down the length of the cock. Rick moaned on the other side of the wall. Simon quickly pulled his hand back.

He could hear Danny cheering him on. "Feels good, doesn't it?"

It did. It felt real good to have another man quiver under his touch, no matter how light that touch was. And it felt... necessary, like this was the one thing that would keep him together for another week, another day, another minute. He was going mad with his sexual seclusion and now, finally, he had the opportunity for a reprieve. That is, if he could go through with it.

But, how could he do this? How could he shun a lifetime of strict relationship-based sex? How could he abandon his own vision of morality?

"Please," he heard Rick whisper from the next stall. He wanted to be touched as much as Simon wanted to touch. Perhaps he needed it as much as Simon. The protective spirit rose in him again. The big brother, here to take care of Rick, to ease his suffering, took over. Rick needed his help, HIS help. No one could take care of him but Simon. No one could do this for him, right here, right now, but Simon.

He took the cock in his fist and felt his courage waver. This was insane, how could he allow himself to carry on like this? How could he dare wrap his hand around a strange man's cock in such a filthy place as this? How could he... then he heard the soft moan from the other side of the partition. An enticing quiver in Rick's voice. Simon slid his hand down over the glans, catching several droplets of pre-come, then slid back to the base, where the tuft of pubic hair curled up through the hole in the wall.

"Suck it," Rick said, a hopeful request with just a hint of aggression. A forcefulness to his voice, a rough demanding.

He couldn't do that. Touching was one thing. Holding it in his hand, stroking it, loving it. But, put it in his mouth? No, that was too much. That was going too far. If he knew him better, was in a safer, cleaner place, like the bedroom in his apartment, then he might be able to. But here?

"Oh, do it man." Rick called to him. The curious lust that had forced Simon to his knees in the filthy bathroom, that had pushed his eye against a hole where perhaps dozens or even hundreds of men had rubbed their filthy crotches or shoved lube-slickened assholes against, now pushed his tongue out to the wanting cock and curled it around the stinky dick-head. He tasted it, let the flavor of the boy dance in his mouth a moment then slid his tongue along the underside of the shaft. He pulled his tongue back up to the head and let it quiver over the head and in the piss-slit, then pulled the entire tool in his mouth.

The mechanics of the act was like second nature to him, and if he closed his eyes he could imagine he was somewhere familiar, back in his apartment, on his bed. But, when he opened his eyes to the wall before him, he could not pretend he was anywhere but there. And the man in his mouth was not someone he knew.

A strange sensation began to blossom inside Simon. The self-imposed restrictions that had guided his life to this point began to loosen, to break apart. The inhibitions that had been his moral grounding for his entire adult life were a sham, he realized. Restricting sex to a relationship did not give him the moral high ground; it was the result of his unwillingness to take a chance.

Yes, this was risky. Yes, this was illegal. *But holy shit,* he thought, *it's the most exciting sex I've ever had.* And he was beginning to feel, perhaps for the first time, free. He could do anything. He could give this man pleasure, and take it in return. He didn't have to know him, because he knew himself. There was no guilt. No need to reprimand or punish himself for this.

Rick moaned, breaking Simon from his own mind and turned his attention back to what he was doing. Simon smiled around the cock. It didn't taste as strong as it smelled. The musky scent from Rick's heavy balls filled Simon's head with a desire more powerful than a hurricane. He pulled the cock deeper into his mouth, letting it slide down his throat until he thought he would gag, then slid it back out. He pushed himself harder and faster down on the cock, soaking up every inch, until his nose mashed against the greasy boy's rank pubic hair. He inhaled deeply, taking in the piss and sweat stench of the wiry black mat.

Simon discovered that he loved this. The real man taste and smell beat the flavor of soap and cologne he had grown accustomed to. He reached down into his lap and found himself as hard as the mechanic. He tugged on his own cock a few times, pulling the thick, rubbery foreskin over the head then gave it up to concentrate on the cock in his mouth. *This is what sex is supposed to be like,* he thought. Raw, urgent, primal. He was beginning to understand Danny's appetite for this.

"Yeah, that's it," Rick cooed. "Take it all." He began to rock his hips, sliding the cock in and out of the glory hole. "You like that big meat in your face, don't you?"

He did. In fact, he loved it. Simon wrapped his fist around the cock and stroked it as he sucked. He wanted to see the mechanic come. He wanted to watch as Rick shot his load, see the shaft flex and jump as streams of warm jism erupted from it, splashing down onto the dirty floor.

Then, without any warning Rick pulled his cock from Simon's

grasp and back through the hole. Simon just sat on his knees and stared as Rick dropped to the floor. They knelt, staring at one another for a second and Simon saw the burning lust in Rick's eyes, the same that Rick probably saw in his.

"Gimme yours," Rick demanded.

Simon stood on shaky legs. He lined himself with the hole, then paused. A thousand scenarios ran through his mind then, with a thousand different outcomes. All of them bad. What if, his mind asked, this was a set-up? What if he pushed through to the other side and Rick clamped something on him so he couldn't pull back out, then called the cops? Or what if he cut Simon, cut his dick off and let Simon bleed to death here on the floor of the out of the way bathroom at this gas station in the middle of nowhere? What if....

"Please man, give it to me," Rick wined from the other side of the wall. He had pressed his face against the hole and his hungry tongue came through, lapping at the air with just the tip making contact with Simon's cock.

A hot shiver ran through Simon. He steeled his courage and pushed his own hard dick through the hole. Rick immediately sucked it into his mouth.

His mouth was hot, wet and velvety smooth. The greasy kid toyed with the cock head, flicking his tongue over and under, and nibbled at the long shaft with his broken tooth. This was heavenly. After six months without another man's touch, this almost felt like his first time all over again. Immediately, Simon's nuts began to tighten, to twist in a hard knot under his slobbering cock. He didn't want to come, at least not yet.

He started pulling his cock back but Rick stopped him. The mechanic tightened his fist around the base of Simon's cock and held him there while he sucked on it. "Stop, man, I'm gonna come!" Simon squealed.

"Can you come again?" Rick asked slowly, his voice deep and husky. He licked the glistening, purple head after each word.

"Yeah. I just want it to last."

"Don't worry. I'm not through with you yet." Rick replied, then Simon felt the hot mouth engulf him again.

Simon gasped and felt that familiar tingle in his belly. His nuts rolled and churned and he could feel the come moving up through his shaft. "I'm coming!" Simon warned him. His entire crotch seemed to explode. He slammed his hips harder against the wall as waves of orgasm washed over him.

Bliss, sweet beautiful bliss. He felt his knees weaken and he grabbed the top of the divider to hold himself upright while his legs pleaded to give out from beneath him. Simon felt the mouth still on his cock as Rick swallowed every drop given him.

The mouth continued to tease his cock, sending spasms through his crotch. Simon wanted to tell him to stop, it was driving him insane, but he could only grunt and pant. Finally Rick pulled his mouth away with a last slurp and Simon pressed his face against the graffiti covered wall to catch his breath.

Simon felt pain then, not in his body—that was still quivering with post-coital delight—but in his mind. He had just participated in an act he had always seen as morally beneath him—anonymous sex with a man he didn't know, or quite frankly, care about. Yet, he enjoyed it just the same. What did that make him?

"It makes you human," he heard Danny's voice say. "You can climb down from your high horse now and join the rest of us peasants down here on Earth."

He heard Rick rise to his feet and then the jingle of keys and coins as he pulled up his pants. The stall door opened and softly banged closed. Simon pulled his dick back through the hole. It was still semi-hard but with the right touch could be fully erect and ready to go in just a matter of minutes. His own stall door opened and Rick stepped in, holding his pants up with a greasy fist. "You came in my mouth." Rick said.

A hot tingle of fear rose up Simon's spine. The mechanic looked pissed. His eyes were pressed into thin slit squints and his hands constricted to hard fists. This, Simon thought, was where he paid for his little fun. This was the retribution for crossing the ethical line, for sexual congress outside the restraints of a relationship. "I know, I'm... I'm sorry," he stammered. "I warned you I was coming. I've been tested, I'm negative."

"I wasn't complaining," Rick said and opened his fist, letting his Dickies fall to the floor. His spring-loaded hard-on bounced up and pointed at Simon. Rick grinned open mouthed, the chipped tooth shining out between his thin lips. "It likes you."

Simon smiled back. "I like it too." He took it in his hands, massaging the low-slung balls. The dark hair on them tickled his palms. Now that they were face-to-face, Simon felt a little less daring, a little shyer about what he wanted to do. There was some power to not seeing the man you were sucking off.

His eyes glanced over his watch as his fingers deftly manipulated Rick's balls. How long had they been in there together, he wondered. Fifteen minutes, twenty? No one could get in there without a key, but how many customers had pulled up to the pumps, then driven off in disgust when no one came out of the station to fill their tanks, or worse, filled up themselves and driven off without paying. This wasn't really his concern, but his unlocked Lexus was. He needed to break this off and get out of there and back on the road before something happened to his vehicle. Then Rick let out a soft moan in appreciation of what Simon was doing to him, and all thoughts of anything other than the man in his hand were gone.

Simon began to drop to his knees but Rick stopped him. "No," he said and opened Simon's shirt. He tugged it off and threw it on top of the toilet tank, then kissed Simon's smooth hairless chest. He took each nipple one at a time in his mouth until they grew as erect as Simon's cock, then Rick stood, grabbed him by the neck, pulled him closer and pressed his lips against Simon's.

Simon opened his mouth to let him in. Their tongues slid over one another and Simon could taste his own cock in Rick's mouth. Rick pulled back and peeled off his own shirt and threw it on top of Simon's. He was thin, but not overly so. His chest was well-defined beneath the wife beater; his nipples, firm and rigid, stood out like tiny mountain peaks. As Simon drew his hand over Rick's belly, he could feel the hard ripples lying just beneath the surface. A tattoo peaked out from beneath the undershirt announced him as BITCH. Grease and dirt stains marked his upper arms.

Rick lifted his right arm and pushed Simon's face in the tangled mass of sweaty hair. "Lick it," he commanded and Simon did as he was told. The pit stunk of sweat both old and new, yet with each pass of his tongue, Simon found himself getting harder. He sucked on the hair, pulling it in his mouth then lapped around the pit until it glistened. He pulled himself back when his glasses became streaked with the sweat and saliva.

Rick gently held Simon's hips and turned them both until Simon's back was against the door. He then removed Simon's glasses, turned and bent to the collection of shirts on the back of the toilet and wiped them on his sleeve. After he did this, he pulled a condom out of his shirt pocket. Rick turned back to him and gently slid the glasses back on his face for him. "Better?" he asked.

"Yeah, thanks." Simon said and swallowed hard. The trickle of fear that had moved through him was now a steady stream. He was nearly naked in a public bathroom with a man he hardly knew beyond the sweet taste of his body. This was a dangerous situation, in the fact they could be caught—though that was slim; a person would need a key to get into the restroom to actually catch them in the act—and that Rick could possibly be something other than what he seemed.

Rick was smaller than Simon, but his hard, lean, muscular body showed Simon that he was strong and could best Simon in any physical competition. If he got it in his head to become physically aggressive, there was not much Simon could do to protect himself, or stop an assault.

But then, Rick had done a stunningly kind gesture by cleaning Simon's glasses for him. He had kissed him, gently, almost lovingly and Simon began to feel more calmness in himself as Rick opened the small condom package and slowly slipped the rubber over Simon's dick, squeezing the end to make sure no air was left in the loose tip. He spat in his palm, rubbed that over the condom, then turned and rested his elbows on the toilet tank. "Fuck me," he said. It wasn't a request.

Chapter 3: Fading Stains

Simon bent slightly to gain access to the greasy boy's ass, found the sweet tight hole and slowly pushed his cock head against it. Rick gasped as the fat head punctured the opening and Simon could feel the boy's muscles tighten, then go completely loose. He was not a virgin and wanted this as much as, if not more than, Simon.

A bright Aztec sun tattoo blazed up between Rick's shoulder blades and after Simon had slowly fed his fat cock into the boy's sweet, tight ass, he rested a hand over the tattoo and began to work his hips. It was like heaven, clamped in the tight channel, the musky stink of ass and sweat and come all dancing around in his head, while Rick moaned beneath him.

"Jesus, that feels good. Fuck me, man," Rick said and pushed back against Simon.

Simon picked up his speed, his hips a blur against the tile background. His balls slammed against Rick's ass. Rick reached up behind his back, took the hand that covered his tattoo and moved it to the back of his head. He squeezed Simon's hand so it closed, entangling his fingers in the oily, black hair. Then he quickly moved his head forward, letting Simon know he wanted his hair pulled.

Simon did as directed. He snapped at the greasy locks, pulling Rick's head back in the process. "Yeah," Rick yelled.

"You like that?" Simon growled, suddenly realizing exactly what he was doing. He was hurting Rick. He was fucking him with the fierceness of an animal and tugging on his hair as though he wanted to rip it from the roots. He was doing to Rick what Peter had wanted done to him. And he realized he liked it. He liked the dominant role Rick had pushed him into. He liked the feeling of power the aggressive sex was instilling in him. "You like that, you fucking bitch?" He grunted, calling Rick by his tattooed name, and pulled on the hair even harder.

"Yeah. I love it. Hurt me, man."

Hurt me, he had said. Just like Peter wanted to be hurt. He would hurt him. He would hurt him just as Simon had been hurt when he walked out on him. He would show him he could be just as vicious, just as cruel as he had been. He raised his palm to the ceiling and brought it down on Rick's ass. The slap echoed through the small room like a gunshot.

The boy began to buck, slamming his hips back against Simon's crotch. Simon slapped his ass again and again until it became red and warm, all the while twisting his cock in and out of the hot hole. "You like it, greasy boy?" Simon said. "Is this what you wanted me to do? You wanted me to hurt you? I'm hurting you know. Right? I'm doing what you wanted. Is this why you left, 'cause I wouldn't do this? Well, I'm doing it now!" He called out then looked down at the Aztec sun beaming out between Rick's shoulder blades and realized it was not Peter squirming beneath him. For a moment he had been lost in his past, lost to a man who no longer loved him.

What am I doing? he wondered. He wanted to stop this, to pull out of this boy and leave. He wanted to get back in his car and drive home where he could sit and hope Peter would come back to him. He wanted to make dinner for two and forget how liberating it felt to have this mechanic under him, how the surge of power over the boy made him feel more alive than he had since Peter left. He wanted to go back to being alone and miserable because that was familiar, almost comforting to him now.

But he couldn't do that because his body was responding to the boy wrapped around his cock right now. The familiar tingle was coursing through his belly and he could feel his balls tightening to a hard fist as another orgasm worked its way through him.

He felt the come rising in him and knew he couldn't hold off. He pushed himself harder and faster, rocking the mechanic until his head almost hit the wall. The tingle spread through his nuts and down his legs, right down to each toe, then Simon's entire body froze as the orgasm came.

Starlights danced before his eyes as he flooded the condom. Simon heard a loud buzzing as the explosive force of the orgasm numbed his other senses, and in the background, like a whisper, his own voice grunting. His entire body went limp and he fell against Rick, his face pressed against the sun tattoo.

Simon kissed the Aztec sun, lapped at the sweat rolling down from the nape of Rick's neck, as his cock jumped and pumped more juice into the condom until it finally faded. He felt Rick's hand on his head, massaging it, running his dirty fingers through the soft blond hair. Simon pushed himself up and slowly pulled his cock from the boy's hole. He peeled the condom off and tossed it in the toilet.

Rick straightened and turned around. His erection jabbed Simon in the belly.

Simon felt the idea of Peter dissipate, slip away. For six months he had been fixed on the hope that Peter would come back to him, that he would see that Simon's love for him outweighed his need to explore his masochistic desires. Now Simon realized it wasn't just the sex that had split them. Peter simply wanted out and he had used the one thing he thought Simon could not do to free himself. He supposed Simon could not be an aggressive dominant lover, and frankly, Simon thought the same. But now he found he could do it. And he liked it.

If Peter had really wanted to stay with him, he would have given up the idea of a rough sex life, and if Simon had wanted him to stay, he would have given a bigger effort to satisfy him. They both had used the sex as an excuse to end their relationship, he realized. Neither wanted to continue with the other.

Simon felt freer and more liberated than he had in a long time. Yet a kernel of his former lover still held firm. He could feel its power inside him, still controlling him. *How could I live without Peter?* it made him ask himself. How could he go on without the one man he had actually felt something for? He knew, to be truly free from his former lover, he had to take charge.

And so, he pushed Rick back against the wall separating the two stalls, dropped to his knees and pulled Rick down into his throat.

The rankness of his dirty cock coated Simon's mouth. Hot sweat, urine and just a hint of the motor oil that spotted Rick forced a wet retch up through Simon's throat. He pushed it back down and forced that much more of the mechanic into him, until his lips met the tangled mat of pubic hair. He inhaled the boy's odor. Raw, pungent, real. There was no perfume here, no scented soaps or finely trimmed bush. This was a tangled mess of funk and bodily fluids.

"Don't," Rick said. "I'm too close." Rick squirmed and pressed his palms against Simon's forehead, trying to push him back. But Simon ignored him and slid one finger along Rick's balls, tickling the wiry hairs, then back, into the battered yet still suckling hole he had just enjoyed. His finger slid up to the second knuckle, a hot, wet hunger pulling him in, then a sudden vice-like clamp as the sphincter slammed shut and Rick came.

The warm seed painted Simon's throat as he swallowed the sweet, watery liquid and felt the last remnants of Peter leave him. He realized, what went on between Rick and himself in this filthy bathroom—a place he never before could see himself engaging in any intimate contact, much less the rough fucking that had just happened—was more than just sex. It was therapy. He had been freed of the illusion that Peter would come back to him. Free of the restraints of his own sexual proclivities. He could engage in more unconventional sex acts without worrying that he might like it, because he did like it and that was okay. He wouldn't take it too far and hurt the one he was with and he found, through Rick's reaction to the slaps and hair pulling, that pain could be as much a sexual stimulant as a kiss.

Simon worked the cock until it began to grow flaccid in his mouth, then he pulled off it with a slurpy plop. Rick leaned against the wall, panting, his legs, pale, covered in a heavy sprinkling of dark hair, quivered with the rush of the orgasm.

Simon stood, pulled his pants back up to his waist and watched Rick as he gathered himself, slipped into his uniform shirt and tucked it into the Dickies. Rick looked up at him and smiled then quickly kissed him on the mouth. "Gotta go back to work," he said, slipping out of the stall and opened the outside door. A heavy blast of sunlight spilled in the room along with a rush of fresh air.

Simon got dressed and went to the sink to wash his face. His hair was sticky with sweat and the greasy taste of Rick's come was turning sour in his throat. He cupped his hands and drank some of the warm sink water. He checked his wallet, pulled out a pair of twenties for the gas and a business card, then scrawled his name and cell phone number on the back and left the bathroom.

Rick stood outside leaning on the gas pump, drinking soda from a can. He looked up at Simon, then let his eyes fall, suddenly sheepish now that the sex was over. "That's thirty-seven dollars for the gas," he said, returning to the real business. Simon handed him the money and the card. Rick looked at the card, flipped it over to Simon's cell number and smiled. He slipped it in his pocket, then pulled out three ones and handed them to Simon. "Looks like we had the same idea," Rick said and nodded at the money in Simon's hand.

Simon opened the bills. There was a scrap of paper with Rick printed on it and a phone number. "That's my home number. I don't have a cell but I work until six. I'm home after that," Rick told him.

"Cool." Simon looked down at the number, then slipped the money in his wallet.

"How long has it been?" Rick asked.

"What do you mean?"

"Since you last got laid. How long?"

"Six months."

"That's too long, man. Give me a call sometime, maybe we can get a few beers, do this again."

"I'd like that." Simon said, thinking about the two-hour drive he still had to get home. Two hours was a long drive to come back for a quickie. If there was a chance for something more between them, well, then the drive might be worth it. A chance meeting like this was one thing. It was hot and fun and now he was beginning to understand Danny's way of thinking. Not every orgasm had to be another step in a relationship. Sometimes a good fuck could be just a good fuck. It didn't have to mean moving vans and a commitment ceremony.

But to drive back there to relieve a hard-on without a possibility of an "I love you" or even an "I like you" hardly seemed worth the effort.

"I live down the road a bit, at the Elm Street Trailer Park," Rick said. "I got lots of toys. I can trust you with handcuffs, can't I? You don't seem like a serial killer or nothing."

"Yeah, you can trust me," he said and slipped into the Lexus. He slid the key in the ignition, started it and rolled his window down.

"Cool. I live alone," Rick replied, taking a step back from the car. "It sucks, sleeping every night alone. Would spending the night interest you? I mean, if not, we can just fool around, or something." He bit his lower lip with the jagged tooth, reminding Simon of a shy kid asking for a new toy.

"It would interest me," Simon said. He looked at the boy. They were very different people, different classes, not that Simon ever really concerned himself with class. What advantages a man had and what he did for a living didn't matter. It was the man that counted, not what he had or what he did. What little he knew of Rick told him that Rick was probably a good man.

Even with that, though, he couldn't really see this going beyond an occasional tryst. And if it did, well so be it. He wasn't going to plan his future any longer; he had done enough looking ahead since Peter left. He wasn't pining for the past either. All that mattered was the here and now. "I would really like that," Simon said.

"See you around, man," Rick said and nodded his head at Simon.

"I hope so." Simon replied, then slowly drove out of the gas station and back onto the highway. He slipped the paper with Rick's number in his shirt pocket, buttoned the pocket closed, then pulled a Camel from the pack on the seat and lit it.

He inhaled the smoke, the sweet tobacco dancing over his tongue. It was a strong flavor, but it didn't overpower the taste of Rick. He could still sense the boy's sweat and come on his tongue. He liked it.

His cell phone rang and he opened the center console where he had stored it before going into the conference that morning. He looked at the screen. It was Danny. Simon grinned and pressed the green TALK button. "Hey Danny," he said. "Boy, do I have a story for you."

If you enjoyed this story, you can sign up for a free membership at ForbiddenFiction.com and discuss it with other readers and the author at the *Greasy Boy* story page at http://forbiddenfiction.com/story/PLR-1.000158.

We do our best to proof all our work, but if you spot a text error we missed, please let us know via our website Contact Form at www.forbiddenfiction.com/contact.

PRIVATE SECURITY
P.L. RIPLEY

Private Security

Chapter 1: The Night Shift

The worst part of this job, Ryan thought, *is easily the hours, but having to wear this damned tie comes a close second.*

He hooked his finger in the knot and pulled on it, loosening the tie enough for him to breathe, and unfastened the top button of his shirt. This could be considered out of uniform, but the only other person here in the security office was old Bill and he didn't care what you looked like, only that you showed up for your shift on time so he could go home.

"I made a fresh pot of coffee for you," Bill said, and clapped Ryan on the shoulder as he grabbed his time card and punched out for the night.

"Thanks man," Ryan replied as he pulled the stack of textbooks from the backpack he had brought in with him and dropped them on the desk. He never had a great deal of time during the night for studying, but every few minutes he could get in helped.

He poured himself a cup of coffee, mixed in a healthy dose of sugar and powdered creamer, then took it with him on his rounds. He was exhausted, and had been since starting the job. When he accepted the position of security guard for the small company, he had hoped for just a few hours in the afternoon, something he could make a few dollars with after classes, but the only shift available was the graveyard at this warehouse.

In his month-long career as a guard he had gotten maybe five hours sleep a day. He tried to make up for it on his days off, but the constant rotation of his sleep schedule, sleeping days half the week then trying to switch to nights the rest of the time, was wearing on him. He found he was tired all the time, no matter how much rest he got. Living in the dorm didn't help matters any either.

The dorms were quiet during the day, when he was at class; but once lunchtime hit the place was nothing but slamming doors and hallway football games, and it stayed that way until ten at night or later.

To top all this off, he hadn't seen his girlfriend, Jennifer, for more than a few minutes at a time since starting work. He was horny as hell and the quick masturbatory rounds in the shower just barely relieved the physical tension. He desperately needed to touch and be touched in return.

He had met Jennifer during his second year at the university through her twin brother, Justin. Justin had lived in Ryan's dorm building, and the two became close friends, sharing a love of science fiction films. Justin was a hardcore fan, though, where Ryan loved it, but didn't live it. Justin would host weekend-long *Magic: The Gathering* games in his dorm room or *Stargate* marathons, and Ryan would show up dragging in a case of beer, or a bag of weed.

He spent entire weekends in that room with him. Often, the other guys left after a few hours or once the beer was gone, but there was a connection between Ryan and Justin that sometimes confused him, made him wonder who he really was. More than once he woke on Sunday morning with Justin's sleeping body entangled with his, his strawberry blond hair filling Ryan's nose with the scent of green apple shampoo and their dream erections straining against one another.

He hadn't seen Justin since everyone left for Christmas break. Justin had quit school, refusing to come back. Jennifer told him their parents were furious, but what could they do? He was over eighteen and could make his own decisions, no matter how bad they might be. Ryan missed Justin terribly, to the point there was an actual physical ache when he remembered their weekends together. Jenn was frantic with worry about her brother. She hadn't seen him since he left school. Ryan tried to calm her, but he was worried too.

When Ryan first met Jenn he was amazed at how much the siblings looked alike. If the two exchanged clothing they might easily pass off as the other. They both had the same blond hair and blue eyes, and they shared the same smile that not only lit their faces, but their eyes as well. They didn't just smile; they emitted happiness, and it made everyone want to be closer to them.

Now, a month into his new job, Ryan was beginning to question what had attracted him to Jennifer in the first place. Was it her beauty, her intelligence, her joyful, almost giddy disposition, or was it that she reminded him so much of her brother? He found himself thinking of Justin when he was in the shower, releasing his sexual needs. It always started out as Jenn, her face beaming up at him as her long, beautifully tanned legs opened and that lovely spot, moist and inviting, called to him. He would lower his imagined self onto, then into her, almost feeling for real the smooth walls of her vagina hugging his cock, pulling him in deeper and caressing him closer to the inevitable finale. Then, the face beneath him would change, it would grow harder, sharper. Blond stubble would appear along the jaw and the smile would become more mischievous. The legs wrapped around him were just as long and tanned but now, instead of smooth and hairless, they were covered in a thick down of blond hair and fierce runner's muscles stood out along the calves and thighs. And his cock was no longer inside her; it was pressed against Justin's cock, the same strong hardness he had felt in the real world pressing against him as they slept on those science fiction weekends.

This was the point he came. When his imagined self realized it was Justin he was with, his real self lost control and came in the shower.

But Ryan wasn't gay; he couldn't be. He loved women and always had. And he loved Jennifer more than any of the women and girls he had dated before her. He loved the way she made him feel: strong, confident, powerful. Like he had earned her love, even though he had never really done anything to warrant her dedication, except return the same affections.

But these thoughts he had been having of Justin were bothering him. He wasn't cheating on her, not really, not physically, but would she see it that way? Would she laugh and tell him it was okay to fantasize about her twin brother while he jerked off? That it meant nothing. That he was just a sexual being and could appreciate beauty, whether in a man or a woman, just as she sometimes mentioned how gorgeous she found certain women around campus.

Would she understand? More importantly though, did he want her to? Did Ryan want her to tell him it was okay? To give legitimacy to his newly discovered desires.

Besides, just because he fantasizes about Justin doesn't make him gay, right?

Right?

The job itself wasn't difficult; the hardest part was staying awake through the night. Every hour he had to make rounds through the warehouse, checking doors and making sure everything that should be locked, remained so. He didn't dare sleep. If anything happened to the place whilst he was napping he would be fired for not doing the one thing he was paid to do: staying awake and patrolling the grounds. The job might suck, but he didn't want to lose it.

He was actually in pretty good shape tonight, though. His American Lit. class had been canceled and he had been able to catch a few minutes of sleep this afternoon before the roar of the other students in the hall pulled him from his nap. It was Friday night and he knew he could sleep all day Saturday if he wanted, then maybe catch a few hours with Jenn before he had to be back here. He might actually get laid this weekend.

Maybe, if he did get lucky, these thoughts of Justin would end. It was just his sudden lack of sex that was making him think the things he thought in the shower. He wasn't really attracted to Justin. Was he?

He shook his head. No, that wasn't right. Getting off wouldn't stop these fantasy images of Justin naked before him. These thoughts were as old as his friendship with him. They had started almost immediately after they had met. *What is it about him that intrigues me?* he wondered.

The warehouse was a monster of a building. Two stories tall and 50,000 square feet of space, the first floor being the actual warehouse, the second housing offices. When he ran his rounds, it took him about 30 minutes to canvass the entire building, upstairs and down.

He finished his first round then went back to the office to finish his coffee and look through his books. He read a few pages of his Psychology textbook then it was time to head out on his rounds again.

The first floor was secure; nothing had changed since he had been there just an hour before. When he got to the second level though, one of the office doors was unlocked. He had checked them earlier and everything had been locked down then, he was sure of it.

"Hello," he called out, his voice shaking and coming out in barky little squeaks, like a cartoon mouse. *Come on, man up*, he thought. He nearly kicked himself for announcing his presence. If there were a burglar in the room, did he really think the guy would answer him back? He pulled the flashlight from his belt and swung the yellowish beam around the room. There were four desks, each set up alike. A small lamp on the left corner with a small metal trash can on the floor on the right side of each desk. A file cabinet as long as a delivery van stood in the back of the room. There was a door at the back of the room leading to an inner office, probably a supervisor and this was his (or her) secretarial pool. It stood open, which was another oddity. These were usually closed and locked as was everything else in the warehouse.

Nothing seemed to be disturbed in here, though. Perhaps he had made a mistake and only thought he checked the door earlier. Perhaps the month of sleep deprivation was getting to him. He might feel rested now, but there could be a layer of madness growing in him deep, deep down that even the few hours of rest he got today could not dissipate. Maybe he would need a week of rest after this was all over, or several weeks, to feel like himself again.

The room was silent; he could hear nothing but his own heartbeat, now slowing to normal with the excitement of finding an unlocked door fading to the mundane realization that it was not a burglar, but his own error. What would he do if there really was someone, he wondered. The only weapon the security outfit allowed was a stun gun. It was effective; its only drawback was how close you had to be to use it; but it would not keep an attacker down for long. But then, that would be all he would need. Time to get the person subdued and get the police on the phone. If he had to, he could club the guy with his flashlight. It was heavy enough and he was strong enough for it to knock him down, if not out.

The room seemed secure and he was turning to close the door and lock it, when he noticed movement out of the corner of his eye. A flash of movement from behind the back desk on his right side. He swung his flashlight in that direction and caught a quick glimpse of a hand and a richly tanned arm covered in a tattoo of the grim reaper. *Justin*, he thought. Just before leaving school he and Justin had gotten stoned and had thought it would be fun to get matching tattoos. Justin wanted the grim reaper. Ryan wasn't crazy about the idea of one so large, but he agreed because, well, he usually did whatever Justin wanted. Justin just had that effect on him. Justin wanted his on his arm, while Ryan, thinking of future career prospects, opted for his thigh.

The man (Justin?) ducked into the back office, the glass in the door rattling as his foot bumped the corner. Ryan reached behind him and flicked on the overhead lights. The florescent tubes crackled and buzzed over his head and the room filled with the sickly weird glow of the unflattering light. "You might as well come out," he said. "I know you're in there."

Quiet followed, and Ryan took a step forward; his balls pulled up into his body and sweat dampened his back, chest and armpits. Fear was taking him and he had to take deep breaths to calm himself. If the guy had a gun he would lie down for him; he knew that. Courage can only take you so far and he was not willing to die for a dollar over minimum wage. He just hoped the burglar knew this, that he wouldn't shoot first and ask questions later.

The smart thing to do was back out of the room and lock the door behind him, trapping the man inside, then call the police. Let them deal with this; let them take the risk. He began to back step, to move out of the room without turning his back on the inner office door when he saw eyes as wide as saucers shining out of the darkness of the other room. "Ryan?" he heard, and the man stepped into the light.

There was a smile beneath the eyes. A beautifully crafted mouth stretched into a grin that was both friendly and inviting. It was a smile he had seen many times, both in the real world and in his shower stall fantasies. A smiling mouth he had kissed in his dreams and parted with his tongue, and heard call his name not with the curious questioning as it had now, but with the simmering passion of impending orgasm, with the lust of sensations that Ryan brought to it in his dreams.

"J-J-Justin?" he stammered and nearly dropped the flashlight to the floor. "What are you doing here?" he asked. Before Justin could answer, however, Ryan ran to him, pulled him into his arms and hugged him. Justin's body was still firm with the lean muscles along his chest and back that Ryan had felt lying on the couch with him back at school. Ryan inhaled deeply, smelling the body wash Justin had used two, perhaps three days ago lying just under the surface of the natural funk of old sweat clinging to him. The combination actually excited Ryan.

"Ryan, oh Jesus," Justin moaned as he accepted the embrace and returned the same, only his was tighter, more urgent.

"Are you a dream?" Ryan asked, not really expecting an answer. This was his fantasy. He had grown so exhausted he was hallucinating Justin. It was the only explanation for his sudden appearance here at this warehouse.

But, Ryan thought, *if this is a dream, it is the most elaborate one I have ever had.* He ran his fingers through Justin's hair. At school, Justin had kept his hair neat, short. But now it spilled down over his shoulders. And it obviously had not been washed in days, just like the rest of him. Dirty or not, Justin was still stunning.

"What are you doing here?" he asked again as he stepped back, pulling himself from what was, he now realized, Justin's firm grip. "What happened to you?" Ryan asked. *You look like hell,* he thought but didn't say. It wasn't true anyway. Justin was disheveled, a little dirty, but far from unattractive. Ryan did not think Justin could ever be unattractive.

He stepped back again and saw the dark clothes Justin was wearing. Not the light, bright colors he usually wore. He was dressed in dark, nearly black jeans and an equally muted shirt. The clothing was tight against his chest, thighs, and crotch. It skimmed his body like a wetsuit. Ryan glanced at the floor, at the leather satchel half hidden beneath one of the desks. The bag was shut tight, but he could easily imagine what implements might be hidden inside.

"You're here to rob the place, aren't you?" Ryan asked.

Justin quickly looked away from him.

"Is this what you have been doing with your time since you left school? What the hell is the matter with you?" Ryan barked.

Justin swung his eyes up to meet Ryan's. His beautiful blue eyes brimmed with rage. "Fuck you!" he bellowed. "You haven't lived my life. You don't know what I've gone through." Justin stood straighter, the muscles in his chest suddenly pushing at the tight shirt. He seemed to be itching for a fight, something Ryan did not want to join him in. He did not want their first meeting in months to end up in a slug-fest.

"You're right. I'm sorry. Why don't you explain to me what you have been through?" Ryan dropped onto the desktop behind him.

Justin sighed. "I fucked up, Ryan. I got involved with some very nasty people and I owe them money," Justin paused and blinked tears from his eyes. "A great deal of money."

"How much are we talking about?" Ryan asked. The quiver in Justin's voice told Ryan all he needed to know. Justin was scared. Even though he assumed it was Justin's own fault, that he was as much to blame for putting himself in danger as the people after him, Ryan still wanted to help him.

"Ten thousand," Justin replied. "By Monday, or I'm not going to be able to walk for quite a while."

"Shit, man," Ryan groaned. "It might as well be ten million."

"I know. Look, Ryan, just walk away. Do your job just like I wasn't here," he said and cocked his thumb over his shoulder to the office behind him. Inside was a safe nearly large enough to walk into. Its door was shut and locked. "It shouldn't take me too long to get the safe open and be on my way." Justin looked pleadingly into Ryan's eyes.

Ryan's head began to throb as a hot rush of rage tore through him. "Yeah, great idea. And what happens later when you get caught and the police figure out I know you? Don't you think they will assume it was an inside job? I could go to jail with you. I won't do that, Justin."

"Why not? It's your fault I'm in this mess," Justin said, shoving his finger in Ryan's face.

Ryan rose to his feet and pressed his chest to Justin's. Justin did not back away, but leaned in against Ryan, edging him back towards the desk he had just been sitting on. "How do you figure it's my fault?" Ryan asked, the ice thick in his voice.

At that moment Justin deflated. His shoulders sagged and he turned from Ryan, the sadness back in his eyes again. "It just is," he said.

"Then let me help you. But not like this," Ryan said as he stared into Justin's eyes, before he let his attention move down to his lips. They were beautiful lips. Red as strawberries, wet, shimmering even in the unflattering glow of the florescent lights. He thought they would be sweet as strawberries as well. Ryan couldn't take his eyes off them. He had to taste them, feel them against his own lips. Nothing else mattered right now. Not his job, not the break-in. Nothing but those lips and his desire to taste them.

So Ryan did just that. He kissed him and held the kiss until Justin finally, perhaps reluctantly, pulled away. Their eyes locked. The flicker of a smile settled on Justin's mouth. It was an almost satisfied grin, as though he had been wanting to do that for as long as Ryan had. Then his face turned hard again. The anger was back. "You bastard!" he screamed and pushed Ryan backwards. Ryan spilled over the desk, caught his foot in the legs of the chair and slammed to the floor. His head bounced off the thin carpeting and the room spun for a second or two. Everything grew as black as Justin's clothes, and consciousness left him.

Chapter 2:
Getting Dirty

"Ryan? Ryan?"

Ryan opened his eyes, looked up at the ceiling. His head hurt, as did his ankle. He had twisted it on the way down to the floor. "Are you okay?" Justin asked, his face suddenly coming into view as he hovered over him.

"What the hell did you hit me for?" Ryan asked.

"I didn't hit you. I pushed you. Sorry about that." Justin grabbed his arm and pulled Ryan to his feet.

"Hey, I've been hurt worse."

"This isn't the football field, though. I really am sorry."

Ryan stood on shaky legs and steadied himself by leaning on the desk. "I know you are. It's okay Justin, really," Ryan said. He waited until he got his bearings back, then grabbed Justin, pulled him close and said, "Now, where was I?"

"Stop. We can't do this." Justin tried to pull himself from Ryan's hold, but could not break free. Ryan tightened his grip and after a minute or so, Justin gave up his attempt to release himself.

"Why can't we do this?" Ryan asked.

"I'm not gay," Justin replied.

"I know you're not gay. I've seen all the girls you were sleeping with back at school. I kind of envied you with some of them. I'm not gay either, but I want to be with you. I have for a long time. And I think you want to be with me as well."

"Just because I want to, doesn't mean I should."

"So you do want to!"

"I do. I don't know why, but I do." Justin began unbuttoning Ryan's uniform shirt, then slid it from his shoulders and let it pool on the floor at their feet. He slipped his hands beneath the crisp, white undershirt, his cool fingers causing a chill to race along Ryan's belly and chest. Justin looked into Ryan's eyes and they both swallowed nervously at the same time. "Is this what you wanted?" he asked. Ryan couldn't speak. His mouth was desert dry, but he nodded his head that this was exactly what he had fantasized about.

Justin's fingers found Ryan's nipples and teased them until they grew as hard as Ryan's cock had become. God, how Ryan wanted him. He resisted the urge to tear off Justin's clothes and ravish him on the desk. To taste his entire body from ankles to eyelids. Ryan tugged on Justin's jeans, pulling the button loose and sliding the zipper down until his bright white underwear shone out at him. He slipped his hand beneath the elastic band, feeling the shock of pubic hair then the rigid stem of Justin's cock. He was hard and Ryan felt a flutter in his belly when Justin moaned at his touch.

He pulled Justin's cock out, gave it a few tugs, watching as his foreskin slid up over the fat, red head, then pulled away again, leaving the crown slick with precome. Ryan licked his lips, wondering what it tasted like. He had tasted his own semen once, when he was very young and just learning how to masturbate. One quick dip of his index finger in his overflowing belly button and Ryan discovered it was bitter, foul tasting stuff. He had never asked any girl he had been with to take his come in her mouth because of that. Some still did, but not at his insistence. But he had never tasted precome and really had no desire to, until now. He imagined it must taste similar to come, yet he wanted Justin's just the same.

Ryan nuzzled Justin's neck, thrilled by his friend's pleasured moans. He nibbled Justin's earlobe while continuing to fist his cock.

"Oh god, Ryan," Justin moaned. He fumbled with Ryan's uniform pants, tugging them open and letting them slide to the floor. Then Justin had Ryan's cock out and was playing with it just as Ryan was playing with Justin. "I'm sorry I pushed you. I'm sorry you hit your head."

"I told you, it's okay. You didn't hurt me. I understand why you freaked."

"Let me make it up to you," Justin said and before Ryan could comment, Justin was on his knees before him and pulling Ryan's cock into his mouth. Ryan gasped at the sudden wet heat surrounding him. His body went limp and he leaned against the desk before he fell again.

It was obvious that Justin had never done this before. He fumbled his tongue over Ryan's cock in an attempt to imitate what girls had done for him. Ryan didn't complain, though. He knew he would do no better, having never even had the desire to give another guy head before. But he wanted to do this for Justin. And the way Justin looked up at him, the smile in his eyes, the way he struggled to pull Ryan all the way into his throat, Ryan knew the desire to please was not his exclusively. "Does it feel good?" Justin asked, pulling Ryan's cock from his mouth just long enough to get the words out, then went back to it before he got the answer.

"It feels great," Ryan replied. It did, too. It was not the best blowjob he had ever received, but Justin's ambition, coupled with the fact it was Justin doing this for him, more than made up for the inexperience. And there was something truly exciting in knowing he was Justin's first.

Ryan nearly came each time their eyes connected. If he didn't stop him now, he would go over the edge and he might not get the chance to perform the same act on Justin. He desperately wanted to go down on Justin. He hooked his hands under Justin's armpits and pulled him to his feet.

"What's the matter? Did I do something wrong?"

"No, nothing is wrong. It's my turn now." Ryan dropped before him, pulled Justin's pants to his ankles—it was a struggle getting the tight jeans over his well muscled, beautifully rounded butt, but Ryan managed—and inhaled Justin as deeply inside him as he dared.

The several days without bathing had left Justin a little musky, a little funky down there, but Ryan didn't mind. It was very much like the aroma Ryan had inhaled during the hug at the start of the evening, only more pronounced. He had liked that scent and found he loved this stronger version even more. There was a primal feel to it. A feral aroma. And it excited Ryan more than anything he had smelled before. Or at least as much as the scent of a woman in full bloom.

He pulled Justin down, deep into his throat. He fought the gag reflex, struggled to keep his lips buried in Justin's blond bush, but he needed to breathe. He reluctantly pulled back, letting inch after inch of Justin's pale, hard-as-stone cock back out into the office air. It glistened with his saliva. Ryan lapped at it, watching with fascination as Justin's dick bounced and flexed under its own power each time Ryan's lips and tongue made contact. Then he swallowed it once again.

"Oh shit, Ryan," Justin moaned as he curled his hand around the back of Ryan's neck and held him still. He began working his hips, pushing himself deep into Ryan's throat, then back out again, slowly fucking his mouth.

Ryan slid his hands into his own lap and took himself in hand. He slowly pumped himself at the same rhythm Justin was working his mouth. He ran the hand not busy with his cock up Justin's legs. The blond hair ticked against his palm and he ran his fingers in the grooves of the thick muscles along Justin's calves and thighs. He reached around to Justin's butt, massaged the thick globes, and slid a finger between the cheeks. A deep moan slipped from Justin's lips and he began pumping his hips faster. Ryan relaxed his throat and let Justin do what he wanted while jerking himself to the new beat.

"Oh no; I'm going to come!" Justin nearly screamed. He started to pull back, to pull himself out of Ryan's mouth, but Ryan wrapped his free arm around him and held tight. A moment later, the warm splash of Justin's seed coated his tongue and tonsils. It was bitter, but Ryan barely noticed the flavor. He was too busy grunting around the cock in his mouth as his own orgasm painted the carpet between Justin's feet.

Ryan leaned back, letting Justin's still-erect cock slide from his mouth and grimaced at the taste in his mouth. He sat on his knees a moment, while he caught his breath.

After, neither man spoke as they dressed. Ryan glanced at Justin, trying to gauge his feelings about what had just happened, but his body language was as mute as his tongue. Justin finally looked over at Ryan and broke into a wide grin. "That was incredible," he said.

Ryan sighed in relief. For him, it had been better than he suspected it could be. The simple act of pleasuring Justin had felt as good for him physically as the blowjob Justin had performed on him earlier. Getting Justin off, got Ryan off.

"It *was* incredible, wasn't it," Ryan said as he pulled a tissue from a box on one of the desks and cleaned the mess he had made on the carpet. He tossed the sticky tissue in the trash. "Grab your bag; I have to go on rounds."

"So I guess you're not going to let me..." Justin nodded his head at the back office and the safe that hid within.

"No. We are going to have to figure something else out. You don't want to do this anyway. Right? You're a better man than this, Justin." Ryan grabbed his tie and shoved it in his back pocket. He didn't want to fumble with the thing right now. As long as he had it back on before the morning crew showed up, he was safe.

"I don't want to ask my father for help, but I guess I have no other choice." Justin grabbed the leather satchel from beneath the desk and left the office with Ryan leading the way. Ryan locked the door closed behind them and they descended to the first floor. "I didn't want to disappoint my parents. That's why I've been living on the street for the last four months."

"Which would disappoint your father more?" Ryan asked. "You asking him for help, or you getting your kneecaps broken because you were too scared to go to him?"

"I'll drive up there in the morning. Can you come with me? You and Jenn? I don't want to go alone."

Jenn. Ryan had forgotten about her. *Jesus, what have I done?* he asked himself. He had cheated on her. And with her brother no less. This could be the end of them if she found out, and she had to find out. He could not keep something like this from her. He loved her too much to keep her in the dark about this... this revolutionary self-discovery. He liked what they had done and hoped Justin would want to do it again and he couldn't keep this from her.

"Will your father loan you the money?"

"I'm sure he will. I've never been in trouble before. I'm sure he is pissed about me leaving school, but Jenn has him wrapped around her little finger. If I can't convince him I need his help, she will."

"*I'm* still pissed at you for quitting school," Ryan said. The smile he poured down onto Justin never faltered though. "If he can't or won't come up with the cash, we can come up with something."

"Like what? A *Justin fucked up his life* benefit?"

"Maybe. We all make mistakes. It could happen to any of us. The guys at school, they ask Jenn about you all the time. They love you, man," Ryan paused a moment, stared into Justin's deep, blue eyes. "I love you."

Justin laughed. "How do you love me? Romantically?"

"I don't know. Maybe. I've never felt this for another guy before. I've never wanted to be with someone as badly as I wanted to be with you. I want to do this again." He leaned in, kissed Justin. "And again," another kiss, "and again."

What does this make me, he wondered. Those long weekends when they barely got out of each other's sight were the happiest he had ever been with another person, and when Sunday evening arrived and Justin's roommate came back to the dorm after spending the weekend away, forcing Ryan back to his own dorm room, he found sleep difficult. He wanted to be back down the hall, back with Justin, and he would press his own clothes against his face and smell the black cherry air freshener Justin scented his room with.

There was something powerful going on between them. He didn't know exactly what it was, but he liked it. What did this make him? Gay, bisexual, bi-curious? Who cared what he was. They were just labels, to pigeonhole people into categories. He might be sexually attracted to women, but he had never felt such an emotional connection to one as strongly as he did for Justin. He had always loved Justin. From the moment they had met, he wanted to be with him. He was a friend closer than any he had had in high school. The more time he had spent with him, the more attracted to him he became. Did that make him gay? Perhaps, but he didn't care right then what that made him. He liked it. He liked being with Justin and he even liked doing what they had just done. Maybe he was just gay for Justin.

"You are going to have to get out of here soon," Ryan said as he glanced up at the clock on the wall. He was late making his rounds.

"You're not going to turn me in? I don't want you to get in trouble if they see me here on the cameras."

"There aren't any cameras. The owner never installed them because it's cheaper to hire me than it is to monitor the feeds. And no, I'm not going to turn you in to anyone. You made a mistake, but you never had a chance to go through with it, so no real crime has been committed."

"The police wouldn't see it that way."

"Fuck the police. They are just here to protect the rich from the poor anyway." He led Justin toward the security office and the door to the parking lot outside.

"Still the angry idealist," Justin laughed."

"Look," Ryan said, his hand on the door handle. "I need to tell Jennifer about what happened here tonight. I can keep your name out of it but..."

"She will understand Ryan. She won't hate you, or me. It might actually turn her on. She's kind of a pervert that way."

Ryan laughed. "I love her, you know."

"I know. She loves you too," Justin said. "I don't think this is going to bother her that much. She kind of already knows anyway."

"What do you mean?" Ryan pulled on the ring of keys, fit one into the lock on the door leading outside.

"Just before Christmas break, Jennifer told me something that...well, it frightened me. I panicked and left school because of what she said. Don't tell her that was the reason, though. I don't want her to feel guilty about it."

"What did she say?" Ryan turned the key, causing the tumblers inside the door to rattle and fall into place.

"She said that when you and I were together, she saw something in my eyes that made her believe I had a thing for you. She called it a sparkle," Justin laughed. "She is such a girl, but that's what made her believe what I already knew was true. I did have the hots for you; still do. But the thing that scared me? She saw it in your eyes as well. Jennifer thought it was adorable. She actually used that word, adorable. I couldn't stay there, knowing something might happen between us. I'm not gay; I'm not attracted to men...except you."

"So why did this just happen?"

"You live on the streets for a few months; you come to realize what is really important. You are my closest friend, Ryan. I love you, man. I don't know what this is between us, but I like it and would like to explore it more. See where it takes us. If..." he sighed heavily, "that is, if you want to."

"I do want to. I don't know what this is either, but we will figure it out, together."

"And don't feel guilty for my leaving school," Justin said. "It wasn't because of you or what Jenn had said. It was me, my own fear that made me run away. I got scared and I quit school. This was my doing. I made the decision to sell drugs for those guys, and it was my decision to use those drugs rather than sell them. I'm sober now and haven't touched anything in a while, but after I get this mess cleared up, I was thinking about coming back to the university."

"That's great. The dorm is lonely without you."

"I won't be at the dorm. I want to get a place in town. I would like you to move in with me."

"Jenn and I were talking about getting a place off campus. Maybe we could all live together."

"What are you going to do? Bounce from my bed to hers?"

"Maybe. Would that bother you? Do you think Jenn might go for that?"

"She might. She is quite the free spirit. It doesn't bother me. I'm still going to date women, you know. I still love the girls, but I will always have time for you."

Ryan pulled the door open, felt the cool rush of night air flutter over his still bare chest. He buttoned his shirt, pulled the tie from his back pocket and draped it around his neck. "I get out at six. Meet me at the dorm. You can take a shower there before we head to your parents."

"Cool," Justin stepped outside into night. Light was just beginning to illuminate the horizon. It would be morning in a few hours. He began to cross the paved lot to the road when he stopped, turned back to Ryan and said, "I love you, man."

"How did I get so lucky?" Ryan called back, then Justin disappeared around the corner of the building. *How did I get so lucky?* he asked himself again. The two most beautiful people he had ever known loved him. The entire situation was crazy, but he hoped things would work out between the three of them. He wondered if Jennifer would really be okay with this. Justin thought she might. Maybe he was right. If not, there could be some serious heartache in the future. But at least he was secure in the knowledge that he loved them both and that, at least for now, they both loved him. He couldn't ask for more than that.

What Goes Down
Must Come Up
A Little Push
P.L. Ripley

A Little Push

Chapter 1:
The Push

"Why is this happening?" Jennifer, my sister, asked, tears streaming down her beautiful face. I stood beside her, holding her hands as we watched the things inside the pen stumble over one another, gnarled fists clutching hungrily at us. They were ravenous.

"I don't know," I replied. I didn't know why it was happening, only that it was. The town preacher said it was God's anger, that the world's sins had finally set Him off. Scientists suggested when the planet passed through the tail of a comet a few weeks ago, that a virus had somehow spread from outer space, bringing the dead back to whatever form of life this was. I didn't know which side was right, if either; nor did I care. One thing was indisputable though: if the brain was destroyed, they couldn't come back. But most people couldn't or wouldn't do that to their loved ones. Kill them forever. I couldn't understand that thinking until now. But I have learned.

The thing that used to be Horace Maplewood, the owner of the feed store and part-time town drunk, tripped over a rock in the pen, fell on his face and shattered his jaw. As he rose to his feet again, the jaw hung like a broken window shutter, creaking and grinding against the dying bones.

"Are you sure you want to do this?" I asked her. "I mean, we could put him in the root cellar. He doesn't have to be here with the others."

"No," Jennifer said, "I think it's best we keep him out of the house. I wouldn't want him getting loose and... and hurting someone else." She pulled little Elizabeth closer to her bosom. The baby cooed, her voice barely overriding the grunts and moans of the things in the pen.

"You're right." I patted her hand and walked back to the wagon where the man who used to be her husband lay, straining against the ropes holding him down. I pulled him to his feet. "Wesley, I'm going to untie you once you are in the pen," I explained, as though he could understand me. He gnashed his teeth and the wound on my bottom lip throbbed in response.

He didn't resist as I nudged him through the gate, slammed it shut behind him and refastened the latch. The clanging of the metal brace bought the attentions of the others. I slid a knife between the thick wooden slats and cut the ropes holding Wesley's hands together. "I'm so sorry, Wes," I said. If I could have taken back all that happened, all I'd done, I would gladly take his place in there. He gave me a mixed look of indifference and sorrow—or perhaps that was just me projecting on him. "I love you," I whispered. The Buffalo Soldier guarding the pen glanced at me, then quickly diverted his eyes as though he were embarrassed at overhearing my endearment.

Wesley grunted. The spot where he'd bitten me gave a slight twinge again. I sucked my lip into my mouth, as though I could hide the wound. No one knew he'd bitten me, least of all Jennifer. She didn't know about a lot of things he'd done to me, or I to him.

We climbed back in the wagon. Jennifer gave her husband a slight wave then glanced my way sheepishly. "He probably doesn't know who I am anymore, does he?"

"Probably not," I replied, but I wasn't so sure myself. There'd been a glimmer of recognition in his eyes a few days ago. The day I killed his mother. My second murder in a week, his being the first.

Back at the farm, Jen carried the baby in the house while I took to the barn. The barn had always been my refuge. Actually, it'd been our refuge, Wesley and I. It was where our story ended, and also where it begun.

It was during their engagement party, Wes and Jen's. After six months of courting, Wesley finally gathered the courage to ask our father for Jennifer's hand in marriage. Dad gladly gave his consent. He knew Wesley was a good man, and would make a good addition to our small family. I'd been their chaperone on all their outings, and Wes and I became close friends during their dates. I knew he was a good man as well.

Our father pulled out the bottle of Merlot he brought here from Boston when he and our mother first came west to start their farm. It was the best wine I'd ever tasted, mostly because of the joyous celebration it represented. When the bottle was empty, Jennifer and Dad retired to their beds for the evening while Wesley and I took to the barn, where we continued the party with a bottle of cheap whiskey.

That was where it first happened, in the hayloft. The bottle grew empty and our courage grew strong and, well, we didn't mean for it to happen, but neither one of us tried to stop it either. I would be lying if I said I hadn't fantasized about this very thing. About his lips, so soft and wet, touching mine. His body, toned from years of farm work, lying naked and strong against my own.

I quivered as his chin stubble tickled my hip, scratched its way down into the groove between my thigh and groin. And when he took me in his mouth, I was hooked.

But it wasn't a love affair, not at first. We were simply two men succumbing to something that had lain dormant between us until then. We didn't pretend we were making love, but were fucking just because it felt good.

When I first entered him, his furry legs on my shoulders, my spit-soaked cock pushing deep inside him, I knew this could not be the only time I experienced him this way. I had to have him again and again. And that night I did. We screwed until the sun came up, then one more time just to get us through the day.

"I love you," he said to me. Not that first night, or even the second, but he said it. "I love you," as his body shook with the force of his climax. "I love you," as he erupted, covering us both with his seed.

He said it, and he meant it. At least, he meant it then, but time and a child have a way of changing a man's perspective, of altering a man's outlook on the world. When Elizabeth was born, he stopped seeking me out for the needs my sister could not satisfy in him.

At first I said nothing. He was, after all, a new father with a father's responsibilities. I understood, and let him care for his new family. But eventually my needs, my manly needs, got to be too much for me, and I cornered him out there in the fields and demanded his attentions.

"I can't do it anymore," he said, his eyes refusing to meet my own. "I can't. I have a daughter now, a wife. I have got to be a man now."

"You are a man, just as I am!" I screamed. "An' your wife's my sister. You think I don't know that? You think I don't worry 'bout that? What this would do to her if she ever found out?" I reached and grabbed his wrist, the dark hair on his arm curling around my fingers. His skin was hot in the afternoon sun, and I felt that heat go into the thick, calloused pads of my fingertips. "Please Wesley, I can't live without you," I pleaded. I wanted him more at that moment than I had ever wanted him. I grabbed him around the neck and pulled him to me, forcing his lips against my own.

He pushed me away with his free hand. "I told you I ain't gonna do this no more!" He turned and began walking away from me, heading back to the farm, half mile or so away. His booted feet threw angry steps, pushing the dust in red and tan puffs. I watched him walk away, his shirt clinging to his back, wet with sweat, the muscles beneath the cloth flexing, pumping with the angry march. And the way his denim pants hugged his body. Jesus, it worked its way into me like a damned virus. Eating at me and making my head, heart, and cock yearn with images of just he and I, alone in my bed or out in the barn. Our naked bodies pressed tightly while the cows and pigs watched and Wes moaning my name over and over, "Oh Jesse, Jesse," while I fucked him again and again. And him shooting come like a volcano and me, lapping it off his hairy belly while pushing him to go again and....

I couldn't take it any longer. I needed him like a thirsty man needs water. I ran up behind him and knocked him to the ground, then dropped and began pulling his pants free. He fought me, but I worked that farm my whole life and was stronger. I had his ass clear in a matter of seconds, and before I knew it, my pants were around my knees. I shoved myself inside him. He always loved it rough. I knew all he needed was a reminder as to how good I made him feel. Once he realized he wanted it as much as I did, things could get back to the way they were before. But, things didn't work out the way I wanted them to. He twisted and thrashed but couldn't buck me off, so he lay still and waited for me to finish. A tear rolled from his eye, cutting a clean swath through the dirt on his cheek. My lust dwindled with that lone tear. He saw me looking and closed the wet eye, shutting me out.

I realized what I was doing. I was hurting the man I loved. Raping him. I pushed myself up from his back, pulling free of his body with a slick plop. He winced as I left him. I stood and hitched my pants, too afraid to look at him. I didn't want to see the hate I knew must be on his face.

He rose, secured his pants, then began silently shuffling off back home. I needed him to understand why I did what I had done. No, not just why I'd done it, but why he forced me to sink this low. I loved him and he loved me. I knew this, he knew this, and if he could just understand I didn't want to hurt him, but he'd made me. He pushed me away, made me force him to the ground. It was as much his fault as it was mine, maybe more so.

"Wesley," I begged, standing in front of him, stopping him with my hands against his chest. "Please."

He pushed me away, looking into my eyes with fire, anger, and raw hatred. I knew I'd lost him. No matter what I did now, nothing would bring him back to me. Right then, something inside me died. I don't know if it was the love I felt for him, or my very soul, but I was suddenly a different man. We were on a ridge with a thirty foot drop. It wasn't a rolling-ground-to-the-bottom of the chasm, but a straight off plummet. I looked at the open air behind him, his feet no more than four or five feet from the edge, and that hard, dead, rejected part of me reached out and pushed him, gently, but hard enough so he shuffled back a few steps. He was still far from the lip of the drop.

That shove felt good but it wasn't enough. "How many years?" I asked.

The anger in his eyes turned to confusion. "What in hell are you..." Wesley grunted.

"How many years you and I been fooling around out in that barn, making love? Now you think it can end all clean and pretty. No one gets hurt? Fuck you Wesley," I was furious and it must have shown on my face because he looked scared. Seeing fear in his eyes felt almost as good as that little push I'd given him.

He started moving away from me, heading towards the house once again. I blocked his way. "You ain't going nowhere," I said, setting my hand in the center of his chest. He slapped it away.

"Get your fucking hands off me," he growled. His anger matched my own. He wanted to hit me, beat me for what I'd done to him. Nothing I did could get him back now. He was lost forever.

How could I survive living and working next to him day and night and not be able to touch him, make love to him. I couldn't live through that. I had to do something so I might be able to move on. So I might find another I could feel the same way as I felt for Wes.

I had no more doubts. He had to go. I gave him another push.

This time his feet found the edge, and he shuffled to hold onto the ground. His arms pin wheeled as he struggled to maintain his balance.

I reached out for him, as though I were going to pull him clear of the fall. I might have done just that, saved him, but then he gave me that look. That arrogant, little grin that said, I knew you couldn't let me go. You love me and I can use that because I own you.

He reached for my grasping hands, but instead of pulling him free, I pushed him, sending him over the edge. The look of fear in those eyes, the same eyes I'd buried myself in time after time, filled me with instant regret. I never wanted to hurt him, never wanted him to be afraid, but he'd done this to himself as much as I'd done it to him. He killed himself the moment he turned me away.

He fell with a low moan rising out of his chest. He didn't yell as I suspected he might, just a quick, rough grumble as gravity took him. The rocks at the bottom of the chasm, sharp and jagged, seemed to reach out of the ground to catch him. I could hear the wet, splintery crack of his bones breaking echo on the ridge.

Nothing seemed to move then. Even the light breeze that'd been blowing all day stopped The air was still, quiet.

I looked down at him, his body lying broken, his left leg jutting out in an unnatural angle, the shin nearly touching the top of his thigh. His face and neck were covered in blood. Even from thirty feet up, I could see small pools of foam rising from the blood at his mouth. It was the last of the air in his lungs leaving his body. I called down to him, "Wesley?" He didn't stir or acknowledge me. His eyes were still open, but there was no clarity in them, no focus. He was gone.

To get down to bottom of the chasm safely, I walked back along the ridge a few hundred feet, to the trail there. It was steep, but once I sat and scooted down on my butt part of the way, I could stand and shuffle down the rest. At the bottom, I pulled off my boots and dumped the handful of gravel that had collected in them, and then joined Wesley at the rocks.

He seemed more pitiful up close than he had from the ridge. His arm had come up in the fall and he looked as though he were shielding his eyes from the sun. The shadow of his fingers fell over the right eye, which popped out of the socket and hung on his cheek. I lifted it onto my fingers, feeling the slick, jelly-like softness of it, and tried to push it back into his head. It didn't seem to want to go though, so I let it settle back onto his cheek. I slid my arms under his broken body and lifted him from the rocks, then set him onto the hard dusty soil.

I knelt beside him, took his hand in mine. Here was the man I loved for what, six years? Seven? Lying in the dirt, dead because he could no longer love me back the way I wanted. I killed him in a rage, and now I was alone. And Jennifer no longer had a husband.

I climbed on top of him, pressed my body to his. He was cooling, but there was still some residual heat there. I opened his shirt, kissed his chest, the hair still tickling my face as it had the last time we were together, then lay there, hearing my own heartbeat reverberate against his silent chest. I felt my chest hitch like I had hiccups, and realized I was crying. The tears felt good, cleansing, like being baptized.

When I was cried out and felt more myself again, I buttoned his shirt, lifted him onto my shoulders, and began the long walk home. The dead weight wore on me and I had to stop every hundred feet or so to readjust him to the other shoulder, when my chest felt ready to split open, then carried him in my arms like he were a baby. His head lolled against my shoulder. The right eye swung on the thin cords holding it to his head, bouncing from his nose to ear.

As I climbed the little knoll to our farm, Jennifer was in the yard feeding the chickens. She saw me carrying a man in my arms and had to know it was her husband. Who else could it have been? She dropped the bag of feed and began running towards me.

"Don't come any closer Jen," I cautioned. "You don't want to see this."

Of course, not only did she want to see it, she had to. She stopped and asked, "What happened?" then took a few tentative steps forward.

I pulled Wesley's face closer to my chest, to shield her from the most gruesome of his injuries.

I entered the barn and set him on the floor, pulled off my shirt and covered his face. Jennifer followed inside. I turned to her and began to cry again. "I'm sorry Jennifer. I'm so sorry. He slipped over the cliff. The same one Dad fell from."

She dropped to her knees beside her husband and wailed. The screech tore through me and I joined her on the floor, my heart tearing out of me. She'd lost her husband, I'd lost a lover. We clung to each other, sobbing, until we could hear the baby inside the house wailing.

Jennifer's duty as a wife was now over, but motherhood demanded her attention. She lifted herself from the dusty floor, her eyes and face puffy with grief, and went to the house to care for her daughter. She was a widow now, but at least had the child to remind her of the man she loved. I only had the ache in my heart and memories. I pulled my shirt from his face and kissed his lips one again, then walked out behind the barn with a shovel and began digging his grave, next to Mom and Dad, in the family cemetery. He began to walk before I could get him buried, though.

Chapter 2
The Push Back

Wesley's mother, Mrs. Danvers, arrived two days later.

I sent her a telegram after digging Wesley's grave. I didn't know if she wanted to see him—she never bothered to come out for the wedding—but she was his only family, besides us. There were five of those things shuffling around in the corral when I passed. I watched them a while and thought about Wesley. I suspected he might rise up like these things, but couldn't really be sure.

I hurried home and when I got there, Wesley was sitting up in the barn. My shirt had fallen from his face, pooled in his lap. He turned his head when he heard me riding up, the right eye still dangling from its hole.

Jennifer ran out of the house with the baby in her arms. "He's been sitting up like that for an hour," she said. "He's become one of them, hasn't he?"

"Go on back in the house," I said, "I'll take care of him."

"You can't bury him now. He'll just dig his way out."

"I know. I just sent his mother a telegram. We can keep him secured until she arrives. Shouldn't be more'n a few days."

"You don't think it would be safer if he were in town?"

"Maybe, but let's just leave him here a while. After his mother comes we can decide what to do," I said. I didn't want to see him in that corral. I wanted him here, at home with me. Even with him being dead, I still wanted him so badly it ached. I couldn't just leave him out there in the hot sun, to decompose with the others. He didn't deserve to go that way.

I grabbed a loop of rope, tied his hands behind his back, then pulled him to his feet. He growled, low and deep, turned his head to snap his teeth at me. "I know baby," I said, running my hand down his back and cupping his still firm buttocks. Shoot, his ass turned me on. Even in his condition, I became erect touching him.

I turned him and part carried, half pushed him into one of the empty pens, then shut and bolted the gate. I knew those things couldn't climb. The corral they were kept in town had fairly low fencing, and none had managed to climb onto the posts to make their escape, even though anyone, even a child, could have done it. Something in them could not make the connection to raise their legs high enough to meet with the lowest posts. We were safe as long as the bolt holding the pen door was not opened.

I went back in the house and held Jennifer while the baby slept in her arms. She wept until the sun fell out of the sky and night called with the howls of the coyotes off in the hills. My sister went off to bed without supper. She was too heartbroken to be hungry.

I dug a few biscuits from the pantry and chewed on them while sitting on the porch. I could hear Wesley out in the barn, growling and slamming himself against the walls of the pen. I wanted to go to him, to talk to him and explain what happened. I wanted him to understand how devastated I was by what had gone on between us. I was sorry not only for his death, but also for his pushing me away. He would still be alive if he hadn't of pushed me away.

Talking to him would have done no good. Not for him, and especially not for me. I would have begged his forgiveness and probably ended up getting myself hurt. There was talk around town that getting bitten by one of those things turns you into one. That whatever was causing this had developed a virus in the inflicted that could be spread through saliva or blood. I didn't know how true this was, but I wasn't willing to take any chances.

On Friday, Mrs. Danvers showed up at the train station in town. I met her there while Jen stayed at home with the baby. Neither Jen nor I had ever met the woman, but what Wesley said about her was not flattering.

She stepped down from the train and I instantly knew she was the one I'd come for. Her head was held high enough she would have drowned if it had been raining. She eyeballed the townspeople like they were dogs with the mange, or lepers. I took an instant dislike to her and she in turn, did the same to me.

"You must be Mrs. Danvers," I said, without the slightest hint of a smile on my face.

"And who are you?" she asked in a clipped abrupt speech that sent shivers into my skin.

"Jesse, Jennifer's brother."

She glared at me a moment, then took her bag from the train porter. "Your hair is red," she said, pursing her lips and breathing through her nose. She sounded like a bull with that heavy wind going in and out of her, ready to strike any moment now, and it was me she wanted to hit.

"My family is Irish. I'm third generation American though," I said, as though her comment needed an answer.

"Wesley had a friend back in Kansas City who was a redhead, Shaun O'Malley, his name was. He was a weasel, too." She glared at me, daring me to confront her insult. Instead, I took the bag from her and led her to the wagon, threw it in the back and watched as she struggled to climb onto the bench. I wouldn't help her even if she had of asked, which she didn't. When she was settled, we started back to the farm.

Jennifer had supper ready when we arrived. It was late to be eating, but she had held off our usual meal time for her mother-in-law's arrival. "What is that smell?" Mrs. Danvers asked the moment we walked into the house. "It smells like cabbage."

"It's so good to meet you, Mother Danvers," Jennifer said, reaching her hand out to grasp the old woman's. "I'm sorry it has to be under these circumstances."

"I am, too," she replied. "If he had stayed in Kansas City where he belonged, instead of this godless country, he would still be with us." Jennifer stood rigid. I knew that look, and if the old lady saw the fire in my sister's eyes, she never let on. I knew if Jenn could actually emit that fire, Mrs. Danvers would be cinders now.

Jenn kept her anger under control, but I could still hear the quiver in her voice as she said, "I'm sure you must be hungry. Let Jesse take your bag to your room and we can have supper, shall we?"

"I don't eat cabbage. If that's what you are going to try to fill me with, you can forget it. Vile stuff."

"Well," Jennifer stumbled, "we have potatoes, ham. I have some carrots I canned last fall."

The old woman huffed, dropped herself in the chair at the head of the table, her son's place, and stared down at the empty plate before her. "I'll take some 'taters and some of that ham. You Irish love your 'taters don't you. I'm not really partial to 'em, but will eat 'em when I have to."

I took her bag to the guest room, thought about opening it and setting a lit match inside, thought against it, then joined the women at the dining table.

"So, how'd it happen?" Mrs. Danvers asked, tiny flecks of potato clinging to her lips, which she refused to lick away. "Was it some animal that got him, or maybe one of them inbreds in town?"

"No ma'am," Jennifer replied. "He fell out in the back part of our acreage. There is a drop off, and he lost his footing. It was the same place that got our Daddy a few years back." She looked up at me, tears filling her beautiful green eyes again. I thought she would be cried out by now, but then, I thought I would be too. "Jesse was out there with him when he fell. He tried to save him, but it all happened so fast, didn't it Jesse?"

I nodded my head. Jennifer loved me, and never once questioned my story. Mrs. Danvers, however, wasn't as trusting. She turned her eyes on me and I could see her sizing me with those coal black, suspicious pits. "What the hell was he doing out there?" she asked, never once taking her eyes off me.

"We was checking the fencing. We let the cows out there to feed off the grass and some strong winds a few days ago pushed some of the wire off the posts."

"Seems to me you need better fencing around that drop off. Better get it done before that baby is old enough to crawl out there, don't you think?"

"Yes ma'am. That's an idea." I stared right back at her, never letting my eyes wander from her pinched, bitter face.

"Is he buried yet?" she asked, still stuffing her mouth with those potatoes.

"He's still moving," I said.

"Yup, they doing that back home, too. Is that what that pen is back in town? I seen it when we went by and thought they looked dead inside."

"Yes, but we have him in the barn."

"After I eat I want to go out an' look at him." She looked first at me then Jennifer. "Alone," she continued.

"I don't know if that's a good idea. He's in pretty rough shape," I said, thinking of that eye hanging onto his cheek.

"I don't care what you think. I'm going out to see him and I don't want no company."

"Suit yourself," I said, finalizing the business.

After supper I sat on the porch, rolled a cigarette and smoked it while the old woman visited her son. She came out of the barn after just a few minutes, her face scrunched with hardly any emotion on it. "He's dead alright," she mumbled as she passed me and went on into the house.

I sat there on the porch a while, listening to the house behind me settle into that hushed quiet of an evening winding to an end. Jennifer had washed the dishes and placed them back in the cupboards. She could never go to bed until the evening chores were finished and the house was spotless. She always said the worst thing in the world was to wake up to a dirty house. She meant it when she said it, but I think her philosophy might have changed since then. Now, the worst thing in the world was having a dead husband who couldn't sit still.

Jennifer stuck her head out the door and wished me a good night. I wished the same for her and she went off to bed. I sat a while, smoked another cigarette then, when I suspected everyone was asleep, walked to the barn to see Wesley.

Wesley grunted when I entered the barn and strained against the ropes holding his hands behind his back. "Hey, Wes," I said lighting an oil lamp, set it on the floor and pulled the milking stool up to the front of his pen and sat. "Did you have a good visit with your mother?" I asked. He slammed his body against the locked gate. I wasn't really sure if he understood me, but his reaction to mention of his mother indicated he might have. "I know," I replied to his unspoken comment, "but she is your mother and she wanted to see you again. She will only be here a few days then things will settle down again."

I rose from the stool and ran my fingers through his hair. He always had beautiful dark hair, as thick as a horse's mane. He snapped his teeth at my arm, but couldn't reach it. "I love you so much," I said then looked around the barn conspiratorially. "We're all alone. We could have some fun while the women are asleep."

He grunted. I took that as approval. I untied his hands then immediately secured them to the walls of the neighboring pens. He stood with his arms stretched to either side, as though he were awaiting an embrace. I climbed in with him, ran my hands up and down his back, kissed his neck and ears, just the way he always loved it. After all these years, I knew what turned him on and I did everything I could to show him how good we were together. He couldn't say it was over after this.

Even if it was incredible making love to him again after our summer-long hiatus, I still had trouble keeping things going. There was a smell to him, not exactly bad smell, but not something that comes from the living. Of course, he'd been dead for a few days.

I reached around and unbuttoned his shirt, exposing his solid chest and belly, ran my fingers up and over him, feeling the ticks of hair count off the inches against my palm. He groaned again as my fingers found his nipples and toyed with them. They were hard and firm and I plucked at them the way he always liked it.

I was getting excited now and stripped the clothes from his body. I massaged his shoulders, ran my hands over his back and down the curve of his spine, my fingers easily slipping inside him.

I pushed my pants down, spit on my palm and rubbed it over my steadily growing hardness, then pushed myself inside him. Wesley turned his head and snapped his teeth in my direction. I pushed in deeper, until I could go no further and just let it sit there a while. There wasn't the sweet warm wetness I was familiar with. It was cold and clammy, like an early morning fog.

"You like that Wes?" I asked, running my hands over his belly. "Please tell me you like this." His flesh did not feel like flesh. It was too soft, too pliable, but with an almost rubber-like consistency, like the skin that grows on the top of Jenn's chocolate pudding. The way it moved over his muscles felt like the flesh wanted to slide right off his body.

I licked his shoulder, and tasted the all consuming rot eating at him. Down further, his cock lay flaccid in a nest of hair that'd grown brittle. Clumps of what had once been beautiful dark hair fell out in patches into my palm. "Oh Wes," I moaned, heartbroken at what death had done to his body.

He let out a low, whimpering moan and began pushing back on me, fucking me as fiercely as I was fucking him. He did like it. He wanted this as much as I did. I kissed his back again, ignoring the unholy flavor of him. I worked him until I couldn't hold off any longer. When I let go inside him, I clung to his normally rock-like frame—now soft, with the faintest hint of squishiness beneath—as my knees threatened to pitch me into the straw at our feet. He growled and snapped his teeth at the air. I pulled out of him with a slimy shiver of iced flesh and noticed some of him still on me. Something that shouldn't have been there. He was coming apart on the inside. I cleaned myself with a handful of straw.

That was when I heard the voice. "Wesley I been thinking about what I said and..."

It was his mother. She stepped into the barn, the lamplight illuminating us like it was day. It didn't take her long to make the connection to what had just taken place here. Her eyes grew to the size of dinner plates. She opened her mouth and uttered the one word that took away all sympathy I might have had for her. "Faggots!" she cried.

I dropped the bloody straw, hitched up my pants. "Freaks!" she bellowed, "Just like that O'Malley boy. I should 'a known marriage wouldn't fix you." She turned to me, hate glaring in her face like a hell born fire. "Sexing a dead man. You monster!"

She turned and ran from the barn towards the house. She was going to expose Wesley and me, demean our love to a dirty sex act. I couldn't have that. It would hurt Jennifer too much. I had to protect her.

I chased after Mrs. Danvers. I had to take her down before she reached the porch so, grabbing the first weapon that came to hand, I scooped one of the chickens from the ground by its legs and struck her in the head. The chicken squawked as its neck snapped against the back of the old woman's skull. Mrs. Danvers pitched forward, face down in the dusty yard. I dropped on top of her, continued to hit her until the air was thick with feathers and the old woman lay still in the dirt. She let out a moan as I dragged her back into the barn. Unconscious, not dead. The old bitch was tougher than I had thought.

"Now look what happened," I said to Wesley.

He grunted and pulled at the ropes. His tongue lolled from his mouth and over his lips with a dry papery shuck. Flakes of skin fell from his mouth like bloody snow.

I picked up the lamp, set it down out of the way, and kicked the stool across the barn floor. Then, I opened the gate to Wesley's pen and rolled his mother in with him. I closed the gate again, cut his ropes, freeing his arms. He immediately fell to his knees and began feeding.

The first bite woke Mrs. Danvers. She began screaming, then screamed even louder once she realized she was being eaten, and who was eating her. She flailed her hands at him, breaking a nail on his stony forehead. She grew weak in seconds and settled into low groaning protests.

When he was finished eating, I pulled the milking stool back over to the stall, opened the gate, and slammed her in the head with the stool a few times destroying the brain, in case that was how they come back. She would not be telling anyone what she saw out here. I slammed the gate closed again. Wesley lunged for me, but he was too slow.

He surprised me when, instead of clawing at me, he stroked my cheek instead. He remembered me. He wasn't lost. Then, with a voice that croaked more than spoke, he said, "Jesse....love."

I couldn't hide my smile. He still loved me. After what happened between us, after him trying to end us and my angry, rejected outburst that sent him over the edge of that cliff, he still loved me. "Oh Wesley," I moaned and jumped onto the gate holding him in the pen. I grabbed his face and pulled him to me, pressing my mouth against his. His face was still coated with his mother's blood, and now mine was as well. I slid my tongue in his mouth and tasted his dry, musty breath. He began to pull away and when he did, I felt a slight sting. One of his teeth had grazed my mouth and opened a small wound on my lower lip.

I thought nothing of it until later. It's always the later that gets us in the end. .

And Wesley had bitten me. It wasn't a large bite, just a tiny pinprick of a wound, but could that be enough to infect me? Was I now destined to become like him. Was I going to die and come back?

I was still awake when the sun rose and I heard Jennifer in the kitchen preparing breakfast. I slid out of bed, dressed then joined her. "Is Mrs. Danvers still asleep?" I asked nonchalantly.

"Oh yes, she probably is," Jen said. "She's something, isn't she?"

"Yeah, something." I pulled a chair from the table, sat and slid into my boots. "I'll get started on the chores, then have breakfast with you," I said and gave my sister a peck on the cheek before walking out the door. I was not going to do any chores though. I was going out to discover what happened to our guest.

I stepped into the barn and my lower lip began to throb. I touched my finger to it and Wesley chuckled low and deep. He slid me a hard, bitter smile. He touched his own lips, that gruff laugh rolled out of him again. I understood then. He had bitten me on purpose. He infected me with that little scratch of teeth over my lip. I was doomed to be like him. I killed him, and now he returned the favor.

"You bastard!" I screamed. I was furious both at him and myself.

How could I have been so stupid? How could I have let his mouth anywhere near me? "You're leaving this place. You're leaving today!" His lips achingly turned upward in a death mask grin and he grunted again.

I stormed back to the house and told Jennifer what I found in the barn, that Mrs. Danvers was dead and Wesley killed her.

"We can't keep him here any longer," she said. "We need to take him to town. Put him in that corral with the others."

I nodded, but was already thinking twice about it. I don't know if I wanted to go on without him close to me. My belly twisted and threatened to empty itself at the thought of his leaving me forever. My lip throbbed and I pinched it between my fingers.

She was right though, and I knew it. We couldn't risk him getting loose and hurting the baby, or Jennifer. I was lost, but they could still be saved. That afternoon we packed him in the back of the wagon and rode him into town.

My lip is throbbing almost constantly now. I can feel the infection moving through my face and the vision in my left eye has gone cloudy as the nerves have begun to die.

Hunger is my constant companion. I cannot manage to keep anything down, though. All of my favorite foods—baked beans, biscuits, even Jenn's incredible Apple Crumble Pie—sit on my tongue like rancid butter. Nothing tastes right. Nothing seems edible... Except MEAT.

I crave it endlessly. I can't stop thinking about it. Not beef, pork or fowl. I have tried them all and have not been able to keep them down. Nothing satisfies me. I need (MEAT) something that I can actually swallow and won't make me (MEAT) retch.

What I want is throbbing inside Jennifer's head. Sweet, delicate MEAT. It would take just one bite. One little bite to break through her skull and get the fresh, gooey MEAT inside. It would be so easy. Just one little...

No! I cannot let this happen. I will not hurt my sister. I will not...

MEAT! Tasty, sweet Elizabeth with her human veal. Baby MEAT. My mouth waters at her infant scent. Her skull is soft. It will take no effort at all to get at all that delicious MEAT inside.

No! What am I thinking? How can I even consider hurting her? Or Jennifer? But I am so hungry. So damned hungry.

I am dying, and I know it. The realization is a tough one, but I know there is nothing I can do about that. I can, however, remove the threat to the last of my living family. I have to leave them. I hurt Wesley, but I will not hurt them. I cannot (MEAT) stay here any longer. I need to be with the one person I can no longer hurt.

This evening, after Jennifer has gone off to bed, I will be taking the wagon into town where I will meet my end with Wesley in the corral. I will rest myself at his feet and let nature take its course and die hoping for another chance with him. Perhaps, he will forgive me for what I have done, and maybe, just maybe we will be together again. This time, forever.

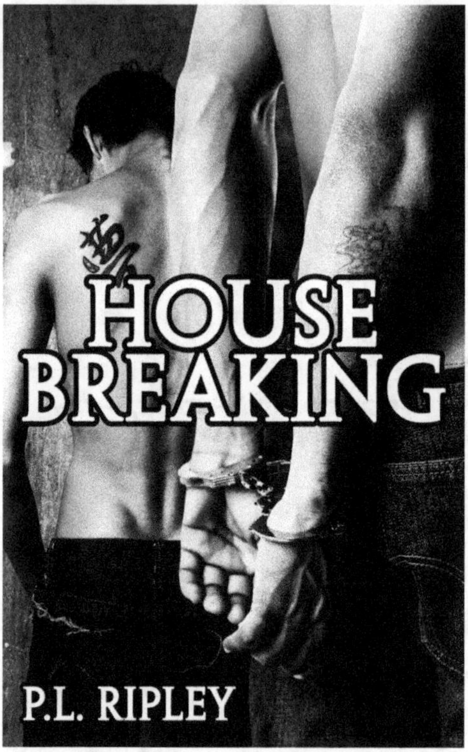
HOUSE
BREAKING
P.L. RIPLEY

House Breaking

Chapter 1: Enter the Brothers

I'm not rich. I tell people this, but they don't believe it. Why would I live in a three-story Victorian in Finnerman Heights unless I had money, they ask. Why would I have a house filled with antiques and a Mercedes in the garage unless I was loaded?

The fact is, I inherited the house, and everything in it, when my Grandmother passed away a few years ago. I can barely pay the taxes on the place. As for the antiques, there is an old armoire in the foyer, but the rest of the furniture is that pre-fab shit you get at WalMart. And the Mercedes hasn't run in years. I have been searching for a buyer for the house a while, but the way the real estate market keeps floundering, I'm going to take a bath on the deal if it ever gets sold. I just know that I have to do something soon, either sell it or get a loan to make some much-needed repairs. The paint is peeling everywhere on the face of the house, a few of the external wallboards are loose and hanging off a single nail, and there is rot along most of the windowsills. It's starting to look like the Addams Family lives here.

The only real alteration I have done to the house is the dungeon I built in the basement. It hasn't seen much action in the last two years though, not since Jimmy left. In a smaller town like this, it's difficult to find someone who shares my particular sexual proclivities. The few I have discovered were novices to the art of submission and several of them left in tears, claiming I had gone too far. Perhaps, Jimmy was a fluke. He was the only man I had found who could take all that I could give, and I love to give. Jimmy is gone now though, he left me for a biker with more toys and a hair trigger temper. I hope they are happy together.

I own my own business, a small bookstore downtown, but the way books sell these days I'm lucky to afford lunch. I have a few regular customers who come in on a weekly basis, and the summer tourists help me out a great deal, but for the most part I'm just getting by.

I'm not rich, but people think I am. Maybe that's why they broke into my house that night.

It happened during the worst snowstorm we had seen in decades. I had arrived home at about six o'clock that night, fighting snow drifts and icy streets all the way. By the time I had dinner at eight, another couple of inches had fallen. I kept thinking—as I ate my frozen pizza in front of the television—that the power would probably go out. If the power did go out, I would have no heat and the old Victorian would cool off in no time. I could have used the many fireplaces to stay warm and keep the pipes from freezing, but I had never had the chimneys inspected. Besides, the only wood in the house was in the walls themselves or the cheap furniture lying about.

I went to bed at ten, piling mounds of blankets and comforters on the bed in case the heat did go out in the night. I didn't want to have to get out of bed to get them if I needed them.

It must have been a few hours later when I heard the noise coming from downstairs. I sat up in bed, cocking my ear to see if I could hear it again. I wasn't really sure the thumping I had heard was real, or just part of the dream I had been having. It came again, this time a bit louder. It was followed by some muttered whispering.

I slid out of bed as quietly as I could, pulled my grandmother's old Winchester rifle out of the closet and slipped into a pair of jeans. I had only fired the rifle a few times, back when I had first moved into the house. It kicked like a mule and it had left a bruise the size of a goat's head on my shoulder. I don't even have any ammunition left for the thing, but it is intimidating enough to make anyone wanting to fuck with me think twice before charging. I padded as silently as possible down the stairs, the empty gun gripped solidly in my fist. There were two men in the living room. One had a flashlight and was waving it around the room, looking for something worthy of taking. The other I could only see in silhouette; he was carrying a large cloth bag that looked half full already. I hadn't realized I had that much of value lying around.

The bag man stumbled over something, nearly falling to the floor. The other shushed him. "Jesus, you wanna wake that asshole up?" he whispered.

"Too late," I called out and flipped the light switch in the wall next to me, hoping the power was still on. It was. The chandelier in the center of the room lit up and the two men squinted against the light.

They saw the rifle I was holding, the business end pointing right at the bag man. "Oh, fuck," he said and the pair immediately threw their hands in the air. The bag clattered to the floor.

They were dressed for the weather. Both in heavy parkas, wool hats and gloves. "Take off your hats and gloves, boys, you are going to be here a while," I said and cocked the rifle for emphasis.

"Might as well take your coats off too," I continued after their heads and hands were undressed. I recognized the pair. They were brothers and they hung out in the downtown area all summer. The older one, the brother who had been carrying the bag, had come into my store a few months ago. He was about twenty or maybe twenty-one, tall, lean and his pale skinny arms were covered in tattoos from the shoulder to wrists. There were large gauges in his ears, stretching the lobes to twice their normal length. He, like his younger brother, had naturally bright red hair that almost looked like his scalp was on fire, and pale eyelashes that were nearly translucent.

Back in October he had come in the store looking for a certain story by H. P. Lovecraft. He had described what happened in the story and I immediately knew which one he was talking about. I had been really into Lovecraft when I was in college and had read nearly everything written by him. The guy had followed me to the *Horror* section and stood close to me as I rummaged the overstocked shelves, looking for the anthology he wanted. I could feel the heat coming from his body; he stood that close. I inhaled and the scent of cigarettes and old sweat coming from him overtook the musty stink of old books that permeated the shop.

"Is this it?" he asked and reached to the top shelf. The air outside had that crisp fall chill to it, but the boy was still wearing one of the sleeveless shirts he had been wearing all summer. I turned to him as he reached up and the shock of light, nearly blond underarm hair waved in my face. The strong stench of sweat assaulted me. It was a gorgeous smell, a manly smell, and the only thing I wanted to do was shove my face in there and suck that stink out of his pit.

But it was the book he had come in for and he pulled his arm back to his side, hiding that sweaty, furry pit from my sight, making me want it even more. I followed him to the counter, watching his tight, near-perfect ass shift beneath the baggy jeans. He paid in cash, then scooped the paperback in his hand and gave me this weird, lopsided smile. "Thanks, man." he said and sent a little wink my way before leaving.

It took twenty minutes for my erection to go down after he left. I felt like a fool going all gaga over the kid. In my eyes he was just a kid. I was easily old enough to be his father and well... shit, with my fiftieth birthday only a couple of months away, I could have been his grandfather. The age difference didn't matter to my dick then, and with him in my house, a virtual prisoner, his age meant even less to the old one-eyed beast.

I picked up their coats from where they had dropped them on the coach and rummaged through the pockets, while balancing the rifle on my forearm. There was a bundle of rope in one of the pockets, but no weapons.

"What's this for?" I asked. "Planning on tying me up?"

"Look," the Lovecraft fan said, "we weren't going to hurt you. That was just for insurance."

"I see. Just beat the fuck out of me, tie me up and leave me for dead. Was that your plan?"

The kid with the flashlight, the younger brother, began shaking. "Jesus Christ, Kevin, is that what you had planned?"

"Don't say my name. Fuck, what's wrong with you?"

"Kevin is it? What's your name?" I asked the younger one. He looked a year or two younger than Kevin and not nearly as rough. He had a few tattoos on his arms and a pierced eyebrow, but no gauges. He also seemed a bit slow. Not mentally retarded, just a little dim. He was the sort of kid who, when he was in school, took the lower level or special education classes and did okay in them, but would have been lost in anything higher. He was the kind of guy who would get a job in a factory or a mechanical shop and live a pretty decent life, as long as no one took advantage of him. I suspected that was exactly what was happening now; the older brother getting him involved in something he would never do on his own.

"Jesse," he replied and looked down at the floor. He seemed really bothered by this situation and I had to say I couldn't really blame him. He seemed like a good kid but he had fucked up, and fucked up bad. Whether his brother talked him into this or not, which was probably the case, the law would see him acting on his own. If I called the police—which I had planned on doing—he could see time for this. He was too old for Juvie and even though he probably wouldn't get a lot of time, he would have a record that would follow him around for the rest of his life. That was, of course, if he didn't already have one.

"All right Jesse." I turned to his brother, "Kevin. Now that we've been introduced I'm going to need both of you to strip."

"What?" Kevin glared, balling his hands into fists.

"I said strip, right down to the underwear. I don't want you guys running off before the police get here."

"No fucking way," Kevin muttered.

"Kevin, just do it," his little brother begged. "We are in enough trouble as it is."

"Fuck you Jesse. You might want this fag checking you out but...."

I threw the rifle onto my shoulder and pointed it at the tattooed punk. "What did you call me?" I said through gritted teeth. I had been called worse by more intimidating people than this kid, but I was not about to tolerate the slight in my own home. A man's home is his castle, as they say. Even if that castle is falling down around them.

Kevin's skin sunk to an even paler shade than it had already been. I had scared him and scared him badly. He immediately shucked off his shirt and bent over to unlace his boots. Jesse had already gotten down to his underwear and he stood with his arms crossed over his chest, shivering. It was cold in the house. I keep the thermostat at a steady sixty-four degrees. Warm enough to keep the pipes from freezing, but not exactly the right temperature to run around in your underwear. He wore gray boxer-briefs and the bulge in the front of them looked like he had a softball shoved in there.

"Okay Jesse, I need you to work with me on this." I tossed him the rope. Kevin had stripped to his boxers and I noticed something very large shifting around behind the material when he moved. "I want you to tie your brother up. You can tie knots right?"

"Yes, I can tie knots. You're not going to hurt him are you?"

"Nobody is going to get hurt as long as you do what I tell you."

He pulled his brother's arms behind his back and tied them, then I told Kevin to sit on the couch while Jesse secured his legs. Once he was done, Jesse stepped away so I could inspect his work. The bulge in the front of his boxer-briefs had pumped up considerably while he had worked, tenting the material out and away from his slim, hairless belly. It seemed to me that tying his brother down might have turned him on a bit. The knots were tight. Kevin was going nowhere.

"Turn around," I said to the young Jesse.

"Yes sir," he said and turned his back to me. I pulled out a pair of handcuffs I always kept in the armoire (if you look around the house you will find all sorts of toys hidden here and there), and locked them around the young man's wrists, then slipped the key in my jeans pocket. He winced when the metal touched his skin. The handcuffs were cold to the touch. I should have breathed on them like a doctor does to his stethoscope before placing it on a patient's chest. I noticed odd marks on the backs of his legs. I knelt to the floor to get a better look at them. There were six ragged strips where the skin had been broken. They were wide, open sores and I could see the gristly meat of his legs shining out through the cuts. It looked like someone had caned him. "How did you get these?" I asked, looking up at the boy.

"I don't know," he said, his voice becoming very soft, almost a mumble. He was lying. I looked over at his brother on the couch. He turned his head away, refusing to look at me. I helped Jesse down onto the couch next to his brother then went behind them to the phone. I still use my grandmother's old phone. It is the type where the receiver lies in a cradle to cut off the connection. It has push buttons to dial, but it is one of the models in which that technology was very new when it was built. I picked up the receiver, and dialed 911, while simultaneously pushing down on the little plastic buttons to hang up the phone. I wasn't really calling the cops, I had other plans for these boys, but I wanted them to think I had made the call. I felt I needed the threat of the police to convince them to let me play. I would never have touched them if they had not wanted me to. I was not that sort of man. I needed them to agree. After all, a yes was still a yes, even when blackmail was involved.

"I need to report a break-in," I said into the phone, giving the best performance I could manage. I heard Jesse groan from the couch. I looked back and he had his head on his brother's shoulder.

"I'm sorry," Kevin whispered to him. "I shouldn't have involved you in this."

I gave my little speech, telling the "police" how I had the attempted burglars secured and they could take their time, what with the storm and all, and then I hung up the phone and went back to my *guests.*

I pulled a footstool before the two boys and sat. "So," I said, "it's going to be a while before the police arrive. How should we spend our time?" I looked from the boy Jesse to his older, meaner brother Kevin and waited for suggestions. When none came, I looked at the younger boy. "I'm going to suppose you don't have a record. Is that right?" I asked.

Jesse nodded, "Yes, I've never been arrested."

"How about you, Kevin?"

"Fuck you!" he barked.

"Two B&Es and an assault," Jesse blurted as he leaned away from his brother and sat upright again.

"Shut up Jesse, you fucking idiot!"

"I'm not an idiot! Don't say that. You promised you wouldn't call me that no more," Jesse whined.

Kevin's demeanor immediately changed. The tenseness had drained from his chest and shoulders and he no longer sat rigid, ready to pounce. His entire body sagged a bit and his eyes had gone from cold, emotionless rocks to gentle emerald pools as he stared at his brother. There was a deep connection between them. They loved each other, deeply. "Is he right?" I asked Kevin. "Is that your record?"

Kevin nodded his head, not looking at me. His eyes never left his brother's.

"I see," I said and pondered how to approach the boys with the proposition I had in mind. I wanted their permission to do what I wanted to do. I already had them secured so they were no longer a threat to me and I could always make a real call to the police and have them taken away, but something told me that I could deal with this my way and have a better outcome. I had never really trusted the legal system. It seemed to me that the prisons just made better criminals than rehabilitated them. Without their permission though, I would be seen as a kidnapper or worse. I had never done anything to anyone unless they wanted me to. "Tell you what," I began, "you boys need to be punished. I don't think criminals should get away scot-free. Even though you wouldn't have gotten away with anything of value here, it's still my stuff you were stealing. It might not be much, but it is all I have.

"So," I continued, "you have a choice. We can sit here like civilized people and wait for the cops, and Jesse will have a record and Kevin will go away for a long, long time, or I can take things into my own hands then release you before they arrive."

Jesse looked over at his brother. "I don't want to be arrested," he said.

"Don't worry," Kevin grunted back. He looked at me and said, "You don't have the guts to do anything to us. I know what you people are. All fucking cowards. You're a nelly little faggot and you don't have the balls to...."

I leaped to my feet and came toward him.

"Don't you fucking touch me!" he screamed, straining against the ropes. "Get your faggot hands off me."

I reached out, grabbed the rope trailing from his hands to his feet in one hand and yanked on his hair with the other. I lifted him from his seat, spun him around and tossed him back down so he was bent over the couch. and yanked his boxers down. I slammed my open palm against his ass. He bellowed and bucked against me but I had a hold of his neck too tightly.

Jesse began whining and pushed himself as far from us as he could and ended up on the floor. I brought my palm down again and again, smacking his smooth, pale ass. Each strike brought a ripple to the flesh like skipping a rock over a lake. It was a lovely sight and it took all my willpower not to knead that flesh and spread the cheeks open to get a good look at—and possibly a taste of—that hole in between. When I assumed he had learned to keep his mouth shut I pulled his underwear back up onto his hips, let go of him and leaned over to help Jesse back onto the couch.

Kevin rolled back so he was in the sitting position again. He glared at me, but didn't say anything. Jesse had that deer-in-headlights look. He was stunned by what had just happened. I suspected he had never seen his older brother bested before. I also noticed the ample bulge in the front of his boxer-briefs had grown again. His underwear stuck out much more now than it had when he was tying Kevin originally. "You liked that?" I smiled at him, nodding my head towards his crotch.

He looked down, noticing the state of his erection and a deep scarlet filled his neck and face. Kevin looked over at him and scowled. "I have to pee," Jesse said.

"Can you hold it?" I asked.

"I don't know," he said.

"Jesus, just let him go to the bathroom," Kevin groaned. "He has a small bladder. He's gonna piss himself." He looked over at his brother and everything in his features softened again. It happened every time he turned his attention away from me and onto Jesse. He seemed to love him more than I ever thought it possible for a man to love his sibling.

"Please," he continued, "take him to the bathroom."

"All right," I said and gently helped Jesse from the couch.

"Thank you," Kevin mumbled, not looking up at us as we passed him. It must have been very difficult for him to humble himself like that. To ask me, a man he had intended to rob, a man he seemed to see as beneath him, for help. But he hadn't done it for himself, he'd done it for his brother. I had a feeling there was not much he would not do for him.

"I'm going to leave the bathroom door open to keep an eye on you," I said. "You can try to escape if you want, but remember, I will have your brother in there with me. He will go to jail if you run and the police will track you down. You will not truly get away." He glared up at me and I could almost see the plan he had in head dissolving. "You seem like a smart guy, Kevin. Don't fuck with me." I then walked Jesse to the bathroom. "Do you want to sit or you want me to hold your dick for you?" I asked before lifting the seat.

He grinned a handsome mouth full of even, white teeth as his cheeks exploded in the same fiery scarlet as his hair. "I'll sit," he replied, sheepishly, not letting his eyes lift from the floor. I slid his underwear down to his ankles; his long, pale cock had lost its erection, but not it's power. It flopped in front of my eyes, nearly hypnotizing me with it's lovely shimmering whiteness. It was like a ghost against the brutal red of the pubic hair surrounding it.

He sat on the toilet and I turned my back to him. I could still see him in the mirror over the sink, but only from the shoulders up. "Did your brother do that to your legs?" I asked, referring to the gashes along his calf muscles.

"He didn't mean to," Jesse replied as the tinkle of splashing water filled the small room.

"How did it happen?"

"We play a game. It just got out of hand."

"How often do you play this game?" I asked.

"A lot."

"And how often does it get out of hand?"

"A lot," he repeated and I could hear the sadness in his voice. He sounded like he wanted to cry but was fighting it off.

I turned back to him. He was bouncing on the toilet seat, trying to shake the last of the piss from his dick. "I'm done," he said and I lifted him by the elbows, bent to pull his underwear back to his hips.

"Tell me about the game," I said. And so he did.

Chapter 2
The Games Boys Play

They were two boys who only had each other. Their father left just after Jesse was born, then not long after Jesse turned eight and Kevin celebrated his tenth birthday, their mother discovered pursuits more exciting than her own children. Mainly heroin and men. Both in great quantities.

The brothers were taken from their mother and transferred from foster home to foster home, but they were lucky enough to be moved together. They were not separated and they grew closer than brothers normally would, or as some said, should. But they only had each other. They relied on each other and their relationship grew from that mutual need.

It began innocently enough in a strange, new bedroom with a strange, new family. A brief touch, a light tickle, a late night hug. The touches turned to pinches, the pinches to something more fierce, more brutal. As the boys grew to men, they realized what excited each other. For Jesse, it was a hard slap, the crack of a leather belt stinging his backside. Pain made him feel alive. It made him feel sexy.

Kevin had learned he liked doling out pain, almost as much as Jesse enjoyed receiving it.

I had thought at first that Jesse had been being manipulated by his older brother; forced into an abusive, incestuous relationship with a man who cared only for his own pleasure. Jesse had convinced me otherwise.

"This is who we are," Jesse said, "who I am. He doesn't make me do anything I don't want to do. It's just that sometimes Kevin goes too far. Sometimes he hurts me too much. He doesn't mean to, it's just...."

"He doesn't understand your limits," I finished for him. He nodded sadly.

"Yeah."

"When I was about your age I was trained by an amazing man, Master Don. He showed me the key to being a great dominant," I said. "It's about knowing limitations. In order to know your partners limitations, you must first know your own."

Jesse giggled. "Master Don. Sounds like a dinosaur."

I didn't understand at first until I sounded it out in my own head. Master Don—mastodon. Pretty clever of him. I wanted to train Kevin, show him control so he and his brother could have the fun they wanted with each other. I liked Jesse, he seemed like a sweet guy and if things continued between them the way they had been, he could end up with some pretty serious injuries. I also wanted to have the fun that Jimmy and I used to have. I could accomplish both in one night.

When I had made the fake phone call to the cops, I had just planned on treating the boys to my expert mouth then throwing their asses out into the storm without their clothes. The blowjobs would have been for me, the naked in the storm was their punishment. It had been so long since I had been with a man in any capacity that doling out a couple of blowjobs would have eased the tension for a while. But knowing that they played the same game I liked to play... well, how could I resist?

"All right, let's see what your brother is up to," I said and escorted Jesse from the bathroom and back to the couch. A wave of relief passed over Kevin's face as I set Jesse down next to him.

"What the hell were you two doing in there? Knitting your own toilet paper?" Kevin groaned.

I ignored him. "Do we wait for the cops, or do we handle this ourselves?" I asked.

"Up yours!" Kevin barked.

"So, I take this as a *yes*," I said and went to the kitchen, grabbed a knife from the block on the counter and came back to the brothers.

Kevin's eyes grew nearly as wide as dinner plates. He squirmed against the ropes and I could see he was holding his breath, waiting for the initial plunge of the knife.

"Settle down. I'm just going to cut your ropes," I said and brought the knife down on the rope holding Kevin's feet together. I kept his hands tied though. I needed him to walk, but that was as free as I was going to let him get for a while. "Can you stand?" I asked Jesse and he struggled to get to his feet. It is very difficult to get up from a low position when your hands are secured behind your back, so I scooped an arm around his waist and pulled him to his feet. I held onto Kevin while I did this, my fingers intertwined with his short red hair. I felt I could trust to let Jesse walk down to the basement, but I wasn't letting his brother have any freedom. Kevin let out a shriek as I gave his hair a good tug.

"Listen to me and do everything I tell you to," I said into Kevin's ear. "We are going to the basement and if you struggle or try to get away, I will push you down those stairs. If you are lucky, you won't break your neck, but you could easily break a bone or two. Do you understand me?"

"Yes," Kevin replied, nodding his head and wincing at the tugs on his hair the movement caused.

"From here on out everything you say to me will be ended in *sir*. Do you understand?"

"Yes," he said.

I tugged on his hair again. "Everything you say will end in sir," I repeated. "Do you understand?"

"Yes sir," he replied.

"Good boy." I looked over to his brother.

"Jesse, I know this is going to be difficult with your hands cuffed behind you, but I want you to open that door on your right. Inside there is a light switch on the left side. Turn that on and carefully walk down the steps. I don't want you to fall, so take one step at a time if you have to. Okay?"

"Yes sir," he replied. He had been listening. He seemed a much better learner than his asshole brother.

Jesse put his back to the door, turned the knob with his secured hands and flipped the light switch on. The switch was low on the wall. I had had it installed that way so Jimmy could get to it when he was in the same situation as Jesse was. I had made him descend these steps the same way more times than I could count over the years.

He took the stairs slowly, just as I had told him to and I followed behind, with Kevin's hair in my fist. When we got to the bottom, the boys saw what await them and they let out small, worried groans. Kevin seemed more worried of the two. He should have been.

The dungeon Jimmy and I had created in the basement looked like a true dungeon, a place in which any of those screwed up priests from The Spanish Inquisition could feel at home. When we first started remodeling the room, we had intended to put up dry wall so that later, when we decided to sell the house, we could easily transform the basement from a dark place to explore our dirtiest sexual desires to a happy family room complete with blue and yellow walls and a large screen television.

However, once we began clearing and cleaning the room, we realized the walls were constructed of large slabs of stone. How could we realistically cover these stone walls when they fit so well with our intended use of the room? So, we left them as they were and simply covered the cement floor with the hard rubber flooring used in gyms. We put in a few Gothic-looking light fixtures and then set up the restraining devices, a cabinet for our tools of torture, and a leather swing, and we had our dream room.

Now, these two boys were about to experience the pleasures of submission.

I directed the little shit, Kevin, to the St. Andrew's Cross set up on the right of the stairs and pushed him backward against it. He began fighting almost immediately, pushing at me with his open palms and kicking his legs out. I stepped on his feet to keep them on the floor while I called Jesse over. I pulled the handcuff key from my pocket and freed his hands. "Help me strap his hands down," I said to him, while I pulled at the ropes securing Kevin's hands together off him and let them coil to the floor.

Jesse ran to us, pushed his brothers hand in place and began looping the strap around his brother's wrist. "Don't you fucking help him!" Kevin yelled, but Jesse just kept working at it. "You do this and I will kill you, Jesse. I will fucking kill you when I get out of this!"

"I'm sorry, Kevin. You need to be here," Jesse replied, his face set in determination. He understood exactly what was happening here. I had underestimated him and felt like a heel for doing it. Just because he may have a learning disability, it did not make him stupid. Not in any way.

I got the strap around Kevin's left wrist then we worked together to get his legs. I held the right one down while Jesse tightened the strap around his ankle, then we did the same for the left. Once he was in and immobile, I turned to Jesse. "Do you want to help me with him or just watch?"

He seemed to think on it a minute, then nodded his head. He wanted to help. I smiled. There was a deviant little Dom inside him screaming to get out.

"It's cold down here!" Kevin barked. Gooseflesh rose on his arms, chest and belly as he strained against his bindings.

"Don't worry," I said, "I'll warm you up in a minute."

I went to the toys cabinet, opened it and pulled out a small cat-o'-nine-tails and left the doors open so Kevin could see the tools that would be used on him. Sweat broke out on his brow and he began blubbering an apology. "Please, please don't do this," he begged.

I brought the leather straps down on his belly, lightly, but he screamed like I was killing him. He thrashed against the bindings and I brought it down again and again, each time a little harder than the last. Red marks rose up on his pale flesh and Jesse moved in and kissed them. He lightly ran his fingers up his brother's body, caressing his nipples as his tongue soothed the red marks from the whip straps. Pain and pleasure was as delectable a combination as salty and sweet. I was amazed at his quick understanding, but perhaps he always had always known.

The boys were still in their underwear and the excitement both were feeling was painfully evident in the swell pushing at the cotton material, Jesse much more so than Kevin. I had left the knife I used to cut the ropes back upstairs but there was a hunting knife in the cabinet. I slid the blade under Kevin's boxers and he shivered at the cold metal touching his skin, then I sliced downward, freeing his cock to the chilly dungeon air.

His cock was long and pale, the head nearly as bright red as the hair surrounding it. I grabbed his balls and tugged on them, hard, and Kevin let out a squeal of protest.

"Shut the fuck up," I growled and gave his nuts a good slap. His cock bounced and grew even harder. He liked this. Jesse smiled, his face only inches from his brother's crotch. He reached out and took a turn at Kevin's balls with his long, graceful fingers, slapping them with just the tips.

"Ow. Christ, Jesse," Kevin whined, but his cock rose to it's full height and a quick drop of pre-come danced over the head. I pulled it into my mouth, tasting the sweet nectar while Jesse slapped and flicked his nuts again and again.

"Why are you helping him?" Kevin asked his brother. There were the first traces of tears in his eyes. He had the look of a man betrayed.

"This is for us, Kevin. You and me. Please understand what we are doing." He pressed his forehead to Kevin's. Their eyes bore into one another's.

"I love you so much, Jess," Kevin whispered.

"I know," Jesse replied and brought his open palm up hard against Kevin's balls. Kevin let out a harsh yelp and struggled against his restraints.

When his sack had grown bright red and his nuts had begun to swell I pulled Jesse away from his brother, threw him over the restraining table in the center of the floor and tied his wrists down. His sweet young ass pointed at Kevin and he ground his crotch into the table, gyrating his hips, enticing me with his hungry butt. I pulled his underwear down and rubbed at the skin. He cooed under my hand as I dipped my middle finger in the crack, feeling his smooth, hairless hole within.

I wanted desperately to get in there, to slide my finger in to the second knuckle and feel his heat surround me, but there was still the matter of his brother to contend with. I gave his butt a quick slap. He squealed and pushed his ass out, wanting more. "In time," I said to him and turned, the whip still in my hand, and flicked the leather straps at Kevin's legs, missing him but still making him flinch and cry out.

"How did he get those marks on the backs of his legs?" I asked for the second time that night.

"Fuck you," Kevin said and I brought the whip down on him again. This time it made contact with his thighs, just inches from his swollen scrotum, and brought a harsh red stripe to the pale skin. He screamed and bucked against his bindings. I hadn't really hurt him and had no intention of doing so. This wasn't about abuse, it was about education. If he had caused those marks on Jesse's legs during a game such as the one we were now playing, then he had to learn not to cause real damage.

"I'm going to ask one more time. How did he get those marks on his legs?"

"And I said, fuck you."

I pulled a steel cock ring from the cabinet, shoved it over his cock and forced the swollen balls through the opening. I stood back to admire my handiwork, then slapped the wet head, hard. It snapped back against his belly with a loud smack. He grunted, but didn't cry out as he had with the much less painful whip. I did it again, then again. He whimpered as I touched his swollen balls and gripped them in my fist.

"Do you like hurting him?" I asked, giving his nuts a good squeeze.

Sweat broke out over his face and his breath came out in ragged little burps. He was in a great deal of pain, but I wasn't doing anything that could injure him permanently. "Answer me. Do you like hurting him?"

"More than you can imagine," he said through gritted teeth.

"Do you want to damage him?" I asked and closed my fist even tighter around his balls. "How old are those marks on his legs? What did they look like originally? I bet they were pretty nasty, weren't they? I bet he bled a lot, too. He could have gotten an infection from those cuts. You could have seriously hurt him. They seem to be healing, but what about next time? He might lose too much blood and you will have to answer some pretty tough questions by the ER doctors or the police."

He turned to me, his brow furrowed, and I saw the look in his eyes that told me I was right.

"I want to help you," I said. "Let me teach you control. I want to help you learn your own limits and help you go beyond them, so you can do the same with Jesse, but safely. You don't want to really hurt him, do you?"

He looked at his brother lying over the table, his ass quivering, hovering in the air. His pale green eyes, which had been brimming with anger and fear earlier, now just reflected his curiosity and something like hope. There were also tears hovering on the edges of his lids. His eyes traced the rough, scabbed lines on the back of his brother's legs. His bottom lip began to quiver as the tears holding steady in his eyes finally broke free and trickled down his cheeks. "I'm so sorry, Jesse," he moaned. He turned to me. "I want to learn," he said. "I don't want to hurt him."

"Do you want me to teach you?"

He nodded. He knew where he was, in the home of a seasoned master. "Please, I want you to teach me." He wasn't doing this for me or even for himself. He was doing this for his brother. When he looked over at him, I could see the love in his eyes for the boy. He felt the same passion and deep burning love for his brother any man would feel for their lover. I had to admit, I felt a little jealous. I had loved Jimmy, but never as strong as what Kevin seemed to feel for Jesse.

I removed the straps holding him to the cross, holding him in my arms until his shaking legs came back to him. I unknotted the ropes holding Jesse to the table with one hand while holding Kevin upright with the other. Jesse slid from the table. "Go over there," I said, pointing at a spot to the left of the table, "get on your knees and do not touch yourself." Jesse did as ordered while I set Kevin where his brother had been. I suspected I no longer had to restrain Kevin; he was there not because I forced him to be, but because he wanted to be there. He was not going to run, he was not going to fight me. He wanted me to teach him the power of control, and the freedom of submission.

And I was more than eager to start his first lesson.

Chapter 3
Breaking Him Down

I turned to the younger brother. "Jesse," I called to him, "I need your help again. You know your brother better than anyone else, am I right?"

He stood next to the table in his underwear, his arms hugging his sides against the chilly basement air, and nodded in agreement. "Y...yes, sir," he said, his teeth chattering.

"You know how much he can handle? Do you understand his limits?"

He nodded again, a smile playing on his handsome face. He seemed to understand what I was getting at. "Good," I said, "because he is not going to be able to speak once we get started. I need you to tell me when he has had enough. When he can no longer tolerate anymore. Can you do this for me?"

"Yes sir," Jesse said.

I looked at Kevin. I had strapped him down on the table, not because I thought he might bolt now, but because securing him down was part of the ritual. It would not have looked or felt right if he had been left loose. "Are you okay with this?" I asked him. "Do you trust him?"

"With my life," Kevin said without hesitation. A lump rose in my throat with the strong conviction in his eyes. He had meant what he said. I was amazed at how strong their connection was to each other.

I filled his mouth with his own torn underwear and covered it with a thick strip of silver duct tape. He tried to spit the cloth from his mouth, but it was going nowhere. The briefs were yellowed with age and they looked as though he had been wearing them for a few days. They probably tasted like his own funk. I often enjoyed the smell of an unwashed crotch, but I didn't think he shared my admiration for sweaty balls. To bad for him. They were in there and I wasn't pulling the underwear out any time soon.

I pulled a set of clamps from the cabinet and showed them to him. "Do you know what these are?" I asked him. He nodded his head, glanced down at his nipples. They stood like pert, pink mountains on his smooth chest. The cold in the basement had pushed them into peaks, but I thought it might have been his curiosity and excited fear that kept them standing. His cock didn't seem to have much problem staying up. It hovered over his belly like a missile.

He seemed confused when I didn't apply them to his tits but moved instead to his crotch. I opened the first one. It's spring was a fierce thing, snapping shut with a hard plastic shudder when I let go of it. I wrapped my hand around his beautifully pale cock, opened the clamp again and let it shut on a small pull of skin along the underside of his root. He bellowed into the filthy underwear. Saliva leaked out around the material and dribbled down his chin. I applied the second clip and received the same reaction.

Jesse let out a small moan from his spot on the floor. His own erection stood tall and proud from the heavy bush of red pubic hair. Long droplets of pre-come dribbled from the head. His hand hovered over his cock, but he didn't touch it. I had not given him permission to do so yet. Jesse knew the rules of the game.

I retrieved the whip I had been using before securing Kevin to the table and brought the leather straps down on his belly a few times. Not hard, just feathery little touches. I increased the velocity of the downward strokes, each strike hitting harder and harder. Red lines crisscrossed the pale skin just under his chest. His belly flamed in a hot rush. I set my hand on him, felt the heat rise off his stomach like he had a fever.

His eyes followed me as I brought the whip up over my head. I could see him preparing himself for another blow to his skin, then relief as I dropped my hand, the whip lying limp over the rubber floor. I'd learned to keep them guessing what I was going to do next so they would not get bored. If I had given them what they expected, they would have been searching out another man faster than I could unlace their ropes. That was what had happened with Jimmy. I had grown predictable.

I reached out to the clips on his dick and flicked the bottom one with my fingers. It waggled against the tight grip of skin. Kevin groaned in pain. It was odd how clamping off a tiny bit of flesh could be far more painful than a hard crack of the whip against the back or belly. When I released that clamp, letting his pinched fold of skin free to move back into its original shape, he screamed into the underwear gag.

I grabbed his swollen scrotum, feeling the firm testicles inside rolling around over my fingers. Kevin whimpered and his legs shifted against the restraints. His groin ached with the punishment Jesse and I had given him, but what we had done was only the beginning. I pinched off a good amount of skin from his nutsack, pulled it away from his body and applied the clip I had taken from his cock to the red, swollen flesh. The whimper turned to a groan. He huffed deep breaths through his nose.

His cock had begun to dwindle. I unhooked the second clip from the underside, secured that one to his scrotum then took his cock in my mouth. I pulled him all the way into my throat until my lips tickled against the bright red bush sprouting from his flat, pale groin. The metal ring I had slipped around his root tingled an icy coolness against my lips. I pulled off him and his cock glistened with my saliva. I blew a light kiss of air at his cock and watched as it seemed to shiver in the cold, then took it in my warm mouth again. I did this over and over again. Warm his cock with my saliva, then cool it off with a burst of breath.

Kevin rolled his head from side to side on the table. He looked like he was going mad from the alternating temperatures on his dick. I ran my fingers through his dense thicket of fire red pubic hair, marveling at the shimmering contrast against his pale as powder belly. It was like the first swirls of cream in a cup of dark roast coffee. Beautiful. Kevin moaned against the underwear gag. He grunted a few things that sounded like he was enjoying what I was doing, although he could have been swearing at me for all I knew. His cock was still very hard, so I had to assume he liked it.

I looked down at Jesse on the floor. He seemed to enjoy what I was doing to his brother as well. His fingers were twitching at his sides and he bounced up and down on his knees. Clear pre-come dribbled from his cock in a steady flow. It trickled down onto his juicy, red balls, saturating them and the spot of rubber flooring under him. He was trying to squeeze his testicles between his thighs, to, I assumed, bring about an orgasm. I had not given him permission to masturbate but if he could get off that way, he would still be following my orders. I looked directly into Jesse's eyes as I lapped his brother's cock. "You want this, don't you?" I asked him.

He nodded his head vigorously. "Yes Sir," he moaned.

"You want to do this, don't you?" I said again and ran my tongue along the underside of Kevin's pale, red tipped dick. I sucked the head between my lips, moaned like it was a delectable stick of sweet candy, then pulled the entire thing into my mouth again. Kevin moaned through the filthy gag. Jesse groaned from the floor. It was driving him crazy. He ached to have this cock that had given him so many thrills over the years. It was just a few feet in front of him, but since he was under my control, by his choice as well as mine, and I had not given him the permission to move from his spot on the floor, he could do nothing.

"You can stand," I said to Jesse. He immediately jumped to his feet. "Keep your hands to your sides," I commanded, "and stay right where you are."

I could tell by the way his eyes darted from Kevin to me to his own pulsating cock, he wanted to jump in and have some fun with his restrained brother. But I was the one in charge and the boys were there to learn. I was torturing Jesse by not giving him what he wanted, his brother's cock. But then, that was half the fun. How could he appreciate what he had if it was always available to him?

I turned and walked to the cabinet where I selected one of my favorite toys. I called it Old Sparky. It was a metal butt plug with wires leading to a control box that looked a great deal like one used for a toy car or plane. I grabbed the toy and a large bottle of lube and brought them back to the table, set the plug on Kevin's belly and asked him, "Do you know what this is?"

"No," he said through the gag and shook his head his head. His eyes narrowed in confusion. I set the narrow end of the plug under his balls and pushed it in between his butt cheeks. He seemed to understand the penetrating capabilities of the device and began to huff wildly through his nose. He shook his head from side to side while uttering what I had to assume were protests to his impending invasion. I had to assume he was a virgin down there.

I looked up at Jesse, silently asking his consent. He smiled and nodded his head to me. "It only hurts for a few minutes Kevin," Jesse said. "Then it feels good."

Kevin immediately relaxed. "This is a special plug," I told him and held up the control box. "I can send a small electrical current through you with this. It will be painful, but I think you are going to enjoy it at the same time." Kevin panted a few more times, then nodded his head. I could proceed.

I loosened his restraints a little, not enough so he could actually work his way out of them, but enough so he could lift his hips when I needed him to. I poured a healthy dose of the lube into my hand, greased up my fingers and slid them between his buttocks. I found his hole with my middle finger and slowly slid it inside him. He barked against the underwear crammed in his mouth. He was tight as a vice. His warm channel clamped around my finger and the deep passage began to milk it, drawing it deeper into him. His body liked the invasion. I added my index finger and pushed both digits as far in as I could, then began fucking his ass with them. Slowly pulling out, then slipping back in again. He began rocking his hips, fucking my hand just as it was fucking him.

I looked over at Jesse standing next to the table, too far away to touch his brother. Sweat had beaded on his forehead and the steady flow from his dick had increased. Long strings of clear fluid connected his jutting cock with the floor between his feet. He was not looking at me or watching his brother's penetration; his eyes were locked on Kevin's, and Kevin's eyes were locked on his. Jesse watched his brother's half lidded, lusty eyes as he pushed his body back to meet my thrusting fingers. He watched the ecstasy roll over his brother's features as I manipulated Kevin's prostate, carrying him closer and closer to that far off orgasm that he craved. This was torture for both of them. They desperately wanted to fuck one another.

I slid my fingers out of him. Kevin groaned as his hole was abandoned. I covered Old Sparky with lube and pressed the tip against his opening. His hole clamped closed against the icy-cold plug. I pushed the top of the cone inside him anyway.

The plug's dimensions started at about the size of a magic marker at the tip, to the width of a wine bottle at the base. It was not the largest toy I had in my arsenal, but it was fat enough to give even the most seasoned bottom a good workout. He squealed as I pushed the toy inside him. His breathing was coming through his nose in rapid pants as he fought against the pain. I worried that he might begin to hyperventilate and accidentally pull the underwear down into his throat where it would block his air and suffocate him. I pulled the duct tape off his face in one quick pull and tore the underwear from his mouth. He screamed. I looked down at the tape and saw small dark ticks of beard stubble that had been yanked from his cheeks when I removed the gag. He could now breath freely. He could also scream very loudly as I worked the plug the rest of the way into him. I covered his mouth again with just the tape this time.

When, after a great deal of time and determination, he had consumed the entire plug and it's base rested against his butt cheeks, I massaged his chest and belly to calm him. He was panting against the pain. A trickle of mucus oozed from his left nostril. I picked his underwear from the floor, wiped his face with it then let it go again. His breathing was slowly coming back to normal. I rubbed him from his throat all the way down to his feet, relaxing him to the point a smile actually entered his eyes. "Feels good, doesn't it?" I asked.

He nodded his head and let out a pleasant moan. I bent over

him, took his cock in my mouth again and sucked on him while flicking the clamps on his scrotum with my fingers. He flinched each time the clamps waggled under my touch, but lifted his hips to push more of his cock down my throat at the same time. Pleasure and pain, so beautiful.

I pulled off him, took a step back and picked up the control box. I was ready now to increase the game. Kevin watched my hand as it hovered over the metal box, sweat breaking out on his forehead again. He knew what was about to happen and I knew he was both excited and scared at the same time. I knew that was good, because fear was an amazing aphrodisiac. They don't call it scared stiff for nothing.

I tuned on the controller and a low hum echoed from his ass as a slight electrical charge ran through the plug. He began to whimper, but the power was low enough not to hurt or even give any sort of shock, just a light tingle. Then I increased it, pushing the knob from 1 to 4. Ten was the maximum the box would let me go but I had never gotten that far with anyone before. I had always wondered what would happen at that power. I didn't think it would be powerful enough to burn anyone, but since no one I had used it on could take that much, I had never truly tested the device.

Kevin screamed as the electricity coursed through him, heaving his hips into the air and his cock, now pulsating with excitement against his tingling red belly, leaked a steady gush of clear fluid, much as his brother's was, over next to the table.

I spun the dial back to zero, letting him lie back on the table. He panted through his nose, snot running out of him again. I wiped his face with the underwear a second time. "You okay?" I asked.

"Yes," he said, his voice muffled through the tape.

"You sure?"

"Do it!" he screamed. Then, just to let me know how serious he was, added, "You fucking faggot." Even through the duct tape I understood every word.

I pulled the tape free, crammed the underwear, complete with snot, back in his mouth, shoved the tape down over his lips and turned up the electricity. He again threw his hips into the air and screamed into his own mouth. I brought the whip down onto him again and again, increasing the force and speed of the blows until my arm was a blur. The basement filled with the sounds of leather hitting flesh, his muffled screams and the low moans of Jesse as he bounced from one foot to the other, dying to get in on the action.

I was so hard in my jeans it hurt. I freed myself and found I was leaking just as heavily as the brothers. I had never really expelled much pre-come in the past, but something about these guys got me going and I found myself more excited than I had been in years.

Jesse was panting like he was about to blow. His cock was bouncing up and down, reminding me of those weird water-drinking bird toys you could get at the novelty stores when I was a kid. Our eyes met. I could see he was going crazy over how excited this scene was making him. I directed him to take a few steps to his left, so his cock was aligned with his older brother's mouth. He smiled at me and did as instructed.

I shut down the electricity again and Kevin drifted back to the table. He looked over at his younger brother and the hungry cock hovering just out of his reach. I tore the gag off him again and asked, "You want that?" Kevin whimpered and stretched his neck out as far as he could, his mouth open, tongue tasting the air.

I flicked the clips on his balls again. He squealed. "Answer me!" I bellowed.

"Yes Sir, please. Just for a moment. Let me taste him, please, Sir." Kevin had fallen into his role as submissive so easily, it was like this was not new territory for him. I had thought their positions had been rigid, that Kevin was the constant top while Jesse was always bottom. Now I was not so sure of that.

I moved around the table, knelt before the younger brother and slowly pulled on his dick. "You want this beautiful cock in your mouth?" I asked while letting my greasy fingers slide over the glistening dark burgundy head. The clear, sticky runoff dribbled down over the back of my hand. I licked it away. "Ooh," I moaned. "So sweet, it's like candy. You want some of this?"

"Please, please," Kevin moaned as he lifted himself an inch or so from the table, as far as the restraints would allow him. He held his mouth open, waiting for me to give the word for Jesse to step forward and feed his brother his cock. But that was not going to happen. Instead, I ran my finger over Jesse's piss slit, retrieved a finger of pre-come and allowed Kevin to lick my finger clean. "More, please sir, more," he begged. He reminded me of Oliver Twist, pleading for more gruel.

"Nope, the rest is mine," I said and pulled Jesse into my mouth. Almost immediately Jesse was pumping his hips, shoving that bright red cock down my throat, his heavy balls slamming my face as I took him right down to the root. His fiery red bush filled my nose with his pissy stink. I could feel him start to throb in my mouth. He was close to coming, but I wouldn't let him go just yet. I pulled off him, stood, then went down on Kevin again. His cock was fatter and a bit longer than Jesse's, but it tasted just as heavenly. When he got as close as Jesse was to blowing, I pulled off him too. I shoved the underwear gag back in his mouth and sealed it with the tape that was losing a great deal of it's stickiness. It didn't really matter if it stuck anymore. We only had a little while to go before the need to get off would be too much for all three of us. They were still young and could spring right back into play. I however would need a few hours rest before even considering a second round. But the end had to come for all of us or I was sure madness would overrun this house. The aching need to come was so evident on their faces it nearly hurt me physically to look at them.

"Ready for more?" I asked and little lines appeared around Kevin's eyes as he smiled behind the tape. He was ready, so I picked up the control box and we began again.

Chapter 4
Final Lesson

I pushed Jesse onto the cross we had strapped Kevin into earlier. I secured him then pulled the table Kevin was currently lying on next to the large X. I took Jesse's scrotum in my hand and gave it a good squeeze. He winced at the sudden pain, but didn't protest or squirm against his bindings. He seemed to enjoy the rough work on his crotch. He had a beautiful sack and I loved toying with his big balls. They were like large worry beads or the rosary my grandmother used to handle when she became nervous.

With my other hand, I turned up the dial on the electrified plug in Kevin's ass. There was a light buzzing sound as the current rushed into the plug, filling Kevin's body with a hum of electricity. He began to whimper. He wasn't in pain yet, but by the worried look on his face he knew what was coming.

I increased the pressure on Jesse's nuts, pulling on the scrotum like it was a cow's udder and I was trying to get milk for my morning coffee. His cock stood tall and proud as a flag pole. Rivers of pre-come dribbled from the tip. I released him, licked my hand clean, then went back to work on them. The brother's eyes locked on one another. They seemed to fall in together. There was no one else there for them but each other. I did not exist at that moment. They were truly, magnificently in love and it nearly floored me. I was jealous of them at that moment. I had been in love before, or at least I thought I had, but nothing I had ever felt for another man could be compared to what these young men seemed to feel for each other. This was one for the ages. And it pissed me off.

They had broken into my house, *my house*, to steal from me. They had been prepared to hold me hostage, probably beat me, possibly kill me and now they were ignoring me while I was trying to teach them the subtleties of rough love. Something they enjoyed with each other but didn't really understand. I was trying to help them and they acted like I didn't even exist. I was furious.

I released Jesse's balls, opened my hand and slapped at them, hard, with my palm. Jesse cried out but it didn't quell my rage. I twisted the dial on the electrical box. Kevin moaned as the white dot on the dial moved past two, then three, then four. He squirmed against the straps as I pushed him further and further. Sweat ran down his face as he fought against the pain. The moans turned to muffled screams as I moved the knob up to the fifth level.

Kevin's eyes stayed locked on his Jesse. There were tears forming along the lids but they were not fat enough to spill out yet. I banged against Jesse's crotch harder; his scrotum began retracting as his testicles tried to pull up into his body where they could be safe. His cock never dwindled though. "Keep going, Kevin," Jesse called out, "I know you can do this."

I turned the knob to six. Kevin was in the air again, screaming against the tape, his firm ass dangling a good two feet from the table, the top of his head pressed against the padded table top. His eyes seemed to bulge from his head, but they didn't turn in my direction to ask me—beg me—to stop. Instead, they continued to remain glued to his brother. There was pain in his eyes, and a small amount of fear, but the overwhelming emotion riding in those gorgeous emerald pools was love. He was doing this for his brother. For his lover.

All the rage inside me died that moment and I was left feeling shaky, weak and frankly, like an ass. This wasn't for me, it never had been. I had started this with the intention of bringing Kevin to his limits so he and Jesse could have a better time together. Sure, bringing him to the edge was exciting as hell for me, and the first time in a long time I had actually used the room as it was meant to be used, but my own pleasure was second. This was for them. I was not being left out of anything. I was the teacher here. Once I remembered that, the anger left and I shut the machine down and he settled back to the table. "You are doing a good job, Kevin," I said. "I didn't think you had it in you. I'm glad I was wrong."

I figured Kevin had earned a little rest, so I turned to Jesse, pulled his balls out of the recess behind his dick and tugged on them again. He whimpered, but his pale, red-knobbed cock began leaking all over again. I lapped at the fluid, sucking it down my throat. Kevin whimpered as I slobbered over his brother's cock. I brushed Jesse's flaming balls with my tongue, bouncing them over my mouth as he struggled to pull away. They were sore from the beating I had given them and I was not gentle as I lapped and sucked on them. He would have crab-crawled up the wall to get away if he could, but he was firmly secured to the cross.

When I thought Kevin had rested long enough, I let Jesse's nuts go with a loud slurp and began turning the dial on the electrical box again, spinning the dial quickly up past the lower numbers and getting back to where we had left off.

I turned the knob up, seven... eight. His entire body shook while the bottoms of his feet met the padded tabletop. His body was so severely curved over the table he looked like a country bridge spanning a stream.

I tugged on Jesse's balls harder. He began grunting and letting out little excited squeals as I squeezed and pulled on him. His cock bounced up and down, pulsating along with his heartbeat. When the dial hit nine Jesse became too excited from watching the electricity course through his older brother and let out a scream as he erupted with a bone-rattling, nerve-shattering orgasm. The thick, white goo shot into the air, raining down on his brother in a sloppy, splattering storm. He slammed his head back against the cross as stream after stream tore out of him. It covered my hand and forearm and saturated the floor between my feet. His beautiful screams of ecstasy and relief overwhelmed his brother's tortured yells.

That nearly did me in. I was so close to losing control that if I had just touched my cock, it would have been the end for me. My breath was coming out as ragged as Kevin's now was. He had made it to nine, but he could make it to ten, the maximum output of the plug, I hoped. Jesse looked down at the box in my hand.

"Almost there Kevin," Jesse yelled to be heard over his brother's screams. "One more increase and you're at the end. Can you take it? Can you do this for me?"

The tears were streaming down Kevin's face now. Pouring out of him as he experienced more pain than most any man could handle. Lines crinkled around his eyes again and I knew he was smiling at his brother. He was doing this for him, and I realized then he would do anything and go through anything for Jesse. Like I said, one for the ages. He nodded his head, giving me consent to carry him to the last level. I flipped the dial to ten.

The screams coming from him were louder than any human being should have been able to produce, even with the gag still in place. The arch his body had formed was now perfect. His feet and the top of his head lie flat on the table. An orgasm as brutal and violent as a bar fight tore through him. His bright red cock and swollen balls heaved against the metal cock ring as rivers of jism raged out of him, spraying his belly, chest and pooling into the hollow of his upturned throat.

Jesse screamed along with him and I lost control then and came right along with him. My legs turned to water and I nearly fell to the floor, but managed to steady myself with my hands on Kevin's spasming body. I could feel the tingle of the electric current flowing through him as I did so. I immediately shut down the controller and Kevin dropped to the table once again.

I pulled the tape off his mouth and pulled the underwear free, then unlaced his straps. I slowly slid the plug from his ass. He groaned as it came free, then sat with his arms and legs quivering. I freed Jesse and helped him down. He immediately went to his brother, jumped up on the table and wrapped his arms around him. Kevin burst into tears as Jesse pulled him close. He sobbed with hard, wracking convulsions, his entire body heaving with each inhalation and expulsion of air. He had done the impossible. He had taken more than I had seen any man withstand. He had probably taken more than even he thought he could. The brothers held one another as Kevin's sobs slowed to snuffling tears, then stopped altogether. Jesse wiped the tears from his older brother's face. "You are amazing," Jesse said to him.

Kevin looked up at me, waiting for my input. I was choked up. I had never had a problem with a man screaming in pain; it actually kind of excited me. But seeing a man cry turned me to jelly. I usually ended up crying myself, blubbering like a little kid who had broken his favorite toy. I wanted to go to that man, pull him into my arms and cry with him. Hold him, make love to him. But Kevin was not my man. I could not do that with him. And he wasn't crying because he was still in pain, he was crying because he had just gone through something that, for him, was revolutionary. He had climbed Mount Everest, traveled to the center of the Earth, moved an entire continent with his bare hands. He had seen the face of God and saw his own eyes staring back at him. His spirit had not died on that table. It had come alive, perhaps for the first time in his life. I pulled a towel from the cabinet, wiped the gooey semen from his throat and chest. Kevin seemed to be holding his breath, waiting for a congratulations or a pat on the back from me.

I wiped the tears from his face with my fingers and fed the salty water to Jesse, who hungrily sucked my fingers dry. "Good job, Jesse. I'm proud of you for what you did for your brother. I envy you both," I said and let them have a few moments together while I wiped the floor with the towel, pulling the mess Jesse and I had left then set the towel on the stairs. The floor would have to be washed, but it could wait until morning.

Afterward, I stood between Kevin's knees, took his chin in my hand and raised his face to meet mine. "I have never met anyone that could take as much as you just did. You are an amazing man and Jesse is lucky you are his brother." The anger that had been in his eyes at the beginning of the night had long since gone, and I suspected it would take quite a bit to make him that angry again. What we had done had given his self-confidence an incredible boost and killed a great deal of the fear inside him. He no longer had to prove he was strong because now he knew he was. "Just rest a bit," I said and playfully tousled his hair.

"Yes Sir," he replied, a slight smile lighting his face.

When he had regained his composure, I helped him down from the table. He sucked air between his teeth as his feet hit the floor. His ass must have seemed like it was on fire. I thought again how this had probably been the first time anything had gone up inside him like that. I know the first time I had ever let a man fuck me, my ass burned for hours after and that was just a dick, no electricity involved.

I grabbed the towel, led the men back up the stairs. They dressed while I dropped the towel in the laundry room. When I entered the living room again, Kevin was holding Jesse in his arms. "I'm so sorry I hurt you," he said. "I know I get carried away and I didn't really understand how much you could take or how much force or... well, I know how much I can handle now. I can use that to see where your limits are."

"Use a safe word," I said. The brothers turned to me.

"A safe word?" Jesse asked.

"Yeah, a word that wouldn't normally come up during play. It can be anything, like elephant or tomato. Agree on the word before you start and when it gets to be too much for you, Jesse, just say the word and Kevin immediately stops what he is doing. It's a good device to use when you don't yet realize how much your partner can take."

"That would work," Kevin said.

Jesse smiled. "That's why we are here. To learn from you."

Kevin and I looked at each other, then turned our attention to Jesse. The confusion was obvious on both our faces. Jesse swallowed nervously. "I... I told Kevin you had shitloads of money hidden around here. It was the only way he would come here. I had heard around town that you had that room downstairs and well... I hoped you could help me."

Kevin took a step away from him. "You lied to me? You tricked me into breaking into this guys house 'cause you wanted... what? S&M pointers?"

"I did it for us, Kevin. I love it when we play. You know I do. And I know you love it as well. But you hurt me. You hurt me pretty badly and you wanted to stop afterwards. I don't want to stop doing what we do. I love it."

"That was pretty risky," I said. "I could have shot you."

"I know. I was desperate though." He looked at Kevin, his eyes pleading for him to understand. "I love him," he said to me. "I know it seems fucked up with us being brothers and all," he turned his attention back to his brother. "But I love you just the same."

Kevin leaned over him and gently kissed him on the lips. "We better get going before the cops arrive." He pulled his hat and gloves on and reached for the door handle.

"Relax, they're not coming," Jesse said.

I looked at him, shocked.

"What?" he smiled at me. "You think I didn't notice your finger on the phone when you were talking to the police?"

I shook my head, amazed at myself for underestimating him yet again. "If you guys decide you want to come back, knock. You don't have to break in."

"Yes Sir," Kevin said. He opened the door and I noticed the snow had stopped falling. The air outside was crisp and bitterly cold, but at least the snowplows were out now and the streets were being cleared. They would have no problem getting home. "Come on Jess, let's go home. I have to get some ice on my ass."

They walked out into the street and headed toward town. I closed the door, leaving the cold air outside and climbed back up to my bedroom before sliding under the blankets. It was warm in there, but lonely. One day I hoped to find a man I could care about as much as those two young men cared about each other, but if not, well, maybe they would return and we could have some fun again. Kevin had taken more than any man I had ever been with, but he was not mine. He was his brother's man. I could teach him to find his wall and, maybe in the process, the brothers could teach me a thing or two about my own limits. After all, you are never too old to learn something new.

If you enjoyed this story, you can sign up for a free membership at ForbiddenFiction.com and discuss it with other readers and the author at the *House Breaking* story page at http://forbiddenfiction.com/story/PLR-1.000169.

We do our best to proof all our work, but if you spot a text error we missed, please let us know via our website Contact Form at www.forbiddenfiction.com/contact.

p.l. ripley
bridging
obsession

Bridging Obsession

Chapter 1:
In the Pines

Clyde was never one to openly disagree with his older brother John, even when John said something stupid, like now.

"I'm telling you, right he-ah having an African American in the White House is the end of this country. We might just as well sign everything over to those godless Muslims, or worse, the French."

John never said the 'N-word', but he could make African American sound just as vile. He didn't speak the words as much as spit them.

"Yeah," Clyde said, not really paying much attention anymore. He had learned a long time ago it was just easier to let him have his say than to argue with him. When John got cornered in an argument, which was easy to do, he started debating with his fists, and in that sort of argument Clyde could never win. John outweighed him by twenty-five pounds and he loved to fight. That was how Clyde had lost one of his front teeth: he had suggested John might be wrong on immigration. That maybe it wouldn't be a good idea to send anyone not born here back where they came from. That maybe this country was founded on immigration and... POP! that was the end of the debate.

Of course John was deeply apologetic after. He begged Clyde to forgive him and even worked a few tears into the apology. Clyde, however, knew he was sincere. The harrowing regret in John's eyes was too shattering to be fake. Besides, John lacked the ability to pretend to be anything other than what he was. So Clyde just kept his mouth shut and felt lucky he still had one front tooth left.

They were sitting in John's truck in front of Millers General Store drinking beer and John was smoking a joint. It was their Saturday afternoon ritual. They worked half a day on Saturday cutting out whatever part of the forest they hadn't finished on Friday, then treated themselves to a few beers on their way home. John was one of many private contractors working for the paper mills; stripping the forests, clearing the land, then replanting trees so, hopefully, future generations could do the same thing. His business was small, just John and Clyde. It could be bigger, he could make a great deal of money, Clyde suspected, though John just did not have the know-how to do that. John knew how to physically work. He busted his ass most days, but to perform any mental task beyond adding single digit numbers or reading further than a fourth grade level was too much for him.

They often shared the joint, passing it back and forth in the truck cab, windows wide open so the stink wouldn't saturate the foam stuffing spilling from the cracked and torn seats. But today Clyde didn't feel like getting high. Pot made him horny and he didn't think he would have time to sneak off to the Route 2 rest area tonight to trade blow-jobs with whoever happened to be there.

It was Clyde's only sexual outlet. He was still in his teens for another year and six months, still too young to frequent the bars in Lewiston or down in Portland. Not that his old Ford Escort could get him there. He was lucky the piece of shit managed to get him to the rest area now and again. He wouldn't have the money to get to the city anyway. What little money he and John made went to the household expenses. Mamma hadn't been able to work for years and so Clyde managed to save enough for the occasional bag of weed and gas money so he could get his rocks off once a month.

He wanted to help John with the business. If they expanded a bit and got a bigger contract with the paper mill, hired a few more men permanently instead of the occasional short timer to deal with deadlines, they could work their way out of the financial hole they were in. Maybe Clyde could actually get a weekly paycheck big enough to afford his own place. But John wouldn't allow him to interfere in the business. Clyde was still a boy in his eyes. "This ain't none of your concern," John had told him when Clyde had suggested ways to increase their income. "I won't have some fucking snot-nosed kid telling me how to run my business." That was the end of the discussion and Clyde hadn't brought it up since.

Clyde kept his trips to Route 2 very secret. John hated gays more than Muslims and immigrants. "Those damned ho-mo-sexuals," he would say, emphasizing each syllable of the word, "are directly responsible for the moral decline of this country." John listened to talk radio a lot and repeated what he heard. John could make homosexual sound more vile than he could African American.

John was a bigot. That was the hard truth of it. Clyde knew this just as he knew the sky was blue, grass green and his small, close knit family of himself, John and Mamma were just a fraction of the enormous Chute clan of Western Maine. A sprawling group that had never, in hundreds of years, spread further than a twenty-five mile radius of this small town of Devon, Maine. Population 1,956 according to last year's town report. A town separated from the rest of the world not only by the wall of heavy, pined hills, but also by its citizen's desire for isolation. Devon's neighbors were small communities like itself: towns wary of strangers and cautious of each other.

It was the perfect town for Clyde. He was a wary man as well. He had lived here his entire life yet had no friends whatsoever. He could recall many of the people of Devon by name, but knew nothing more about them. And he didn't want to know about them. Clyde did not trust people, because Clyde had a secret.

John's bigotry was a hard thing for Clyde to take. John, his older brother, a man he loved and admired for as long as he could remember, was controlled by his own fears.

Prejudice, Clyde understood, was fear masquerading as

something more heinous. Fear of the unknown, fear of the different.

This terrified him, because Clyde was different. He was as different from John, Mamma and nearly everyone he knew as a bat is different from a bird. His secret was his difference from his family and neighbors.

"You want to go to Sparky's tonight?" John asked.

Sparky's was a roadhouse John spent most Saturday nights at. Clyde had gone a few times, but there were too many fights and he often had to walk home after John hooked up with some woman or another.

"Naw. I think I'll just stay in and watch T.V."

"That's all you ever do," John said. "You stay in every Saturday night jerking off like that, you gonna go blind."

"I'll just do it 'till I need glasses," Clyde replied.

John laughed, nearly spitting his beer over the dash. "That's a good one Clydey-boy. You a funny guy. 'Do it 'till I need glasses.' I gotta use that one."

A car pulled up in front of the store. It was a Lexus, black with bright shining chrome rims. John stopped chuckling and watched the sleek, dark vehicle park between their cousin Bobby Chute's motorcycle and a pick-up older than John's. John's eyelids nearly closed as he glared at the vehicle, his face growing pale, mouth dropping open like the hinge in his jaw had sprung. It was the look of jealousy that had grown more familiar to Clyde as he had seen it on his brother's face more and more often as each year passed. It was a look that asked, "Why can't I have something like that? Why do I have to work so hard for so little?"

A man climbed out of the car. He was young—about John's age—with short cut blond hair and a face as pretty as a sunset. He was wearing shorts that showed off his golden tanned, muscular legs, and an Abercrombie and Fitch T-shirt. A company that John called Abercrombie and Fag. The guy in the Lexus was beautiful and Clyde watched him walk toward the store and felt his mind wander up next to the man.

Clyde's sex life might be sporadic, but his fantasies more than made up for it. Scenarios of sexual encounters filled his head during the mundane, day to day activities. Scenarios that he used later in the night as he lay in bed. His hands, working himself up, then off. The fantasies sometimes came hard and fast, overriding everything else going on in his head. The glimmer of a muscled arm in a sleeveless shirt, a pair of hairy, muscled legs, a few stray pubic hairs peeking out over the waist of low-slung jeans. Little nuances like these set his mind in gear and he was having trouble controlling the daydreams. He would sometimes snap out of the fantasies, slack-jawed, chainsaw buzzing in his hand, saliva pooling in the corners of his mouth. It was beginning to scare him.

"City boy," John grumbled. "Fucking faggot city boy."

"Hey," Clyde said turning John's attention away from the blond, away from the danger of another temper flare, "let's go home and get something to eat. Maybe going to Sparky's will be fun tonight."

"You really want to go out tonight?" John replied, the excitement in his voice raising it a few octaves.

"Sure. I can always beat off later." Clyde grinned. "I'm gonna need some of that joint though."

John pulled the roach from the ashtray and handed it over. "Smoke up buddy, we gonna have fun tonight." He pulled the truck away from the store with a squeal of tires, pushing a cloud of dirt behind them. The blond turned and watched them go. Clyde smiled at the man as they left, the man scowled back.

When they got back to the trailer park, their mother was in front of the television watching cartoons and eating a bowl of ice cream. She was always eating something, that is why she couldn't leave home. She hadn't been able to fit through the door in almost a decade. "That you, boys?" she asked when they came in, turning her head as far as she could. The rolls of fat on the back of her neck mashing against one another.

"It's us, Mamma," Clyde said and went in to give her a kiss. Layers of grease and old sweat clung to her cheek and she smelled musty, like the beaten down recliner she sat in. She sniffed the air like a bloodhound.

"You boys been smoking pot again? I told you that God-damned hippie weed gonna get you in trouble someday. You just wait, it's gonna get ya'."

"It ain't gonna get us in no trouble," John argued. "If anything it's gonna keep us out of it."

"How you figure that?"

"It just is," he said.

John couldn't argue with their mother. She was the only person he wouldn't fight with, even when she said something he disagreed with he always backed down and dropped the subject as soon as possible.

"There's last night's pizza in the oven if you boys are hungry," Mamma said.

Clyde pulled the box from the oven, slid the pizza on a pan and set it back in. He turned to oven to 400 degrees and set the timer for twenty-five minutes. The microwave oven had died a few weeks ago. It still sat on the counter, the inside a thick sludge of dried-on butter, spaghetti sauce and other food-like substances that Clyde could not identify. Mamma hated to clean. The pile of dirty dishes flowing from the sink evidence of her lack of ambition. Clyde would occasionally give a half-hearted attempt at getting the kitchen in order, but when John and Mamma refused to pick up after themselves, well... Clyde just gave up trying. When the timer went off he pulled the pan from the oven and set the pizza on plates. Two pieces for John, one for himself.

John sat at the table, glanced at the two plates and asked, "You only having one?"

"There's only three left."

John pulled a knife from the sink, rinsed it off, cut a slice in half and dropped one side on Clyde's plate. "Eat up. You don't want to go out drinking on an empty stomach."

"Thanks."

They ate with Tom and Jerry playing on the television in the other room. "This is good warmed up. You're going to make someone a good wife one day." John laughed and tousled Clyde's hair.

"Funny."

When the pizza was gone John went to the bathroom to take a shower. Clyde sat with Mamma, listening to her breathing and watching television with her. She held the remote control in her hand like a scepter and flipped the channels so fast he couldn't tell what he was missing. She stopped on one of the religious channels the basic (very basic really, less than thirty channels but hey, it was only ten bucks a month) cable provided its small customer base. Brother Jim, a fat preacher with hair as tall as the pine trees Clyde and John cut down every day, screamed at the audience they were all going to hell if they didn't do what God, through him, commanded. They were all sinners and damned but if they would just send him ten or twenty dollars or whatever they could afford, they might find salvation.

"Amen, you god-damned asshole!" Mamma screamed. Mamma had a bible and even glanced through it once in a while. She believed in God, but didn't believe He was an ugly, angry monster Brother Jim and men like him claimed—perhaps hoped—Him to be.

John stepped into the living room wearing a new pair of jeans. Darlene, one of the women who frequented Sparky's as often as John did, had bought them for him in the hopes John would become her exclusive boyfriend. It wouldn't work and Clyde nearly told Darlene this, that she had wasted 120 bucks on a dream that will never come true, but he didn't want to dash her hopes. She would find out on her own eventually. John, of course, accepted the gift happily, not realizing they came with strings.

The jeans clung to his hips as though afraid of falling, clutching madly to the high, tight swell of his butt. The denim hugged his thighs, showing off the thick slabs of muscle in his powerful legs and Clyde's eyes were drawn—as the jeans were designed to do—to the bulge in his crotch. The thick roll of John's cock reached for his right hip, stretching out for the one spot on his body bone could be felt not covered in overworked muscle.

"Jesus Christ," Mamma blurted, "you wearing them jeans or

fucking 'em."

Clyde laughed. He looked up at John's face and found a grin there as well. He was modeling the jeans for them and Mamma's exclamation was the approval he needed. The jeans were doing their job, showing him off.

Clyde let his eyes drift down to John's naked chest and belly. The rough-cut muscle carvings were softened by a thick weave of dark hair covering his torso. His nipples peeked out of the near black swirls like sweet fruit on a vine, ready to be plucked or tasted. Clyde saw in his imagination's eye, doing just that: pulling the puckered nipples, one at a time, into his mouth. He could feel the hard ridge on his tongue and taste the shower water on John's skin, still laced with the hint of Irish Spring. And his imagined self let out a small chuckle as John flinched when he brought his teeth together, delicately pinching the sensitive flesh.

In his head he buried his face in John's chest. It was warm there and he could smell, under the minty soap, the aromas of the forest. John always smelled of fresh cut wood. You couldn't spend as much time as he does out there amongst the thick oaks and pines without it becoming a part of you. John's heartbeat, a strong and regular thumping, lulled the daydream Clyde into a comfortable numbness and when John wrapped his arms around him, Clyde knew he was safe. This is what Darlene and half the women at Sparky's wanted. They knew John was a good man. Yes, he had his violent outbursts. Clyde's missing tooth was evidence enough of that, but those moments were rare ones.

"What do you think, Clyde?" Mamma asked, pulling Clyde from his daydream. "You think John's ever going to have kids wearing pants that tight?"

He looked up, his eyes met John's and he saw there, in his brother's pale hazel irises an angry questioning. John had seen Clyde taking him in, absorbing his body like a sponge sucking up water. He had seen the lusty wandering of Clyde's eyes over his chest, belly and crotch and he glared at Clyde as though he had actually felt the sharp nips Clyde's imagination had taken at his nipples, felt his younger brother's fingers running through the hair on his body.

Beneath the anger though, Clyde saw fear in John's face. Whether it was fear *of* him, or *for* him, he wasn't quite sure.

Instead of answering Mamma's question, Clyde mumbled it was his turn to shower. He ran to his room, gathered the clothes he would wear out to Sparky's and locked himself behind the bathroom door. He leaned over the sink staring at himself in the mirror. *What the fuck is the matter with you?* he asked himself. He had been having these visions of John for years now. Had been fantasizing John not as brother and father-figure, but as a lover. He dreamed of John, not only when he was awake, but when he slept as well. The fantasy had spread its roots through his quick daytime imaginings and down into his subconscious.

Clyde stripped, showered, shaved and when he was dressed and presentable, stepped out of the bathroom. He hoped John wouldn't question him about what had just happened between them, that he would just let it go. Clyde couldn't come up with a viable lie to explain why he had been mesmerized by John's half naked body, or at least not one John would actually buy.

"Well, ain't you all spiffed up," John said when Clyde presented himself before John and Mamma. He was wearing khakis and a pale blue dress shirt buttoned nearly to the top. They were not only his best clothes, they were the only clothes he had not ruined from sweaty days working in the woods.

"Ayuh, that's my handsome boy," Mamma declared in her thick New England drawl and lifted her house dress a bit to scratch at her leg. Clyde noticed her leg was bright red from mid-shin down. There were also splotchy patches of purple along the backs of her calves. It was poor circulation and the last time she had been to a doctor, more than ten years ago, she had been warned that it could become life threatening if she didn't get some exercise. She hadn't taken the advice and hadn't been back to the doctor since.

"He sure is, Mamma," John said while reaching out to adjust Clyde's collar. He unfastened the top button of Clyde's shirt to reveal the thin pattern of hair that had been coming in on Clyde's chest. "Almost as handsome as his brother. Right, Clyde?"

"Right, John," Clyde replied. John had donned a black tee-shirt while Clyde had showered. It was tight around his chest, but it put emphasis on his strong pectoral muscles. The wariness had left John's eyes and when Clyde looked up at him, he saw nothing there but the amused admiration John usually had for him. Clyde was John's kid brother and John often looked on him in just that way, like Clyde was just a kid. Honestly, Clyde often felt that way about himself. Like he was not a boy but not quite a man either. He was trapped between the two worlds.

They headed for the door and Mamma rose to her feet, leaning on the walker frame that never left her side. "You boys be careful," she said. "You drive if he has too much," she told Clyde.

"I will, don't worry."

She followed them to the door and stopped as John and Clyde walked out to the truck. Mamma was wider than the narrow trailer doorway. She hadn't tried to leave home in more than a decade. It was doubtful she could even fit through the door, then of course she would have to maneuver down the three small steps to the ground. With the walker in tow and the fact she could not see her feet while standing, those three steps might as well be a thousand. Mamma waved goodbye to them from the doorway.

They went out to the truck, hopped in and headed for Sparky's Road House.

Though Clyde didn't know it, before the night was over he would find himself in bed with John.

And, by the end of the week, his secret would be out.

Chapter 2
Honky-Tonk

Sparky's was wild that night. A local band called "The Buzzsaws" was performing covers of Def Leopard and Aerosmith hits. The small honky-tonk bar was filled to capacity and the only thing louder than the redneck rock music, as Clyde thought of it, was the buzz of a hundred different conversations fighting to be heard.

The last time Clyde had been here he'd watched a man stabbed to death in front of the stage. He didn't know the guy or his assailant but heard it was a disagreement over a woman. Apparently the victim had been banging the other guy's girlfriend. It was a terrifying thing, to watch a person's life extinguished like that in front of him. He'd dreamed about it for weeks after, waking up in the darkness of his room, screaming, seeing the light fade from the man's eyes as the knife plunged over and over again into his chest. He hadn't been back here since and, looking around the crowded bar, wondered why he had agreed to come back.

John, that was why he had come here. John had asked and he had agreed because Clyde would do nearly anything to make his brother happy. Even come back to this shit hole that had given him nightmares.

They had come to Sparky's early enough to nab a table, but if they wanted to keep it one of them would have to stay with it during the evening. Which meant that Clyde would have to stay with it. John would be busy socializing. That was fine by Clyde. He didn't dance and the few people he actually knew here he didn't really like. These were John's people, his crowd. Clyde only came here to make

John happy.

John was at the bar ordering a pitcher of beer for them to share and a couple of shots of whiskey for himself. Sparky's never checked I.D.s, or at least not Clyde's. John had been friends with the owner, Sparky LaChance, for as long as Clyde could remember; Sparky let certain things slide for his friends. Of course, if the place had ever been raided he would claim ignorance that minors were drinking here. There were only a handful of sheriffs to patrol the entire county so the odds of that happening were minimal.

A blond woman Clyde had never seen before was talking to John at the bar. She wore a skirt so short Clyde could see her pink panties each time she bent a little over the bar. John was laughing at something she said, then gently rested his hand on her bottom. She giggled and gently removed his hand, then set it on her breast. His fingers immediately began working at the flesh, digging in hard enough to leave marks. The woman laughed and John let his hand drop.

"Jesus Christ, look at that asshole," Clyde heard. He turned to the voice. It was Darlene. She pulled a chair from the table, sat and watched John with the blond woman. "I swear, he fucks anything that moves. He'd stick it in a pile of rocks if he thought there was a snake hidden in them."

Clyde laughed with surprise. Darlene had recently had a hair perm and her head was covered in tight, dark curls. She still smelled of ammonia. "So, how are you doing, cutey?" she asked.

"Good. I'm doing fine," Clyde replied. He had always liked Darlene, but kind of felt sorry for her. She was spending her youth pining for a man who wouldn't give her something she wanted: commitment. But then, Clyde was pining for the same man. He wanted something different from him—or at least he thought he did—but he was no more likely to receive what he wanted than Darlene was.

"You seeing anyone?" she asked.

"No. I'm busy working all the time and..."

"That motherfucker!" Darlene interrupted. John was whispering something in the blond's ear and she tipped her head back and laughed out loud at whatever he was saying. Clyde could hear her laugh, high pitched with a squeak curling off at the end, cut through the music and chatter of the place. It was an annoying laugh, he thought. It seemed fake, like she was forcing a semblance of humor to impress John. John's hand was busy under the blond's skirt. He was working at something in the front. This was what had set Darlene off. From where they were sitting it looked like John had his fingers inside the woman. He probably did.

"Hey," Darlene said to Clyde, "want to make him jealous? We can go out to my Monte. The back seat is kinda small, but we could have some fun in the front."

An immediate rush of heat rose up Clyde's neck and he felt it sear into his face. "I don't think... I mean, I... I can't," he stammered.

"Not your type, huh. Well, that's all right. How about her?" Darlene indicated a red-headed woman in shorts and a tube top that strained to hold itself together under the force of her large breasts. A thick spattering of rust-colored freckles covered her chest and arms. Clyde's eyes passed the redhead to a man leaning over the pool table about to take a shot with the cue. He wore a sleeveless shirt that showed off the tattoos running down his lean, muscled arms. An unlit cigarette hung from his bottom lip. The law prohibiting smoking in public places was one of the few rules Sparky actually enforced. He was rough-looking, tough and angry. He reminded Clyde of John.

Fucking hot, he thought.

Clyde looked back at Darlene. There was a thin sliver of a smile on her lips. She had seen where his eyes had taken him. "Do you like that one?" she asked.

Clyde swallowed, hard, and looked down at the table, not daring to meet her eyes. Afraid that if he did she would know the truth about him. "Hey, honey," she said softly, perhaps noticing how uncomfortable Clyde had become. "Whatever you're into, it's okay. As long as it's between two consenting adults, there's nothing to be ashamed of. Got me?" Darlene set her hand on his arm, the long press-on nails, painted a deep purple, shimmered against his well tanned skin. He pulled his arm away, sliding it out from under her hand and hugged it to his chest. Darlene gave him a curious look.

"Sorry," he said. "Personal space."

"It's okay, cutey. We all have to build our own bridges. You're just putting yours together a little slower than most."

Clyde nodded his head, not daring to speak. Afraid if he did, he would either admit to her that he was gay or start crying. And he would not cry. He would not show weakness, no matter how much he felt it inside. It's a difficult thing to realize something about yourself that others might find repulsive. Especially when that other person is your brother, the one you love most in the world. Even though Darlene could not be sure Clyde was attracted to other men, she had told him that he was not a bad person for doing so.

He wondered though, how accepting she would be if she discovered those desires were directed at his own brother. She would probably be as disturbed by the revelation as he himself often was.

John finished with the blond and carried the pitcher of beer with two frosted mugs to the table. He filled a mug, handed it to Clyde, then poured one for himself. "Hey Darlene." he said, taking the seat opposite her.

"Hey yourself," she grumbled. "You might want to go wash your hands. No telling where that whore has been."

"Well, she seemed fine to me. Smell," he said and shoved the finger that had been buried within the blond's skirt under Darlene's nose.

"Get that out of my face!" Darlene screamed, shoving his hand away.

John laughed and nudged Clyde with his elbow. "She acts like she ain't never smelled another woman's pussy before."

"Shut up, John, you idiot," Darlene grumbled.

The smile died from John's face. He turned his attention to her, his mouth a hard grimace, eyes cold, fierce. "What the fuck did you say to me?"

Darlene instantly realized her mistake. Of all the things that could set John off, and there were many, nothing worked faster than to question his intelligence. Words like *stupid* and *idiot* were like waving a red flag in front of a bull for John. "What the fuck did you say?" he asked again, rising from the table. His fists clenched, then relaxed, clenched, relaxed.

Darlene looked up at him, her face hard, terrified. Her mouth hung open. Clyde could see her dry tongue rasping over her lips while her eyes glistened with unshed tears. "John, she didn't mean it," Clyde said, feebly attempting to calm his brother. John could easily strike out at Darlene; he wouldn't care that he had hit her in the middle of a crowded bar with a hundred witnesses. If Clyde tried to protect her, if he got between Darlene and John's fists, then he would be punished just as severely as she. He would be just a minor obstacle that John would have to punch out of the way.

"I'm sorry, baby. I don't know what I was thinking. You know I don't think that about you. I don't know why I said it. Please forgive me, please," Darlene begged.

As suddenly as the rage took him, it disappeared. A smile stretched over John's face and the light, happy glimmer returned to his eyes. He sat, nodded his head at the beer before Clyde and said, nonchalantly, as though he had not just scared the shit out of Darlene and Clyde both, "Go slow with that. You only get two, remember."

"I know." Clyde lifted the mug. His hands were shaking, but he managed to get the glass to his mouth and take a sip anyway. It was cold and delicious and he felt his body relax the moment the beer slid down his throat. He looked over at Darlene. She was shivering as if she was cold, even though the hard press of a hundred bodies in the road house had the temperature hovering near eighty. Sparky had propped the door open, but all that did was let the insects in. A mosquito buzzed near Clyde's ear and he swatted it away. Clyde set his hand on Darlene's and nodded his head to her. "It's okay," the gesture said. She gave him a weak smile in return, then dabbed at her eyes with her other hand.

Clyde was allowed two beers, which meant John was going to get drunk tonight. John never drove while intoxicated. That was what had killed their father.

Dad had been on a night out with his friends from the mill. They had gathered at a little tavern in Lewiston. Clyde never found out exactly why they had chosen a place so far from home, but he had heard rumors that prostitutes frequented the place. He thought the stories were probably true. That would be a draw for his father. He never really knew the man, not like a boy should know his father, but he was only five when the accident happened. He thought his father would be drawn to the Lewiston bar with the ladies of the evening because everyone said John was just like him. John definitely would have gone.

Dad had attempted to drive home after an evening of drinking and who knows what else, probably getting a scorching case of herpes to bring home to Mamma. He'd never made it home though. His car was found by an early morning commuter. He had driven into the river. There were no skid marks or any indication he had attempted to stop or swerve. He had just driven right into the water. The car was standing nearly upright, nose in the thick mud of the Androscoggin River. The ass end of the car had pointed at the sky. It must have looked like some weird doorway to another world, Clyde thought. The tall, dark, oblong object hovering there in the water like the monolith in that Kubrick movie.

That was when Mamma had started eating. She had always been heavy, a little thick in the middle perhaps, the puffy beginnings of a second chin, but not fat. Not like now. In thirteen years she had gone from 180 pounds to just over 500. She was eating herself to death and there was nothing Clyde or John could do but watch. The poor circulation in her legs had discolored them to the red and mottled bruising that looked painful, but Mamma said they didn't bother her. Clyde knew that the color of her legs was proof that her heart was getting weak. She hadn't been to see a doctor in ten years, using their finances as an excuse not to go. They all had MaineCare, the state's low-income health insurance and it would pay for the visit, yet she still refused.

"Don't you worry there, Clyde. Mamma's gonna be 'round for quite some time," she had said when Clyde confessed how worried he was for her. He knew it wasn't true. She won't be around much longer if she didn't get help.

The roadhouse suddenly erupted in the excited squawks of a scuffle. Clyde looked up at the source of the noise and saw the handsome tattoo kid he had been admiring earlier standing his ground against a pissed off biker brandishing a knife nearly as long as Clyde's forearm. The kid held the pool cue in his hand like a baseball bat, swung it a few times at the biker's fist, attempting to knock the weapon free.

John looked over at the action. His eyes widened excitedly, his expression exactly like a kid's on Christmas morning. He jumped from the table and started towards the fight. His fists flexing and relaxing, pumping themselves into a frenzy. Clyde could hear a low, rumbling laughter rising from his brother's chest. This is why John loved this place. It wasn't just the booze or the women that drew him here. It was the nightly prospect of a good fight that kept him coming back.

Clyde grabbed John's arm before he moved too far from the table and into the chaos building at the pool table. "Please, John, don't," he said.

John glanced down at Clyde, looked over at the scuffle, back to Clyde again. Clyde could almost see the gears turning in John's head. He was working it out in his mind. Should he have fun and join in the fight, or stay at the table with Clyde and Darlene? Have a good time or take the responsible route?

The decision was made for him. Sparky put an end to the fight: he pulled out the only weapon he had on the premises, an old cattle prod he had bought at a farm auction just after the stabbing that nearly closed him down six months ago. It was a monstrous long pole with a fat metal ball on the end and when he fired it up, crazy blue electric arcs danced around the ball, letting everyone know he meant business. He pressed the ball against the biker's back and pulled on the trigger. The biker, a thickly muscled man with blond hair pulled back in a ponytail, immediately dropped to the wooden dance floor. A puddle of urine quickly formed under him. The band stopped playing and the entire road house grew quiet.

"That's enough, you dumb fucks!" Sparky bellowed, then everything went back to the way it was before. The band picked up where it had left off and the biker's friends helped him to his feet. Blond ponytail staggered to a table in the corner, grabbed a glass of beer and downed it, shook his head and was fine.

The dancers before the stage began bumping and grinding again. "Let's dance," Darlene said, jumping from her seat. She grabbed John's hand and pulled him to the small dance floor. Clyde watched them from their table, still nursing that first beer. John was a good dancer, moving across the floor with a grace that seemed out of character for him. He held onto Darlene's hips and ground his pelvis into her, grinding his crotch over her rear end, then turned her and did the same to the front. Clyde felt a twinge of jealousy, then blinked with shock. He should not be jealous. He was John's brother, not his lover. When they came back to the table, Clyde noticed John's cock had shifted down his right leg and had grown considerably.

When closing time came, John was all but passed out. Darlene helped Clyde get him out to the truck and into the passenger seat. Clyde stretched the seat belt around John, snapped the fastener to the lock, then gently closed the door. "Thanks for the help, Darlene," Clyde said.

"Not a problem. You know, he doesn't deserve you."

"Maybe. Maybe I don't deserve him."

"It's sad that you think that," Darlene said, then turned and shuffled over the dusty parking lot to her Monte Carlo. She climbed in and waved to Clyde as she drove off.

When Darlene was gone, Clyde realized John still had the truck keys. He opened the truck door and tried to fish them out of John's pocket, but the jeans were too tight. He would not have been able to pull a single strip of paper from the pocket, let alone the ring of keys. He unfastened the seat belt and pulled John from the truck, leaned him against the side and slid his hand into the pocket. John groggily opened one eye. It trained on Clyde, but didn't seem to focus on him. "Wha... doing?" John mumbled.

"I need to get the keys," Clyde said. He pushed his hand in further and felt the fat head of John's cock brush against his fingers.

John sucked in a deep rush of breath and his head dropped onto

Clyde's shoulder. His lips found Clyde's ear and he let out a soft moan, sending an excited shiver up Clyde's spine.

Clyde found the keys, pulled them out, then maneuvered John back into the passenger seat. Once he was secured again, Clyde went around to the driver's side, started the truck on the third try, then drove home.

Twenty minutes later they were back in the trailer park. Clyde brought the truck to a shuddering stop in the driveway and cut the engine. He looked over at John snoring lightly, face pressed against the side window, mouth gaped open, dirty scruff of stubble on his jaw. He was handsome when he slept. Probably because his eyes were closed, hiding the anger that was usually in them and light snores fell from his mouth instead of the usual bullshit. Yeah, John could be a prick, but Clyde loved him.

Now, though, he had to get John into the trailer. He thought at first he would leave him in the truck. Let him sleep the rest of the night there. They were home and safe... but he couldn't do that. It would piss John off to wake up in the truck, but more importantly than that, Clyde needed John inside. He wouldn't feel right sleeping in his small but comfortable bed while John slept in the truck, either secured upright by the seatbelt or sprawled across the cracked and worn bench seat.

Besides, it wasn't like this was new territory for him. Carrying his brother to bed after a long night of drinking was becoming almost a ritual for them. He would just handle this the way he had managed it the many times before. He opened the passenger door, unhooked the belt and pulled John from the truck. Wrapping his arms around John, he half-carried, half-walked him to the trailer, directed him when to lift his leg for the three short steps up to the door, calling out, "Step... step... step." John followed his directions, but burped a sleepy protest each time Clyde called for him to lift his leg.

Mamma never locked the door when they went out. They never worried about anyone breaking in. What did they have to steal, anyway? An old television with one of the government issued digital converters and a sixty dollar DVD player from Walmart? Even the thieves had better stuff than this. He dragged John down the hall, turned him into his room and dropped him on the bed. John held onto Clyde as he fell onto the bed, pulling him down with him. Clyde struggled to get up. "John, at least let me get your shoes off you."

John released him and Clyde unlaced his shoes for him, then pulled them off. The warm stink of his sweaty feet filled Clyde's face. It was a harsh smell, but not unpleasant, Clyde thought. John sat up and struggled to get his shirt off. His eyes were still closed and he seemed to be drifting off again even as he worked to undress himself. Clyde helped him with the shirt, then unfastened John's far too tight jeans and pulled the fly down. He gripped the top of the jeans and pulled them down, dragging John's underwear with them. He was wearing the familiar cheap, white briefs.

Clyde laughed to himself. *Leave it to John to wear 120 dollar jeans with two dollar underwear*, he thought. John's cock lay across his hip, the thick foreskin still damp with sweat from his dance with Darlene. Clyde slid John's underwear back into place, covering him, when John grabbed his arms and pulled him onto the bed with him. Rather than fight, Clyde settled in. This is what he wanted anyway, to lie in bed with John. To feel his strong arms around him. Feel John's chest, thick with hair and muscles, press into his back. He felt safe, protected. Loved.

No matter what this looked like, Clyde thought, it was perfectly natural. They were simply brothers falling into bed together after a long night of drinking. *There's nothing sexual about this*, Clyde thought, even as he pulled off his own shirt to feel the heat of his brother, and pressed himself back into him. He felt John's cock begin to stiffen and felt it, through John's underwear and Clyde's jeans, rub against his ass. It seemed to be digging in, as though it wanted to chew its way through the denim. He pushed his hips back feeling the strength in John move through him. Clyde's own cock strained against his pants, threatening to burst out of the material. John pulled him closer, his mouth gently caressing Clyde's neck. *Completely innocent*, he thought as the warmth of John's breath ruffled the stray hairs, tickling his ear. "I love you, John," Clyde said, softly, so as not to wake his brother.

"I love you, Dar," John moaned. Clyde frowned a moment, then realized he probably meant Darlene. John had said that he loved her.

Clyde suddenly felt an overwhelming shame. He was where Darlene should be, in John's bed, with John's arms around her. He didn't belong here. This was his brother. It wasn't right what he was feeling, it wasn't natural. He lay in the bed with John's arms wrapped around him, John's body pressed against his, and tried to feel nothing. Tried to suppress the desires he had for his older brother, these awful, disgusting desires. But he failed. His erection kept him up through the night and each time John shifted his weight a bit, or moaned in his sleep, Clyde felt his heart race just a bit. Just enough to keep the blood flowing into his dick.

Finally, when the sun began to fill the small bedroom with its morning heat, telling Clyde that this day, just like the past week, was going to be a hot one, sleep came to him. He did not dream.

Chapter 3
Dreaming in the Woods

It was Monday morning. John and Clyde were in the truck long before the sun had managed to climb the hills to the east. They each had travel mugs filled with hot coffee, the emblem from the credit union Darlene worked for etched in red and gold letters on the sides. Clyde took his with four sugars and enough half and half to turn the black liquid white. John pulled out of the driveway, taking a left towards town, the opposite direction of their work site. "Where we going?" Clyde asked.

"We have to pick up something first," John replied, not elaborating.

When they got to town, John pulled the truck in the credit union parking lot. There was a truck already there, parked sideways across two clearly marked spaces. A big man sat behind the wheel, a thick black beard covered his face. John pulled his truck next to the other one and nodded his head at the bearded driver.

"Good morning. This is Clyde," John said, cocking his thumb at Clyde. "Dale and Evan."

The driver, Dale, nodded his head in greeting. Clyde leaned forward to see past him, to the passenger, Evan. There wasn't enough light yet for him to make Evan out very well, but he looked young. Evan gave Clyde a quick smile, nodded his head hello as Dale had. "You guys all geared up?" John asked.

"Ayuh, looking forward to it," Dale replied, giving a sideways smirk through the thick bush of facial hair.

"Just follow us then," John said, then slid the truck back into gear and pulled out of the parking lot. The other truck followed close behind.

"I hired them to help clear the lot," John told Clyde. "Henderson will give me a twenty percent bonus if it's done by the end of the month. Of course that will just cover the wages for these guys, but it puts me in good standing with the mill."

John didn't have to explain and Clyde was a little surprised he did. The business was John's and he wouldn't allow Clyde to interfere with it, or even make a suggestion how things might be better managed.

"Dale and Evan are brothers. They're Darlene's cousins or something. Some relation to her, anyway." John sipped his coffee and glanced into the rearview mirror every few minutes to make sure the other truck was still there. When they arrived at the work site, Clyde checked the gas and oil in the skidder, a big, tractor-like machine with a claw for moving felled trees extended out from its front on a long I-beam, and he officially introduced himself to the new men. Evan was about Clyde's age. He had a handsome smile that he flashed around constantly and a lazy eye that unnerved Clyde at first. It was weird, his looking at you and the trees behind you at the same time. As the day progressed, however, Clyde began to find the flaw endearing. It made him think that maybe the eye had taught Evan sympathy.

Devon, Maine was not known for its financial power. In fact, most of the people here could easily be called poor. But Clyde's family was more than poor, they were seen as near destitute even to the most impoverished families in town. Which of course made Clyde's years in school lonely. No one wanted to associate with the poor kid. He was mocked, ridiculed and friendless during his high school years. Nothing, he thought, brings people together like a common enemy.

When Clyde saw Evan's lazy eye he thought that maybe Evan understood what it was like to be the butt of other people's jokes. That perhaps he, like Clyde, had been ridiculed and teased and that perhaps this had taught him one of the most important characteristics a man can posses: humility.

Maybe this crazy eye would make Evan more accepting of other people's differences and he and Clyde could become friends. That maybe Clyde's abnormality, as John would call it, his attraction to other men, would not lessen his appeal of friendship for Evan.

Clyde needed a friend. He needed a friend like a man lost in the desert needs a drink of water. It was almost a life-or-death urge and he felt like he was dying without company. If he couldn't have a lover, and he didn't think he could—not now at least, not here—then he would like a friend.

It would be nice, he thought, *to have both in Evan.*

Beyond the lazy eye, or perhaps because of it, Clyde found Evan very attractive. There was that friendly smile shimmering from him, as welcoming as a fog-splitting shine from a lighthouse. The unruly mop of curly black hair that stuck out of his head in every direction possible, suggesting that when he woke that morning he had splashed some water on his face and called it good. It wasn't a slobbish look though, but indifferent.

Working in the woods is a tough job. Evan didn't really have the body for it, at least not yet. He was skinny, weak-muscled and because he hadn't really had a physical job before, Clyde decided, he seemed to tire easily. Yet, he kept up with the others just the same. And he did it all without complaint. But when nine o'clock came and John called for a break, Clyde could tell Evan was near beat for the day.

Clyde pulled the gallon jug of water he brought to work each day from the cab of John's truck and climbed in the back. Evan dragged his feet over to the truck, then pulled himself into the back with Clyde. He had a two liter bottle of Coke with him that he cracked open and guzzled a quarter of it in one drink. Clyde watched his Adam's apple bounce in his throat. "I think I should have brought some of that instead of soda," Evan said, indicating the jug Clyde was currently tipping up to his mouth. Clyde let the cool liquid flow down his throat, breaking up what felt like clods of sawdust in his mouth.

"You can have some of this, if you don't mind drinking after me," Clyde said, holding out the plastic jug.

"Am I going to catch anything?" Evan asked, smiling when he said it.

"Just a little trench mouth. Nothing to worry about," Clyde replied, keeping his face as emotionless as possible.

Evan stared at him a moment, then began laughing. "You're kidding, right?"

"Of course I'm kidding. I don't have trench mouth. Hoof and mouth disease, maybe. But not trench mouth."

"You're weird." Evan laughed.

"Good weird or bad?"

"There's no such thing as bad weird," Evan said and gave Clyde's foot a little tap with his own. Clyde surprised himself by not pulling his foot back. He never even thought about retracting his leg. Usually Clyde avoided being touched; he hated the intimacy of a casual acquaintance invading his personal space. But it had seemed so natural, as though they had known each other for years instead of just a few hours. It felt nice.

John and Dale leaned against the truck, each downing their own drinks. Like Evan, Dale had a bottle of soda as well. They were discussing the newest scandal to hit Washington, both quoting, nearly word for word, exactly what Clyde had heard on the right wing talk radio station John listened to. Evan smiled at Clyde and rolled his eyes. Clyde shrugged his shoulders. *What you gonna do*, the movement suggested. *They might be full of shit, but they are our brothers.*

"Hey, Dale," Evan called out, "it's funny you hate this spying shit, but you were all for the Patriot Act."

John spun around, glared at Evan. "What the fuck you mean by that?"

"I'm just saying maybe it's not the fact we are being watched, but who's doing the watching."

"You think the Democrats are going to keep us safe?" John said, his face growing suddenly very red. The arteries in his neck pulsating in abrupt rage. "You think those fucking pussies will do anything with that information but bring Communism down on us?"

"Communism? What is this, 1956?" Evan laughed.

John came around the back of the truck, lifted one foot in the air and set it on the tailgate. His fists flexed and relaxed again and again. Clyde saw what was coming. Evan was about to be beaten and he didn't think Evan's brother Dale, though being a very large man, could do anything to prevent it. When John got mad he was like a blind, mindless gorilla. Unstoppable and often undeterred.

Clyde jumped to his feet and placed himself between John and Evan. "John," he said with his hands at his sides. He wasn't going to try to hold him back, not like he could have anyway. He simply placed himself between the two in hopes it would deter John from doing what they all knew he wanted to do.

"John?" Clyde repeated, a light lilt added to his voice this time. A questioning. *Don't do this John*, it said, *please*. He was standing in the truck bed not only protecting Evan, but John as well. If he went through with this and hit Evan, not only might he lose his contract with the paper mill if the administration discovered an employee, even a contracted one, was fighting on mill property, but also Evan could file assault charges. They were struggling financially as it was, but if this happened they would be ruined and probably homeless by the end of the year.

More than that, he liked Evan. In just the few short hours they had worked together, Clyde found himself very comfortable around him. He trusted Evan. It was not just because they shared political views or only Evan's breezy attitude, but a combination of them. These things also turned Clyde on with as much ferocity as these same things made John angry.

And he had let Evan touch him. It was just a casual brush of booted foot that would not have even registered to someone else. But for Clyde this was revolutionary. Evan had entered his personal space and Clyde didn't even realize it until several minutes after.

John glared at Evan, looked into Clyde's eyes and held his stance for a moment. His shoulders back, legs spread wide, fists flexing. Then suddenly he let his eyes drop and turned away. He jumped down from the truck bed and stepped into the brush for a moment. Clyde watched John's back, rigid with tension. He heard John softly counting. "One-one thousand, two-one thousand..."

John wasn't smiling when he returned, but Clyde could see the fire had died from his eyes.

Clyde huffed in relief and squatted down next to Evan. "What the hell was that about?" Evan asked, keeping his voice low as though John were a wild animal and any loud noises might startle him into another rage.

"He has anger problems. Are you alright?" Clyde whispered.

"Yeah."

John had made his way to the trees they had dropped that morning. The pines lie on the ground, large red X's splashed across the rough bark. They had fallen on an ant colony and the tiny black insects crawled over the trees in such large numbers, the pines almost looked like they were shivering. John looked up at them. "Clyde," he called and motioned him over. Clyde jumped from the truck and ran to his brother. "Dale and I are going to the next lot to clear out them pop-lahs we started last week. You and Evan strip the branches from these pines. After that, I want you to show him how to run the skidd-ah and get this wood loaded in the truck." He nodded his head to the logging truck parked at the entrance to the road. "The driver will be here at four and I don't expect him to have to wait. Got me?"

"Yes, John, and thank you for..."

"I know," John interrupted, "just get this work done."

"We will."

At noon, they broke for lunch. John and Dale were still in the other lot with the poplars and wouldn't be back until quitting time. They had taken Dale's truck. Evan had managed to grab his lunch cooler just before they had left, which was good because Clyde had only packed a pair of sandwiches and bag of Dorito's. He would have shared, of course, but would have been starving by six o'clock when they quit for the day.

"So, how long you been doing this? Cutting wood, I mean," Even asked, pulling the plastic wrap off a bologna sandwich.

"About five years. I worked with John when I could through high school, and for a year full time since graduating."

"This is tough work. I had a job at the paper mill, but with the cutbacks, well, last one hired first one fired, as they say." Evan fiercely devoured his sandwich, taking bites so large he seemed to have trouble chewing what was in his mouth. Clyde ate his peanut butter and jelly more leisurely.

"John gives us a half hour. You don't have to choke down your food," Clyde said.

"Sorry. I'm starving I guess. I don't think I've sweat as much in my entire life as I have today."

Clyde laughed. "You get used to it."

After eating, Clyde and Evan stretched out, backs leaning on the sides of the bed, legs parallel to one another so Evan's feet were in line with Clyde's right hip. "So, you think John is going to fire me? Because of this morning?" Evan asked.

"No. I thought he was going to pound the shit out of you though."

"Is he normally like that?"

"Like I said earlier, John has issues. He's a good guy, but if something sets him off, well, look out is all I can say. I was actually surprised he backed down today. I've never seen him do that before."

"Maybe he's mellowing. Old age does that."

Clyde laughed again. It felt strange to laugh, foreign. Like suddenly speaking a different language. It felt good though. "John is only twenty-five."

"See, he's ancient," Evan said, picked a piece of birch bark from the truck bed floor, twisted it around his fingers a moment. "I'm going to apologize to him when they come back. I know this job is temporary, but I don't want any hard feelings between us after the work is done." He pulled his knees up to his chest, hugged them.

He was wearing insulated coveralls that were a bit too short for him. The pant legs rode up, exposing his shins. His legs were very hairy, with curls of wiry black hair cascading over the tops of his socks. Clyde thought what it would be like to run his fingers through that hair, to feel it quickly ticking against his palm as his hands slid up over his shins, past the knees and into the warm grasp of his thighs. He wondered if the amount on his legs was any indication of the rest of his body. Was he covered? Would it be rough, scratchy or soft and downy like he imagined John's to be?

He could feel his body reacting to his imagination and he quickly covered his lap with the bag of chips, resting it in the V of his crotch. He wondered if Evan noticed because he began to smile at him.

"Do you smoke?" Evan asked.

"Cigarettes? No, but if you want one I..."

"No, I mean pot."

"Oh, yeah. Occasionally," Clyde said, but what he thought was, *every chance I get.*

"You wanna smoke one? I got a couple of joints right here," Evan said and pulled a hard pack of Marlboro's from his pocket. He shook out a joint, lit it and handed it over to Clyde. They smoked it down to a roach that Evan snuffed out and dropped back in the cigarette pack. The comforting buzz surrounded Clyde, like being buried in feathers. It was soft and beautiful.

"I gotta piss," Evan said, slid off the tailgate, walked a couple of hundred feet away and turned his back to Clyde. The hot, wet splash of his emptying bladder echoed against the forest floor.

Clyde's overactive imagination took over then. He watched as Evan, who was not really Evan, but an Evan of his fantasy, shook his cock but didn't slip it back in his pants buried beneath the coveralls. He let it hang out, fat and uncircumcised. A thick fold of skin hung over the head. He hadn't pulled it back to piss and the rim of foreskin glistened with moisture.

Clyde stared while the imagined Evan shook the cock in his palm. It was stiffening, swelling like a cooked sausage. Clyde remembered the last time he had been at the Route 2 rest area, down on his knees before an older man with silver streaked hair. As he choked down the man's oversized cock, he had looked up into his face and seen the same look Evan now had on his: desire and painful desperation.

Clyde slid off the back of the truck, approached the Evan who wasn't really there, and gently took his cock in hand. It was warm and fat and still growing. He pushed back the foreskin and the raw stink of sex and piss hit him. He liked the smell. Evan smiled at him, that crazy eye off in the trees. Clyde moved in and kissed him. His mouth tasted like pot and bologna.

Evan's hand slid down between Clyde's legs. His fingers fumbled with the fly of Clyde's coveralls. Clyde pushed his hand away. In his fantasy, Clyde was a bottom. A groveling, pig bottom who was here to service, not to receive any pleasure except the satisfaction in the other's orgasm.

This is also the way he was in the real world, out at the Route 2 picnic area. He was there to please, not to be pleased. He serviced the men there, but felt he didn't deserve to be served in return.

The fantasy Clyde dropped to his knees, on the same spot of ground Evan had just pissed on (that dirty pig bottom), and put the piss stick in his mouth. The taste was harsh and brutal, a morning's worth of sweat and funk trapped there under the skin, but it excited him, enthralled him in its fantasy filth. He slid the pants down and ran his hands down Evan's hairy muscular legs, then up to the smooth, blemish-free buttocks. A fine mist of hair covered each cheek.

He buried his nose in the thick, sweaty, black bush. Evan began to swing his hips, his cock sliding deeper and deeper down Clyde's throat. He twirled his fingers through Clyde's hair and face fucked him, grinding his pelvis against Clyde's face.

"You like my cock? You like it down your throat don't you, you fucking cock-whore," Evan grunted, slamming harder and deeper until Clyde thought his nose was going to break.

He did love it. Evan was right about that. He loved the hot-as-iron pole ramming his throat. He loved the sweaty man-stink, that funk of exertion and hormones and piss. He loved those heavy, goose egg sized balls covered in thick, wiry black hair, bouncing off his throat. And when Evan came, which he did just moments later, Clyde loved the taste of his oily semen, something that was only true for him in fantasy.

Clyde swallowed and swallowed, his belly swelling from the

massive amount of come. He held onto Evan's shaking legs, twining his fingers through the thick, black hair on the backs of his thighs.

With his balls completely drained, Evan pulled out, his cock slimy with come and saliva.

"You alright?" the real Evan asked, walking back from his quick pee break.

The daydream dissolved as quickly as it had come. Clyde looked up at Evan, then down at his own crotch where the Doritos bag hid his still raging erection. "Sorry, daydreaming," he said. "I guess it's time to get back to work."

"Okay, you gonna show me how to run that skidder?" Evan excitedly looked over at the machine. The cab was small, about the size of a short phone booth. "Is there enough room in that for the two of us? Am I going to have to sit on your lap?" he laughed.

Clyde could almost hear his erection let out a nervous, "Eeep."

Chapter 4
Picnic in the Dark

"Hey, I want to thank you for getting that truck loaded," John said. They were on their way home from the long day in the woods. Clyde was hot and sticky, just as he was every evening after work. He badly needed a shower. His armpits felt like they were stuck with old chewing gum and his back itched from the coat of salty, dried sweat.

"It had to be done, right?" Clyde replied.

"Evan worked the skidd-ah okay, I take it."

"Yeah. He caught on quick."

"Good. You guys got along?"

"Yeah," Clyde said, then wondered what was going on with John. When John and Dale came back from the poplar lot, Evan and Clyde had the truck loaded and were waiting for the driver to show up. He was supposed to be there at four, but was an hour late. While they were waiting on him, they were tuning their saws, tightening and oiling the chains, cleaning the sawdust from the grooves along the motor housing, getting them ready to use the next day.

The buzz Clyde had from the joint they had smoked after lunch had long since worn off. Usually he felt doggy coming down from a high, sluggish like he needed a nap, but he didn't feel that way this time. Perhaps Evan had some really good bud, or maybe it was the company that kept Clyde feeling so upbeat. While they worked they talked about the video games they liked to play—Clyde didn't have a gaming system, but he had played quite a bit at his cousin Fred's—and the movies they had recently seen. Occasionally politics made its way into the conversation: they were both very similar in their progressive leanings, but after the incident with John earlier in the day they moved their conversation quickly out of the political arena.

John had climbed out of Dale's truck and moved so quickly towards them, Clyde thought John was furious at Evan all over again and was about to make him pay for his outburst earlier. Clyde placed himself between them once again and prepared himself to be struck down. Instead, John stuck his hand out to Evan and said, "I want to apologize for what happened earlier. If I scared you, I'm sorry."

Clyde simply stood there, shocked, mouth hanging open like he was a simpleton. He had known John to apologize just once, when he knocked Clyde's front tooth out. He had performed kind gestures after saying or doing something bad—buying Clyde a beer, dancing with Darlene even though he claimed to hate it—but only that one time had Clyde heard his brother actually say that he was sorry for something he had done. Until now.

Evan took John's hand, shook it. "Thank you," he said, "but I'm the one who should apologize. You are passionate about this spying thing. I shouldn't have mocked you. It was childish. I'm sorry as well."

"Apology accepted," John said. He glanced at Clyde, then quickly averted his eyes. He seemed almost embarrassed caught being civilized. Clyde felt a rush of pride that moment. Pride for both his brother and his new friend, Evan.

Clyde wondered what John's real motivation was for the apology and, perhaps even stranger, why he hadn't pounded the shit out of Evan to begin with. Restraint was as rare for John as it was for a hog with a full trough. Why would he not do the one thing he was known for? Why didn't he give Evan a thrashing?

Is John trying to be a better person, Clyde wondered. *If he is, who is he doing it* for?

"You want something at the stoe-ah?" John drawled as they neared Miller's.

"Naw. I just need a shower."

When they got home Mamma was in the kitchen, leaning on her

walker. She was in a sleeveless dress and her enormous upper arms jiggled and flapped like sheets on a clothesline. She had made a kettle of boxed macaroni and cheese with tuna and peas. It was one of her specialties.

Clyde showered, then sat down to eat. It was cold. He went to heat it in the microwave oven, then remembered it was broken. He added some pepper and ate it anyway.

"I'm going to Fred's," Clyde said after washing his plate and fork in the sink, then setting them in the plastic strainer to dry. The sink was full of dirty dishes and he knew he would have to wash them soon. They were starting to attract flies. John or Mamma wouldn't touch them, but it would have to wait until tomorrow.

Clyde ached and he knew it was time to visit the Route 2 rest area. The Evan fantasy that had worked its way through his head earlier was still tearing hell with his body. He had been struggling with a semi hard-on all afternoon and he needed to relieve it. The climax free jerk-off he had in the shower only made it worse. And he needed to touch a real person, not a fantasy. He needed real human contact.

John didn't like their cousin Fred, which was why Clyde used him as his destination when he went cruising. John said Fred was a leech, that he had convinced his own parents to buy him the small house he owned and that his parents, now in their seventies, were killing themselves working to pay the mortgage off.

It wasn't true, of course. Fred had bought and paid for his own house a year after getting his real estate brokers license and Fred was now paying off his parents' third mortgage on their home. If anyone was a victim in this situation, it was Fred. But John couldn't be convinced he was wrong in his assessment of their cousin. Clyde believed John was jealous.

John busted his hump every day and had nothing to show for it. Their trailer was hot in the summer and cold in the winter. The pipes froze every year. They had replaced the floor in the kitchen and bathroom twice in the last ten years and now there were soft spots in them again. He worked and worked and things just kept getting worse for them. While Fred seemed to breeze through life, selling overpriced houses to people who couldn't afford them and filling his own house with every toy imaginable. He had a four-wheel ATV, snowmobiles, a new truck every few years, a large screen television with a surround sound system and every movie one could think of on DVD or Blu-Ray.

Yes, John believed Fred was a leech because he wanted to believe it. That the only way a person could have so much was to gain it dishonestly. So, when Clyde wanted to go out, he said he was going to visit Fred because he knew John would not check on him. He wouldn't ask about Fred when Clyde returned and he never spoke to Fred when he happened to see him around town. Clyde never had to worry that the truth he *hadn't* visited Fred would come out.

Clyde didn't like doing this, though. He didn't like having to lie to John. But what could he do about it, he reasoned. Tell John the truth about where he went and what he did? Tell John that no, he wasn't at Fred's getting high and playing video games, but out at the little picnic area on Route 2, down on his knees, back against a tree with some fat, tourist's cock in his mouth?

He drove through town, up Main Street, took Route 26 and in less than an hour saw the picnic area on the downward slope of Piker's Hill.

The light was fading from the sky as he pulled into the narrow drive. Shadows filled in the spots not occupied by mottled sunlight, giving the small park a sensation of camouflage, as though the place were hiding from the rest of the world.

The drive was a large paved oval that took him around the picnic area, past the half dozen picnic tables shielded by shaky wooden roofs, then back out onto the main road.

The small island in the center of the drive had a few more picnic tables, a barbecue grill cemented into the ground. There was low, scrubby brush that seemed to attract the travelers' family dogs, aching for a piss. The only feature needing maintaining by the state were two outhouses. The cheap green plastic walls were dotted with graffiti and large fist-sized holes let anyone who happened to stroll past the back of the outhouses a crotch level view of whoever occupied the toilet.

Clyde drove around the oval, noting the parking spaces separated by bright white paint lines, were empty. He rounded the curve and found the same situation heading out of the park as coming in, empty. He was the only person here. If there happened to be an empty vehicle or lone motorcycle Clyde would know that its owner was either in one of the foul smelling outhouses, or somewhere along the walking trails in the thin forest surrounding the place, and there was the possibility he might get in on some action. But there were no other vehicles.

Clyde parked his Escort, slid out from behind the wheel and walked to the picnic table at the mouth of the main trail leading up into the steadily darkening woods. He sat on the table, over the carved sentiments of undying love (T.B. + A.D. 4-ever), his feet on the seat and waited for someone to show up. If there were others here, like the old men that brought their own lawn chairs because they were more comfortable than the picnic tables provided by the state, he would at least have someone to chat with while he waited for an arrival that met his sexual requirements. Namely, the requirements being, they had to be under fifty with a dick that stuck out further than their belly. Other than that the only other necessity was their willingness to dance the dance.

Once the sun had completely descended into the west and the woods surrounding the picnic area had grown as dark and foreboding as Hansel and Gretel's breadcrumb trail to the gingerbread house, Clyde began to think that he should just go home.

The picnic area had no street lights to guide weary travelers into its restful arms, like the highway rest stops had. There were no sodium arc lights, shimmering in their weird orange glow, over the small outhouses reassuring women and the occasional nervous man that they were safe here, no one was going to attack them in this place. The only light available was from the moon and the dim glow of the stars blanketing the sky over Clyde's head.

He should just go home, lock himself in his room and finish what he had started in the shower. Jerk-off until his dick became tired and flaccid and every dirty sock littering his bedroom floor became gummed with his labor. He should... then headlights strobed over the small park as a vehicle entered the drive.

Clyde's belly suddenly twisted nervously. This place was dark, dangerous. He could see just a few feet before him. If this car held another man like himself, a man on the make, he might have someone to dance with. Or at least a conversation. But if this was a car full of less friendly types; bashers, young men with a father-sized chip on their shoulders, he could be in very serious trouble.

It had happened before. He had listened to a group of the old men sitting out here in their lawn chairs, daily newspapers folded over their pale, bony knees, tell about incidents in the late eighties and early nineties. Incidents where men were clubbed with baseball bats and tire irons. Where young men, the same age as Clyde, lashed out with a self-righteous hatred and impudence seen only in boys this age. Where they broke arms, legs and rib bones, cracked skulls and gleefully spit and urinated on their victims. The accounts reminded Clyde of Nazi stormtroopers cleaning out the Jewish Ghettos, or the fervent rage of the Hitler Youth he had seen in flickering black and white films shown during history class in school.

He sat upright on the table. Back arched, head held high, attempting to seem bigger, less vulnerable. He shoved his hand in his pants pocket and pulled out his car keys, ready to make a run for it if things turned ugly.

The vehicle made the slow run around the oval, pulled in a parking spot a few spaces down from Clyde's Escort and Clyde heard the heavy THUNK of the transmission shifting out of gear and into Park. The motor cut off and began to tick as the oil settled back in the pan under the chassis and the engine cooled.

Clyde watched the car and waited for the occupant (*please let it be occupant and not occupants—plural usually means trouble*) to emerge. Minutes went by. Hours, it seemed. He began to suspect perhaps the driver pulled in to get a few minutes sleep before moving on to wherever he was going. Travelers did that occasionally here. Stop for a few hours to get a catnap rather than risk falling asleep behind the wheel or spending the money on a motel room.

Clyde thought about leaving, getting out before his worst fears were realized and a lynch mob climbed out of the car. Just make a run for it. Get to his car, jump inside and tear ass out of the park and on the road to home. He had the car keys in his hand and just stepped down from the table when the driver's side door to the vehicle opened.

The dim glow of the car's dome light illuminated the only occupant as he emerged. He looked tall, muscular standing next to his car, the pale sliver of moonlight giving Clyde just a silhouette of the man. He could make out the wide shoulders, tapering in a gradual slope to his waist. There seemed to be some extra pounds on the man. He didn't look fat, just a little comfortable. Like a man who had never truly been hungry, but had never wallowed in gluttony either. The man cleared his throat, sounding like a gunshot in the near silent park, then he began walking towards Clyde, his footsteps echoing off the pavement like the beat of an executioner's drum.

Clyde could feel his own pulse racing, thrumming through his head in time with the man's footsteps. Blood pressure rising as the flight or fight instinct began to build in him. It was now or never, he thought. Run or prepare for battle.

Chapter 5
Dancing in the Dark

"Good evening," the man said. His voice was deep, but gentle. Soothing, fatherly. Clyde immediately settled back onto the table. His pulse slowed to normal and the sweat that had been forming on his brow, dried in the cooling night air. The man was still a good thirty feet away, still time enough for Clyde to run, but the man didn't seem threatening. He seemed a man just looking for a little companionship: a partner to dance the dance with, the same thing Clyde was searching for.

He was black. African-American, as John would have spit, as though the politically correct language he seemed compelled to use fouled his mouth. The man's skin was the color of the sky over their heads; dark, shimmering with a light coat of the day's sweat. Beautiful.

"Hello," Clyde replied, encouraging the man to approach, which he did with a hint of trepidation. He was as nervous as Clyde, which meant he was not here for any other reason than to give (and take) a little pleasure. He was not here to hurt or intimidate. "Nice night, ain't it?"

"Yes, very nice." The man stepped closer and came within touching distance. He was older than Clyde, perhaps by as much as ten years, maybe more. He might even be thirty; it was hard to tell in the dark. He was handsome, though. Clyde could tell that easily enough. "My name is Oscar," he said and stuck out a muscular, dark arm. His palm was paler than the rest of his hand. Clyde took the hand, shook it and felt the hard callouses along the pads at the base of Oscar's fingers. He must work with his hands, just as Clyde did.

"I'm Clyde," he said, giving his real name, something he rarely did out here. "So, what brings you out on a night like this?" Clyde asked, taking the lead in the dance. The thinly veiled questions, the probing as they waltzed around and around, working their way to the aggressive Tango, or a gentle ballet. Whatever they agreed upon could be performed on the picnic table, against a tree or perhaps in one of their cars.

"Just out looking to meet a handsome friend. I'm glad I found you," the man said and took another step closer. His shins touched the seat of the picnic table, straddling the tips of Clyde's well-beaten boots. Clyde could smell the peppery scent of Oscar's skin. It smelled nice, comforting, like a rich beef stew bubbling away on the stove on a winter's evening.

"I'm glad you found me, too," Clyde said and before they could talk each other out of doing what they had come here to do, Clyde slid his hands between Oscar's legs. The firm knobs of Oscar's testicles filled Clyde's palm. He could feel each nut, firm but with a sponge-like give to them, and the leathery sack enclosing them through the thin sweatpants Oscar wore. Clyde squeezed, his grip tightened around Oscar's balls, not enough to hurt, but enough to let the other man know Clyde meant business. Oscar's face split into a mischievous grin.

"That feels good," Oscar cooed as he reached out and fondled Clyde between the legs. Clyde pushed Oscar's hand away. He didn't like to be touched, even when he had sex. Oscar gave him a confused look.

"Just let me play with you for a while," Clyde said. Oscar smiled, pulled his hands back, let Clyde have his fun.

Clyde set his car keys on the table, then moved his fingers up, above the scrotum, to the root of Oscar's cock and traced the length. It seemed to stretch forever down into the baggy right pant leg. He finally found the head and gave it a little pinch with his fingertips, feeling the tight foreskin shiver over the glans. He grabbed the waist of Oscar's sweatpants and pulled them down. The fat, musky cock jumped from the thatch of thin, neatly trimmed curls of dark hair and he marveled at how wonderfully dark the skin was. Almost as dark as the night surrounding it. Clyde saw a pearl of glistening moisture at the piss-slit, winking out through the puckered ridge of foreskin. He pushed the skin back, revealing the lighter colored head. He lapped the drop of fluid onto his tongue. It was slick, greasy and just the lightest hint of sweetness.

Oscar moaned in appreciation, lifted his hands like he wanted to touch Clyde again, then dropped them to his sides and let Clyde do what he wanted to do. Because what Clyde wanted was what Oscar wanted. The dance.

Clyde slid from the picnic table down to the seat he had been resting his feet on and dipped his head down to taste the warm, black balls he had touched with his fingertips. He pulled each one into his mouth, one at a time, and felt the flesh of Oscar's scrotum settle into the space where his front tooth had once been. The salty tang of sweat and the shivery delight of hormones wrapped around his head like a turban, enveloping him in the wonderful smells and flavors of sex. Clyde's entire body quivered at the feel of the large, black cock rubbing against his face. He inhaled deeply, absorbing the smells of the crotch that had not felt soap and water since that morning and the faint traces of the piss that had been expelled since Oscar last showered. He worked each testicle, feeling them bounce over his tongue and move around his mouth like one of those everlasting gobstoppers he used to get at Miller's General Store when he was a kid. Then, he let Oscar's balls leave his mouth with a wet PLOP. The hair on the scrotum wet and clumped in downward pointing tangles, like stalagmites in a cave.

He opened wide and pulled the fat, black cock into his mouth. "Oh Jesus, boy." Oscar whispered as though this place was a sanctuary, a cathedral instead of a quick stop for a weary traveler to rest a moment or take a much needed shit. Perhaps, it was a church of sorts for him. Much as it was for Clyde. A place Oscar could be himself, without the cold, questioning eyes of family, friends and, more likely than not, wife.

After all, most of the men who frequented this place were married. Clyde knew this. He knew that nothing meaningful could come from the casual associations here. Knew that although they had fun, most of the men wouldn't even look him in the eye if he happened to meet them on the street. That, however, was a safety of its own. He didn't have to worry that one of his dance partners would confront him elsewhere, forcing John to ask how he knew this man. Clyde was as much in the closet as the married men he sucked off in the dark.

Clyde rolled his tongue over the head, curling it around the edge of the mushroom tip, then flattened his tongue to a hard plane which he pressed against the underside of the cock as he pushed himself down on it again.

"You like that, don't you?" Oscar grunted. "You like that big..." and here Oscar said something that shocked Clyde. It was a word so vulgar that even a man as angry and bigoted as John would not utter, the N-word.

Oscar said it though. He said it and he wanted Clyde to repeat it. "You like that nigger dick, don't you?" He leaned in, forcing more of himself down Clyde's throat and said it again. "You like that nigger dick. Say it. Say you like that nigger dick."

But Clyde wouldn't say it. He wasn't afraid of offending Oscar, the only black man he had ever really met, and the first he had been with. Oscar obviously wasn't offended by the word, but Clyde couldn't do it. He couldn't cross that line.

Instead, Clyde pulled open his own pants and freed his erection. He tugged on himself while Oscar pumped his hips, shoving himself further and further down Clyde's throat, toying with the gag reflex that filled Clyde's mouth with fresh saliva. Clyde could feel Oscar's cock grow even more rigid until it felt as strong as steel. It flexed and throbbed and Clyde knew that Oscar could not hold on much longer.

He pulled on himself harder, wanting to reach orgasm when Oscar did. He wanted to feel the rush of his own seed leaving him down below, as Oscar's seed filled him above. He wanted savor his first taste of a black man's semen. *Does it taste like a white man's?* he wondered.

In less than a minute after he thought the question, he found out. It did taste like a white man's semen. It was bitter with a mild, sweet aftertaste, just like every other man he had tasted. His own orgasm came a moment after Oscar's. It came with such a force, he nearly pitched forward, nearly rammed the last few inches of Oscar's massive cock down his throat. Come littered the grass between Oscar's feet, spraying several feet out, across the lawn until it met with the base of an old oak guarding the path entrance to the woods.

Clyde pulled himself free of Oscar's quickly softening cock, turned, leaned over the top of the table and spit the oily wad of semen into the grass. He shoved himself back into his pants, turned back to Oscar, who was pulling his sweatpants back up over his slightly husky hips, and picked up his car keys he had set on the table when the dance began.

"Well, that was incredible," Oscar said. "You sure do know what you're doing."

"I try," Clyde said, smiling. "I'm sorry I didn't, um... say that word you wanted me to say."

"What word is that?" Oscar replied, his brow furrowing in visible confusion.

"You know, the N-word. I just can't bring myself to say it."

"Oh," Oscar said, his head dropping slightly. "I use that word too much. But, I guess it's different for me, isn't it?"

"I guess. Yeah, it probably is."

"Look, you are a good man, uh... Clyde, right? Yeah, you are a good man for not saying that word even though a black man wanted you to say it. You are a good man for standing with your principals and not backing down even though the only person that would have heard you, is me. And I didn't give a shit if you said the word. I requested you to say it. But you didn't. Your Daddy must be a proud man. He did a fine job raising you."

"Actually, my brother raised me."

"Then he is a good brother. He must be a good man," he said and pressed a button on the side of his watch. It glowed a florescent green, showing him the time. "I have to go, but this was fun. Maybe I'll see you around again sometime."

"Yeah, that would be cool," Clyde said, but he knew the chances of them ever meeting again were slim to none. Not that he ever wanted to get together with him again. It was fun, he had gotten off, but there was no spark there, no connection. Oscar seemed like a nice guy, but he wasn't someone Clyde could actually see himself spending any real amount of time with.

Then he thought of Evan. They had a good time today working together, getting to know one another. They had so much in common, their choices in movies and games, their political and social beliefs. And he found Evan so very attractive. He could see himself spending a great deal of time with Evan. He could even imagine a lifetime with him. Not that it would ever happen. Evan seemed smart, witty. He was handsome and an all around nice guy. What the fuck would he want with Clyde?

Besides, he didn't even know if Evan was even gay. And, if he was, would he actually want something with Clyde? Could Clyde actually be that lucky?

Chapter 6
Vices of Men

It was just after midnight when Clyde arrived back home to the trailer. He pulled the old Escort in the drive and parked next to the garage. He pulled the keys from the ignition, climbed out and quietly closed the door.

The living room lights were on in the trailer and he expected to see John alone on the couch when he walked in. Instead, Mamma was sitting in her chair. She was wearing the same dress she had been in all week: brightly colored muumuu with large Hawaiian flowers covering whole sections of the dress. On her feet were faded pink slippers. "What are you doing up, Mamma?" Clyde asked, quietly. John was on the couch, sleeping, his stockinged feet propped up on the coffee table. "Are you feeling alright?"

"Oh, just a little trouble with my breathing. You know how this humidity gets to me," she said, her thick hand waving the air in front of her face as though trying to push more oxygen into her lungs. "Lying down makes it worse. I hoped I could sleep in my chair, but I'm wide awake now. Maybe now that you're home I can go back to bed."

"How are your legs doing?" Clyde asked and squatted down to look at them. Her legs were still bright red, but the bruising on the backs hadn't seemed to spread any. Her legs were dry though and large streaks of flaky white skin ran up the shins. "You want me to put some lotion on them?"

"Oh, could you, deah? They itch wicked bad and you know how hard it is for me to get down there to scratch them."

"You probably shouldn't scratch them anyway. It might get them bleeding." Clyde grabbed the bottle of lotion from the coffee table, pumped a quarter-sized gob in his palm, then rubbed that onto Mamma's left leg. The lotion was greasy and smelled like coconuts, but the white patches immediately disappeared.

"That feels better already," Mamma said.

Clyde glanced over at John. His head was resting on his left shoulder and a soft snore whistled through his nose. A can of beer sat on the coffee table next to his feet. A makeshift coaster of paper towels separated the can from the wooden table. "John's been drinking in the house?" Clyde asked. As long as Clyde could remember, Mamma had a rule about drinking. "Do it if you want, but not in my house." After their father had died, Mamma became somewhat of a teetotaler, rallying against the drink that had killed her husband.

"I changed my mind," Mamma said. "Women can do that now. We got the vote and the pill, now we can even have an opinion." She chuckled softly. "No, I realize we all have vices. Everyone has 'em, 'cause we need 'em. If we didn't have 'em, we'd go crazy. I got my food. I didn't work my way up to five hundred pounds 'cause I like to run, that's for sure." She let out another little laugh, clapped her hand down on her enormous thigh, causing a little breeze of warm air to flutter Clyde's hair. He could smell old sweat in that air. Sweat and something more organic. A smell he sensed was coming from under Mamma's muumuu. "We all need something bad for us, something that wouldn't be bad if we didn't have so much of it.

"And men," she continued, "well, men need more vices than women. They got more worries, more problems. A man needs to take care of his family. Needs to support them. A woman can stay home with the kids, take care of the house. She does that and no one says a thing. But, if a man stays home while the woman works, why, he's no better than a gigolo.

"John's got his drink and his dope. I know you like that dope too, don't you?" Mamma laughed again and ran her thick fingers through Clyde's hair. "It's alright that you smoke that shit. I hear it ain't no more harmful than beer. Probably it ain't, but it's illegal and that's what worries me. I'm so afraid you boys gonna get caught with it. I can't have either one of you in jail. That would kill me, seeing you or John penned up like animals."

Clyde looked up at Mamma and felt the long, heavy drawl of resentment begin to build in him. She hadn't been there for them when their father died. She allowed John to quit school long before he should have to feed her and Clyde. Had forced John to become a man even before he knew what being a man was. Now she was concerned about how much he drank and smoked? He opened his mouth to voice his protests, but stopped himself. Mamma had weaknesses, just like John did. Just like he himself. He couldn't be angry with her for being weak, for being human.

"And John," Mamma continued, "well, he has his women too. Oh, I know he been seeing Darlene for years now, but there been lots others during them years as well. He loves that Darlene though. I can see it on his face. He loves that girl more than he loves himself. That's why he fools around with them others. He don't want to lose himself. That's what happens when a man falls in love, you know. He loses who he is, becomes, I don't know, part of that other person. Happens to women too, but we don't mind it as much. But that's why men need more vices than women. They need them to keep hold of themselves, remind themselves they are men."

Mamma glanced up at the television where a 'reality' show was playing, the volume so low Clyde could barely hear it. The show featured a group of has-been celebrities living in a mansion together and the viewer had the privilege of watching their daily lives. A process which consisted of getting drunk and nearly breaking their necks when they fell down the stairs, or erupting into fist fights with each other. Mamma shook her head, gave the television a disapproving look. "Such foolishness," she said. "Why do these people get paid so much for acting like assholes? I know lots around here that do it for free."

Clyde laughed out loud, then clamped a greasy palm over his mouth before he woke John. He could taste the coconut oil in the lotion and wiped his lips on the back of his hand.

"John said the men he hired started today," Mamma whispered.

"Yeah, they did." Clyde ran his hands up to her knees, then back down to her ankles, spreading the lotion over the worst, driest areas.

"Are they good men? The youngest is your age, right? Evan, is that his name?"

"They seem like good workers. I worked alone with Evan most of the day. He seemed beat by the work, but he kept going. He's a pretty cool guy."

"You like him then?"

"Yeah, I do."

"Good. You need friends, Clyde. You need people your own age. Me and John are family. A man can't survive on just family. You need friends, but you need to start trusting people first."

"I do trust people," Clyde said.

"No you don't. I can tell it in your eyes. You're wary around 'em. Scared almost. I know that look. I see it in my own face every morning when I look in the mirror. Scared, angry. It don't get you nowhere neither."

Clyde pumped more lotion into his palm and began working on the other leg. He felt his cheeks burning and he wouldn't look up at his mother. She was right, he didn't trust people. He was afraid of them because he knew that if he got to know them, they would either leave, like his father, or end up disappointing him, like she did. Or beat the fuck out of him. That's what worried him with John. He knew John loved him, but knew his temper as well, and his hate.

"When your father died," Mamma continued, "I was so mad. I was mad at him for leaving me and mad at God for taking him away. I turned my back on everyone; my friends, family, even you and John. I didn't want to live no more, so I tried to kill myself with one thing that gave me pleasure: food. I thought it would be a beautiful way to die. Eating anything and everything I wanted. I just didn't realize it would take so long.

"Now, I don't want to die, but all this weight has taken it's toll on me. I'm 42 years old and can't walk one end of this trailer to the other without help from this goddamned walker. I can't sleep lying down half the time and haven't seen the outdoors in ye-ahs.

"This is what all that anger and fear has done for me. Don't, Clyde, please don't let it twist you like it did me. Be friends with Evan, don't push him away. I know it's your nature to do that, but you need him. And you know what? He probably needs you, too."

"I'll try, Mamma," Clyde said and he meant it. He would try to trust Evan.

Clyde finished with the lotion, rubbed the film on his hands into his arms and stood. "Thank you, baby," Mamma said.

John stirred on the couch, let out a little snort and turned his head to the right shoulder. "I think I'll go on to bed now. Maybe I can get a few hours sleep. Oh, this humidity is awful." Mamma set her walker in front of the chair and heaved herself upright, her hands gripping the walker so tightly her knuckles turned white. Then, once she was stable, made her way down the hall to her bedroom. The walker clicking like a stopwatch that badly needed winding. Her hips and shoulders brushed both walls of the hallway.

Once, when Clyde was a young boy, there had been pictures on those walls. Framed photographs of Mamma, Dad, John, Clyde, their grandparents and the many, many cousins. It had been a sea of faces. But as Mamma grew wider, the pictures began falling from the walls when she passed by them. To ensure the frames would not be broken, Mamma packed the photos in cardboard boxes and stored them in her bedroom closet. For ten years now the smiling eyes of their family stared into the dark. The memory of what everyone looked like, who everyone was then, were now just memories for Clyde. There was nothing on display to remind him.

"It ain't true, what she said about Darlene." Clyde looked over at John, startled by his voice.

"You're awake."

"Yeah, I heard you two old women gossiping 'bout me. I ain't in love with Darlene. Mamma's wrong 'bout that."

"Are you sure?" Clyde asked.

"No. I'm not. Maybe I do love her. All I know is she gives great head," John said, a smile stretching over his face. He patted the couch cushion next to him. "Come sit with me a minute. You want a beer?"

"Sure," Clyde replied and took the can John had pulled from the plastic bag on the floor. It was warm, but felt good going down his throat. It washed the oily coat of semen from his tongue that had grown bitter in his mouth. A rank flavor that reminded Clyde of raw potatoes kept him wishing for a bottle of water or a soda to rinse his mouth all the way home. He had only two dollars in his wallet and didn't want to spend the last of his money on something as frivolous as that, so he drove past all the gas stations and convenience stores on the way home. It felt good to have his mouth washed clean again.

John was wearing an old pair of sweatpants. They had a hole as big as Clyde's palm in the upper thigh, near the crotch. Clyde glanced down at John's bare leg shining out through the hole. At his muscular leg with the sprinkling of coarse, dark hair. He wanted to set his hand on that bare leg. Feel the heat and strength surging through his brother's flesh into his own. He wanted to massage that thigh, feel it lift and move off to the side, giving him access to the heavy basket it walled. Clyde could see John's underwear though the hole. Briefs that had been white when new, now yellowed with age, bleach and piss.

Clyde drained the can and watched as John scratched his leg though the hole in the sweatpants. His fingers running just under the underwear. When he pulled his fingers out a thick tuft of pubic hair stuck out under the leg band, curling around it like a beckoning finger. Seeming to say to Clyde, "What you want is in here. Come and get it." Clyde looked at it and felt the familiar ache growing in him again.

He saw himself moving in between John's legs, pushing his brother's thighs apart while his mouth worked at that hole in his pants, widening it, tearing strips of the material free. In his fantasy he was like a hungry dog, snuffling at John's body, snorting and lapping his way into John's crotch. He could taste the salty tang of the thin layer of sweat coating John's thighs and when he worked his way into the crease of his brother's leg, had the first glimmer of the heat and raw power of what awaited him beneath the underwear.

"Jesus, look at the tits on that one," John said, his eyes glued to the television.

On the television screen the reality show played on. A former porn star, wearing just a tee-shirt and panties, laughed uproariously at the little-person actor—whose most famous role was playing a serial killer troll—who had just fallen off the dining table in a drunken stupor. The porn star's massive breasts bounced like helium-filled balloons as she clamped her fists to her sides to calm herself.

"Oh man, I'd like to give that one a good titty fucking," John said and squeezed his crotch through the sweatpants. The underwear lifted slightly as he did this and the wrinkled flesh of his scrotum peeked out through the worn leg hole. Clyde could feel the snuffling dog in him begging to get back to work again. Could hear it whimper as Clyde held it back by it's collar. "Bad dog," he silently ordered it.

Clyde downed the rest of the beer and clapped John on the leg. His hand smacking the bare flesh through the hole in the sweatpants. He could feel the rough hair against his palm, sense the heat coming off his brother and Clyde felt the surge of his own blood rushing into his nether regions. "I'm going to bed," he said and rose from the couch, keeping his back to John to hide his growing erection.

"Me, too," John said. "We have to be up in four hours." John turned off the television and followed Clyde down the hall. "Good night, bro," John said as Clyde entered his bedroom while John continued down the hall to his own.

Clyde stripped to his boxers and slid into bed. He thought about Oscar and the taste of his cock. Thought about how it felt when Oscar pushed himself down Clyde's throat, going deeper than he had allowed any man to get. It hurt and scared him a little, having his air choked off like that. But he liked it as well. It had tested his boundaries, like a runner testing his limits in a marathon.

He slid his hands into his boxers, felt himself growing hard at the memory. He ran his thumb over the head of his dick and caught a drop of pre-come, pulled it up to his face and let it string between his thumb and index finger a few times, then slid his fingers into his mouth. He liked the taste of it, much more than the fluid that came after. This was light and sweet, almost like corn syrup. He pulled on his cock, working the liquid flowing out the urethra to coat his palm, then slowly slid his hand up and down, working himself closer to orgasm.

He thought about Oscar wanting him to say the N-word and his erection dwindled. John would have said it. If a black man wanted John to say the word, he would probably do it. John never said it because even he knew it was one of the most socially unacceptable, most vile of words. Of course, John would say it if asked, but he would not have been in the position Clyde had been. He would not be on his knees with a black man's cock down his throat, or any man's for that matter. Clyde imagined the look on John's face if he happened to see Clyde down there, on his knees, sucking off Oscar in that picnic area. He imagined John would go batshit seeing Clyde go down on any man, but a black man? Jesus, it would be like the end of the world. He would probably do more than knock one of Clyde's teeth out. He would probably kill him, beat him to death.

Yes, John was controlled by his fear, but then Clyde realized he was, too. He avoided people in town because he was afraid: if they found out about him, about his unorthodox sex life, he would be shunned. It was better to shun them first.

But he knew John wouldn't find out. It was best if he didn't because there are some things that just have to stay secret.

He thought about John and that hole in his pants, the leg beneath it and the old underwear holding him in. His erection sprang back to life. He had fantasized about John so long, for so many years, it was almost second nature to him. The moment his hand wrapped around his dick, images of John's body, hot and sweaty, naked with his arms spread wide, waiting to take Clyde into his loving embrace, filled his head.

He imagined now, his face buried in John's hairy chest, smelling the pine and sawdust on him. He imagined John's cock pressing against him, grinding into his own dick as John lay on top of him. John's mouth moving in for a kiss, which Clyde would gladly give him, but the moment their lips touched, John was gone. In his place was another man. The lips were just as delectable though, just as soft and tender. The body just as beautiful as well. He looked into the new man's eyes. They were a pale hazel, like John's, but one was looking at him, the other to the left. "Evan," Clyde whispered.

That was when he came.

Chapter 7
The Invitation

All morning Clyde felt as though he were walking through some weird, translucent goo. Encased in a strange jelly-like substance that was there, in his bedroom when his alarm clock pulled him from what turned out to be a two hour nap at four o'clock and followed him out to the kitchen where he downed his first coffee of the day with a bowl of corn flakes. A second coffee followed after a quick shower, but before brushing his teeth. A third went into his travel mug and journeyed with him to the work site off Pine Hill Road.

"You look like shit," John said as he checked the gas and oil levels in his chainsaw. It had been a mostly quiet ride, except the yammering of the right-wing nut on the talk radio station John nearly always kept the radio tuned to, and Clyde actually felt himself drift off to sleep at one point. His face pressed against the door glass like a lonely puppy in a pet shop window.

"Thanks," Clyde replied. He and Evan had completed their saw checks the previous afternoon in preparation of this morning, so Clyde sat on the tailgate and watched his brother work.

"That's what you get for wasting your night getting high with a douchebag like Fred."

The excess of caffeine couldn't seem to shake the odd out-of-body feel the lack of sleep had on him. Everything seemed to be moving in slow motion, like a scene in a movie where the film is slowed down to capture every nuance of a particular action sequence. It seemed like minutes passed from when Clyde thought about lifting his arm and his hand actually appeared before his face.

It was a little frightening, with his mind moving this slow and knowing he had to run a chainsaw most of the day.

When Dale's truck pulled into the lot and Evan climbed out of the passenger side, a travel mug of his own firmly gripped in his hand, Clyde's mind seemed to snap to attention. His penis sat up and took notice as well. He now felt more alert and rested than if he had twelve hours sleep instead of just two.

He watched Evan grab his gear from the back of Dale's truck. Hard hat, ear protection and chainsaw—fluid levels already checked —then juggle them along with his coffee cup over to where Clyde and John stood. "Morning," Evan said, his right eye looking directly into Clyde's left. A long, slow smile spread over his face. He quickly glanced over at John. "Good morning John," he said with almost casual disinterest, then turned his attention back to Clyde. The smile grew wider and Clyde felt himself return the smile.

"You guys ready to cut some wood?" John asked, then threw on his own helmet, pulled the screen visor down over his face and marched up the narrow trail to the spot they would be working. Dale raced ahead to walk beside John while Clyde and Evan lagged behind.

"Are you okay, Clyde? Your eyes are wicked red. You aren't high already, are you?" Evan asked as they walked along the hard, crusted path.

"No, I..." Clyde started. He was about to give Evan the same lie he had handed to John, but he couldn't do it. He couldn't lie to Evan. That was strange because he had no problem spilling the lie to his older brother John, a man who had raised him from the age of five, who had sacrificed his own education and future so Clyde could possibly have a better life than he did. He couldn't lie to Evan, but couldn't tell him the truth either. So he simply gave the excuse, "I couldn't sleep."

"Oh, this is going to be a rough day then."

"Nah, I can handle it. I've done it before."

"I was going to ask you... um, if you wanted to... uh, hang out or something after work. If you want to do that, but are too tired tonight, we can do it some other time," Evan said. He took large swallows during each pause as though he were nervous. As though something very important weighed in Clyde's reply.

"What did you have in mind?" Clyde asked, feeling his pulse suddenly slam through his veins, his heart speeding so fast he grew dizzy. He could almost see himself fainting into Evan's arms, like some southern belle in an old black and white melodrama. *He likes me!* he thought. *Enough to want to hang out with me. Maybe not the way I like him, but it's something.*

"I just picked up the new *Battlelines* game last night, *Wars of Our Fathers*. I haven't had a chance to check it out yet, but I thought I'd order a pizza and we could try the game together. But... I mean, if you didn't get much sleep last night, we can always do it another time."

"No, it'll be fun," Clyde quickly replied, doing his best to keep too much excitement from pouring out of him. He didn't want to seem desperate to spend some alone time with Evan, even though he really was.

Evan stopped walking, the chainsaw dangling from his hand, blade pointed at the ground. "It's okay Clyde, we can do it another time."

"Evan, tell me where you live because I'm coming over tonight. I'll sleep when I'm dead. Besides, days like this are what caffeine is for."

"Cool." Evan gave Clyde directions. He lived on Pleasant Lake Road. Clyde knew the area: it was on the west side of town and the road was paved for the first two miles, then turned to dirt. Evan lived a mile onto the rough, dusty, unpaved section. In the four miles of dirt road, there were only about six homes. It was isolated and rural compared to the trailer park Clyde lived in.

With the excitement of his impending evening with Evan shining ahead, time slowed to a tongue dragging crawl for Clyde. When lunch finally arrived, after what seemed an eon had passed, Clyde and Evan sat together on one of the trees they had brought down, gobbling their sandwiches and guzzling from gallon jugs of water. "No soda today, huh?" Clyde said as Evan tipped back the water jug, the liquid spilling out the corners of his mouth, saturating his

Chapter 8
With Evan

Clyde was startled when the pavement of Pleasant Lake Road abruptly ended and the dirt and gravel section began. It seemed to come out of nowhere, like he was driving off a cliff. Clyde had only been out in this neighborhood a few times—if a small collection of six abodes in a four mile stretch could be considered a neighborhood—and when the rough, narrow dirt road loomed ahead of him he instinctively slammed on the brakes. The road narrowed from a mostly smooth two lane stretch of blacktop, rough and cracked, but still paved, to a single lane potholed dirt path.

Clyde slowed his Escort down to crawling speed, the needle hovering around the 15 MPH mark as he wove all the way to the left side of the road, then back to the right to avoid the most ominous looking potholes. He still managed to hit the majority of the smaller ones. The car rattled and banged against each small drop and he began to sweat the suspension system. He wasn't sure what condition it was in, but after traveling up this road he might need to have it looked at.

The houses along Pleasant Lake were mostly old farmhouses. Evan's home was the only new one. It was a double-wide trailer on a single lot set here in just the last year.

Clyde saw it as he rounded a very sharp and very terrifying corner. If another vehicle had of been coming the other way neither Clyde or the other driver would have seen one another and they might have collided. But there was no other vehicle and as he made the hairpin turn, he saw in the distance on a flat stretch, the double-

shirt.

Clyde watched the water cascade over Evan. Stared as it soaked the thick fistful of hair sticking out of the top of the teeshirt and he saw himself licking Evan dry. Even with the sweat and muck covering him, Clyde still wanted to pull that water from Evan with his tongue.

"No. I think I was getting dehydrated yesterday. I felt kind of light headed, sort of like I was high, but not in a fun way. Like when you're stoned at a family get-together or something and have to act sober."

"Do you do that often, puffing before a family party?"

"I try not to. Do you know what it's like trying to carry on a conversation with your grandmother while you're stoned off your ass? It's not fun, I can guarantee you that."

When six o'clock finally came, the four men left in two directions: Dale to drop Evan off at his car in the credit union parking lot, John and Clyde for home. John stopped at Miller's on the way home to get a single beer, using the last two dollars in his wallet. Clyde grabbed a two liter of soda, using the last of his money. It was only Tuesday and they were both now officially broke.

"So, what were you two girls giggling about all day?" John asked once they were back in the truck.

"We weren't giggling," Clyde said, though he did feel a giggle coming on in anticipation and expectation of the coming evening with Evan.

"Tee-heeing then."

"Evan invited me over to play video games," Clyde said, forcing his voice to sound as nonchalant as possible.

"Ooh, you guys are really hitting it off. Should I be jealous?" John laughed and clapped his palm onto Clyde's leg. Clyde felt the sting, even through the insulated coveralls.

When they arrived home, Clyde quickly kissed Mamma hello, then ran to the bathroom to shower. Standing in his room wearing just a towel, he grabbed a clean pair of jeans from the closet and dug through the small dresser built into the wall for a shirt that wasn't threadbare or had holes. He found just two that fit the requirement. One was tight around his chest, which had grown much harder and more muscular in the last year working with John in the woods every day, the other featured a group of cartoon characters dressed like 1940's G-Men. He stood debating for a moment, should he go with tight and sexy, or goofy and fun? He decided on sexy.

He thought about sneaking into John's room and using some of his cologne, then thought against it. He didn't want to seem like he was actually trying to impress Evan. Evan had, after all, invited him to play video games, not a candle lit dinner and dancing. Yet, he hoped tonight would be the start of something between them. If not something sexual or—*gulp!*—romantic, then at least another step in their friendship. Mamma was right, he needed friends his own age. He couldn't be happy with just family.

He stepped into the living room, keys in hand. Mamma gave him a wolf whistle. "Don't you look nice. Is that a new shirt?" she asked.

"No, I just haven't worn it in a while."

"Well, it really shows off your arms. You got some muscle on you now. How did that happen?"

John stepped in from the kitchen. He leaned against the wall, arms crossed over his chest. "All set for your big date, huh?"

Clyde felt the heat rushing into his face. He could feel embarrassment creeping up on him, ready to lay him out with his own shame. He had nothing to be ashamed of, though. They were just two guys getting together to play video games. If something happened—*please, please, please let something happen*—he would let it happen. But he wasn't going to anticipate or expect anything. And if they did happen to fool around, John never had to know about it. "Fuck you, John," he said, letting the guise of anger cover his embarrassment.

John pushed himself from the wall and stepped up to Clyde. Their faces just inches apart. John's face hard and stern, Clyde forced his features to match his brothers. He was scared, but the anger he had just feigned, was becoming real. John was trying to intimidate him, just as he had their entire lives and it occurred to Clyde then, he didn't have to allow John to threaten him any longer.

He had as much right to live his life his way, just as anyone else.

Clyde's hands were at his sides and he felt them moving. He looked down and saw the fingers curling in on the palms, then opening. He was involuntarily flexing and relaxing his fists, just as John did before throwing himself into a fight. He took several deep breaths, calmed himself and prepared himself to feel John's fis striking his face. Instead John laughed, reached around Clyde an gave him a playful pat on the bottom. "Remember, if he tries t touch you, tell him you are not that kind of girl. Nothing until yo get a ring," he said, then stepped out of Clyde's way.

"I'll be home later, Mamma," Clyde said, bent over the reclin and kissed her cheek.

"Have fun, De-ah," Mamma said as Clyde walked out the dc and gently closed it behind him. He jogged out to his Escort, start it, then noticed his gas gauge hovering just above the quarter t mark. It was only about eight miles to Pleasant Lake and back. knew he had plenty of gas. *The only thing that matters though* thought, *is getting there.*

shirt.

Clyde watched the water cascade over Evan. Stared as it soaked the thick fistful of hair sticking out of the top of the teeshirt and he saw himself licking Evan dry. Even with the sweat and muck covering him, Clyde still wanted to pull that water from Evan with his tongue.

"No. I think I was getting dehydrated yesterday. I felt kind of light headed, sort of like I was high, but not in a fun way. Like when you're stoned at a family get-together or something and have to act sober."

"Do you do that often, puffing before a family party?"

"I try not to. Do you know what it's like trying to carry on a conversation with your grandmother while you're stoned off your ass? It's not fun, I can guarantee you that."

When six o'clock finally came, the four men left in two directions: Dale to drop Evan off at his car in the credit union parking lot, John and Clyde for home. John stopped at Miller's on the way home to get a single beer, using the last two dollars in his wallet. Clyde grabbed a two liter of soda, using the last of his money. It was only Tuesday and they were both now officially broke.

"So, what were you two girls giggling about all day?" John asked once they were back in the truck.

"We weren't giggling," Clyde said, though he did feel a giggle coming on in anticipation and expectation of the coming evening with Evan.

"Tee-heeing then."

"Evan invited me over to play video games," Clyde said, forcing his voice to sound as nonchalant as possible.

"Ooh, you guys are really hitting it off. Should I be jealous?" John laughed and clapped his palm onto Clyde's leg. Clyde felt the sting, even through the insulated coveralls.

When they arrived home, Clyde quickly kissed Mamma hello, then ran to the bathroom to shower. Standing in his room wearing just a towel, he grabbed a clean pair of jeans from the closet and dug through the small dresser built into the wall for a shirt that wasn't threadbare or had holes. He found just two that fit the requirement. One was tight around his chest, which had grown much harder and more muscular in the last year working with John in the woods every day, the other featured a group of cartoon characters dressed like 1940's G-Men. He stood debating for a moment, should he go with tight and sexy, or goofy and fun? He decided on sexy.

He thought about sneaking into John's room and using some of his cologne, then thought against it. He didn't want to seem like he was actually trying to impress Evan. Evan had, after all, invited him to play video games, not a candle lit dinner and dancing. Yet, he hoped tonight would be the start of something between them. If not something sexual or—*gulp!*—romantic, then at least another step in their friendship. Mamma was right, he needed friends his own age. He couldn't be happy with just family.

He stepped into the living room, keys in hand. Mamma gave him a wolf whistle. "Don't you look nice. Is that a new shirt?" she asked.

"No, I just haven't worn it in a while."

"Well, it really shows off your arms. You got some muscle on you now. How did that happen?"

John stepped in from the kitchen. He leaned against the wall, arms crossed over his chest. "All set for your big date, huh?"

Clyde felt the heat rushing into his face. He could feel embarrassment creeping up on him, ready to lay him out with his own shame. He had nothing to be ashamed of, though. They were just two guys getting together to play video games. If something happened—*please, please, please let something happen*—he would let it happen. But he wasn't going to anticipate or expect anything. And if they did happen to fool around, John never had to know about it. "Fuck you, John," he said, letting the guise of anger cover his embarrassment.

John pushed himself from the wall and stepped up to Clyde. Their faces just inches apart. John's face hard and stern, Clyde forced his features to match his brothers. He was scared, but the anger he had just feigned, was becoming real. John was trying to intimidate him, just as he had their entire lives and it occurred to Clyde then, he didn't have to allow John to threaten him any longer.

He had as much right to live his life his way, just as anyone else.

Clyde's hands were at his sides and he felt them moving. He looked down and saw the fingers curling in on the palms, then opening. He was involuntarily flexing and relaxing his fists, just as John did before throwing himself into a fight. He took several deep breaths, calmed himself and prepared himself to feel John's fist striking his face. Instead John laughed, reached around Clyde and gave him a playful pat on the bottom. "Remember, if he tries to touch you, tell him you are not that kind of girl. Nothing until you get a ring," he said, then stepped out of Clyde's way.

"I'll be home later, Mamma," Clyde said, bent over the recliner and kissed her cheek.

"Have fun, De-ah," Mamma said as Clyde walked out the door and gently closed it behind him. He jogged out to his Escort, started it, then noticed his gas gauge hovering just above the quarter tank mark. It was only about eight miles to Pleasant Lake and back. He knew he had plenty of gas. *The only thing that matters though,* he thought, *is getting there.*

Chapter 8
With Evan

Clyde was startled when the pavement of Pleasant Lake Road abruptly ended and the dirt and gravel section began. It seemed to come out of nowhere, like he was driving off a cliff. Clyde had only been out in this neighborhood a few times—if a small collection of six abodes in a four mile stretch could be considered a neighborhood—and when the rough, narrow dirt road loomed ahead of him he instinctively slammed on the brakes. The road narrowed from a mostly smooth two lane stretch of blacktop, rough and cracked, but still paved, to a single lane potholed dirt path.

Clyde slowed his Escort down to crawling speed, the needle hovering around the 15 MPH mark as he wove all the way to the left side of the road, then back to the right to avoid the most ominous looking potholes. He still managed to hit the majority of the smaller ones. The car rattled and banged against each small drop and he began to sweat the suspension system. He wasn't sure what condition it was in, but after traveling up this road he might need to have it looked at.

The houses along Pleasant Lake were mostly old farmhouses. Evan's home was the only new one. It was a double-wide trailer on a single lot set here in just the last year.

Clyde saw it as he rounded a very sharp and very terrifying corner. If another vehicle had of been coming the other way neither Clyde or the other driver would have seen one another and they might have collided. But there was no other vehicle and as he made the hairpin turn, he saw in the distance on a flat stretch, the double-wide.

His pulse immediately began to quicken and sweat beaded on his forehead. *This isn't a date*, he told himself, but it sure as shit felt like one. He was sweating like a virgin on her honeymoon. His palms were slick, sweat trickled down his back, collecting in his underwear and his heart was beating like he had run a mile.

He pulled in the driveway and sat for a few seconds trying to calm himself. The lot around the trailer had been cleared. The shrubs, trees and wild scrub had been pushed back at least thirty feet from all sides of Evan's home. The lawn—which was not really a lawn yet—was covered in hay to protect the grass seed sewn into the soil from hungry birds and squirrels. When the grass eventually made an appearance, Clyde could see this would be a beautiful piece of land.

He pulled the key from the ignition, exited the car while wiping his nervous palms on his jeans and, with slightly shaky legs, climbed the few steps up to the front door and raised his hand to knock. The door opened before his knuckles could connect. Evan stood on the other side of the screened storm door, that gorgeous smile pouring from his handsome face.

"You made it," Evan said with a voice that sounded as excited and nervous as Clyde felt.

"You give great directions," Clyde said, holding up the 2-liter bottle of Coke he bought at Miller's on the way home from work. "I remembered you brought Coke to work yesterday, seemed like a safe bet."

"You didn't have to bring anything. But since you did, let's get it in the refrigerator." Evan opened the screen door, inviting Clyde inside. Evan was shower fresh, his curly black hair still wet and lying over his head in moist rings. When Clyde stepped inside could smell the strawberry shampoo in Evan's hair. He smelled good and Clyde wanted to press his face into the thick mop, inhale him like a drug.

Evan had changed into a baggy tee-shirt and loose shorts. His thin, furry legs bare from just six inches below his hips down to the short crew socks at mid-shin. Instantly Clyde's body responded and he held the bottle in front of his crotch to hide the evidence.

Evan took the bottle from him, glancing down as he did. A smile quickly flickered over his face before he turned to set the soda in the refrigerator. A large pizza box took up the majority of the small kitchen table. *Donovan's,* the box exclaimed in bright red letters, *The best pizza east of Chicago.* Clyde had a Donovan's pizza once, long ago and honestly couldn't remember if it was good enough to proclaim it was the best east of Chicago, and didn't really care. He wasn't here for the pizza. He could feel the heat coming from the box as he turned away to glance around the room.

Clyde was surprised at the kitchen. It was small, but clean. The walls were papered with tiny blue cornflowers against a shimmering white background and even with night coming and only two small windows in the walls and a skylight in the ceiling, the room had a bright and sunny feel to it.

The living room was equally impressive. The ceiling stretched up 12 feet to a cathedral ceiling. A fan slowly pulling the warm air up to the mock rafters. A gas fireplace held the prominent position in the room though. A mantle over the fireplace held framed photographs of Dale and his wife, a black and white still of a handsome, middle-aged couple that Clyde assumed was Evan's parents and a shot of a German Shepard, its tongue lolling out of its happy mouth. Evan looked just like his mother. He had the same dark, curly hair and twinkling smile she did in the photo.

"This place is gorgeous," Clyde said, thinking of his own trailer, a 1982 model that hadn't had a proper cleaning since before he could read.

"Thanks. I bought it last year. Had it moved in here to be closer to Dale."

"Where are you from originally?" Clyde asked, feeling a little self-conscious asking, like he was prying.

"Vermont. Our parents still live out there. Dale's wife is from here though."

"Cool."

They looked at each other a moment. Clyde was unsure if he should direct the conversation from here or even what he should say. Finally Evan broke the silence. "I was hit by a car when I was a kid. That's how I got this," he said and pointed at his lazy eye. "Head trauma. The doctors said it might come back to normal eventually, but it never did. Anyway, that's how I bought this place. I got a settlement that went into a trust fund until I turned eighteen."

"I like it," Clyde blurted out before he had a chance to reconsider what he was saying.

"You like what? My fucked up eye?"

"Yeah... I mean, yeah, I do. It gives you character."

"Most people think I'm simple because of it. You know, like I'm mentally retarded or something."

"Those people are morons," Clyde said. He wanted to tell Evan what he really thought. He wanted to tell Evan how intelligent, witty, and clever he was. How Evan was unlike nearly everyone Clyde had known in his eighteen years. And how special Evan made him feel just by associating with him. But, he didn't say any of that. Instead he stood with his hands in his back pockets and struggled not to undress Evan with his eyes.

Evan pulled a couple of paper plates from the cupboard, handed one to Clyde, then opened the pizza box. Heat radiated from the food in humid streams. Evan had apparently just returned from Donovan's Pizza before Clyde had arrived. "Dig in," he said. "We can eat while we play." He tore a dozen paper towels from the holder hanging near the sink, handed them to Clyde, then tore another dozen free for himself.

Clyde dropped a single slice of the pepperoni pizza on his plate. The crust was golden brown, and when he lifted the slice from the rest, the bubbly mozzarella cheese clung to the rest in long stringy strips. The combined smells of cheese, tomato and greasy pepperoni made Clyde's belly growl in anticipation of the food. He hadn't realized how hungry he was until now; the sandwich he had at lunch had long since been digested. He stood back to let Evan fill his own plate. "Take two," Evan said, pulled a slice from the box and dropped it on Clyde's plate, then grabbed a few for himself. They took their food into the living room, sat on the couch, then Evan dashed back to the kitchen to grab the bottle of Coke Clyde had brought, along with a set of plastic cups.

Evan grabbed the television remote control, hit the power button, then fired up the gaming console. They both ate while the welcoming screen started on the game. *Battlelines: Wars of Our Fathers* exploded in bright splashes across the screen, in gray letters like the iron body of a battleship, complete with rivets and in hot red slashes resembling flesh wounds. Evan handed Clyde a game controller. Clyde took it after thoroughly wiping his hands on the paper towels. Clyde had played one of the *Battlelines* games before at Fred's and was familiar with the controls and the general object of the game. It was a first person shooter and the goal, like most games like this, was to kill everything in sight.

They played, taking bites of their pizza, washing it down with Coke and rubbing their fingers incessantly on the paper towels to clear them of the orange pizza grease. All the while, Clyde sneaked glances at Evan. Evan had a bright smile and the intense squint at the television as he fired and fired and ran his character through obstacles and danger zones revealed how much he enjoyed playing the game. Nearly as much, Clyde thought, as he enjoyed watching Evan. He snuck looks at those gorgeous legs, pale, hairy, faintly muscle toned, adorable knobby knees bent. He wanted to run his hands up those legs. He wanted to feel them as they spread for him, press his face between the furry thighs, feel the bulge in Evan's shorts expand with his touch.

As they played and Clyde's peeks became more and more common, his eyes would catch Evan's face turned to him, looking at him in the same way. Quick glances at Clyde's firm chest in the too tight shirt, rapid peeks at his muscled biceps, the thick blue veins in his forearms as his hands flexed with the manipulation of the game controller. They were studying each other, Clyde realized. Watching each other with the intensity of two predators in the wild, but each hiding their examinations with the guise of human civility. He glanced at Evan with thoughts of lust weighing on his mind. But, he wondered, how was Evan looking at him? Was it the same? Was it sexual curiosity that drew his attention or was he simply watching Clyde, a new friend, for signs of his deeper emotional makeup? To see if Clyde really was worth his friendship.

Their eyes met and each quickly turned away, a nervous laugh erupting from both of them. It happened once, twice, then on the third encounter they did not turn away. They kept their eyes locked to one another, held their stares. Evan grinned, a quiver of nervousness on his smiling face. Clyde stared at those lips, shiny with pizza grease, those beautiful lips he wanted to touch with his own. Lips he wanted to taste.

So he did. He leaned in and pressed his mouth to Evan's mouth, gently yet firmly enough to taste the pepperoni, gooey cheese and Coca-Cola on his lips. He felt each wrinkle, each line in Evan's lips on his own, felt the ridge of his thin, red mouth. The connection was heavenly. The most beautiful moment of his life so far. Kissing a man he not only found so stunningly attractive, but also a monumentally extraordinary person. A beautiful man in and out.

That is, until Evan snapped away from Clyde's touch, a look of shock on his face. Shock and yes, was that disgust he saw there in Evan's eyes? Disgust and repulsion at Clyde's mouth on his. And was there anger in the mix? Yes, it was there. He knew he saw a near uncontrollable rage flash over Evan's face.

How dare Clyde think Evan would want him? How much gall did Clyde have to think that Evan, bright, handsome, wonderful Evan would ever want someone as lowly and fucked-in-the-head as Clyde?

Panic erupted in him with volcanic pressure, tearing him from the couch, pushing him to the door. "I'm sorry... I... I'm sorry," he stammered, his head spinning in terror.

You fucking idiot, his mind screamed. *You screwed this up, you screwed yourself with your fucked up abnormal lusts. You don't deserve Evan, or anyone for that matter, as a lover or a friend. You deserve to be alone. Fucking idiot!*

"I misread... oh, I'm sorry."

"Clyde," he heard from behind him, but he ignored the voice. Ignored the gentle understanding in the voice.

Clyde reached the front door, grabbed the handle and turned it. It spun uselessly in his fist. His hands were slick with pizza grease. He wiped them on his pants and tried again. His hand still slicked around the handle, frictionless, spinning around the metal knob.

He felt the tears coming then. His eyes filling with exhausted self-depreciation. He had slept only two hours in the last thirty-six and his tired mind and body struggled to hold them in, yet a few escaped and trickled down his cheeks.

"Clyde," the voice behind him again. Hands, on his back, gentle, caressing hands. They touched his shoulders and turned him. He allowed himself to be turned, but kept his head low. He wouldn't look at Evan, wouldn't let Evan see him cry. He would not show weakness. He would not allow Evan to see him crying like a boy who lost his favorite toy... or a man who has destroyed his first chance at happiness.

Mamma is right: I push people away. I am alone because I secretly know I deserve to be alone. If I can't push potential friends away by normal means, I throw myself at them, ensuring they will leave me in disgust. I am repulsive.

"Clyde, look at me," Evan said. But Clyde wouldn't, even when Evan took his chin between his thumb and forefinger and lifted his head. He kept his eyes focused on the floor. Stared through the rippling tears at the tiles. If he looked up and saw the hate he knew must be there in Evan's face, he would shatter like a pane of glass. He would be destroyed and like Humpty Dumpty, would never be put back together again. He would be lost forever.

"Clyde, look at me. Please." He heard something in that voice. A shaky quivering, a sad pleading. It hurt him to hear it. Hurt that maybe he had not enraged Evan, but struck him on some other level. Had perhaps, caused Evan to hurt as Clyde now did.

He took the chance and turned his eyes up to meet Evan's. He was ready to feel his brain explode, ready to see the disappointment on Evan's face, effectively ending their very short-lived friendship. He saw instead, wet, red rimmed eyes looking back at him. "I'm sorry I pulled back like that. You just surprised me, that's all," Evan said, still holding Clyde's chin in his fingers. "I've wanted to kiss you all day. You beat me to it."

Clyde let himself go then, let the tears flow. But, there was no need for them now. Evan wanted him. Could this actually be possible? Could this be real? Then he felt Evan's mouth on his, felt his own mouth open and Evan's tongue slide inside. Felt his tongue touched by Evan's tongue. He tilted his head, their lips hungrily worked against, then with each other. The kiss went on for minutes, hours, days. A lifetime of unrequited crushes and secret longing smashed against the draw of this beautiful mouth.

Chapter 9
Building the Bridge

The kiss carried Clyde and Evan, still connected, back to the couch. The pizza, soda and war game forgotten. They had something better to eat and play with. Clyde hooked his fingers in the base of Evan's shirt, pulled it up, exposing his furry torso, and broke the kiss just long enough to clear the material past their faces. He tossed the shirt behind him, hearing it flutter to the thick carpet somewhere on the living room floor, then dove back into that warm, inviting mouth. He ran his hands along Evan's body, feeling the thick mat of hair on his belly and chest brush his palm. He had to see it. He had to see what his hands saw, had to see the body that he knew needed to be explored further with his eyes and hands and mouth.

He felt Evan tugging on his own shirt. He sat upright, lifted his arms so he could be freed of his clothes and heard a groan of appreciation from Evan. He felt Evan's mouth on his chest, teeth at his nipples and a wet tongue lapping at his armpit. "You are so fucking gorgeous," Evan said and Clyde was pulled down on top of him. Hands clamped around Clyde's back, ankles crossed over his buttocks as he was firmly secured to this beautiful man. Their cocks, separated by Clyde's jeans and Evan's shorts pressed against one another, attempted not only to excite one another, but to meld into one fat organ. Each man sharing pleasure and quivering, physical excitement.

Clyde reached down between them, tugged on the cotton shorts clinging to Evan's hips. He lifted himself from Evan to free the garment. He pushed them down over those beautiful legs, pausing only to caress the thighs, to feel his fingers dance through the thick, dark carpet covering those legs and tossed the shorts as carelessly as he had the shirt. Evan wore white briefs underwear, the same type John wore. These came off even more quickly than the shorts. The hard ridge of Evan's cock, hot and pulsating, sprang loose once the confining underwear met the floor. Clyde stared at it a moment. Long and fat with a dark circumcision scar ringing the bright red, nearly purple head. His balls dangled low in the heat of the day, covered in curls of dark hair. Clyde immediately dipped his face into them. The raw, musky man stink filled his sinuses. His head swam, drunk with want. He let each big, sweat-coated ball bounce over his tongue and he lapped down below them into the recesses of the furry ass crack.

A sweet moan escaped Evan's lips. A shuddering groan. Fingers forcefully tugged at Clyde's hair, pulling him up to the fat cock head. A steady stream of clear, wet pearls dribbled from the tip. Clyde lapped at them, the sweet nectar coating his tongue. The cock tensed with each touch of his tongue. Bounced against Evan's furry belly, then back against Clyde's lips as though wanting to dive between them. Clyde opened his mouth and pulled it in, savoring the control he had over Evan. He pushed himself down, swallowing the fat pole until his lips met the course, wiry patch of hair at Evan's groin, then pulled back up again, suckling at inch after inch as it left his mouth. He savored the pleasured groans, reveled in the quivering ticks rippling through Evan's body as he drew him closer to orgasm. He wanted to feel him erupt in his mouth. Wanted to taste his seed as it coated the back of his throat.

But Evan wasn't ready for that now. He pushed Clyde off his cock. Clyde fought him, refusing to give up his prize. "Clyde, stop. I'm too close. I don't want to come yet," Evan said. Reluctantly, Clyde did as requested.

Evan stood. "Sit down on the sofa."

Clyde complied without protest. Evan dropped between Clyde's feet and pulled off his boots. The tan, Herman Survivor steel toe work boots—the only shoes Clyde owned—slid off his feet and Evan gently set them on the floor beside the couch. He handled them like they were fragile, like they were valuable idols to worship. He pulled Clyde's socks off him, then slid up the length of Clyde's body, dropping wet, sucking kisses along his belly and chest. He lapped at Clyde's nipples again, teasing them with his teeth until shivers ran up Clyde's back and goose flesh rose along his neck and arms.

"You like that?" Evan asked. Clyde nodded his head that he did. He didn't dare speak. Tears were dangerously close to filling his eyes and spilling down his cheeks again. Not because he was afraid or hurt this time. It was because he had never allowed anyone to touch him like this before. It was too dangerous. If he enjoyed being with someone like this he might start to have feelings for them beyond the sex. If he had feelings for someone, then his world would change, forever.

Clyde realized then, it didn't really matter what he and Evan did together. He already had feelings for him. Evan's hands and mouth on him only intensified those feelings.

Evan leaned back and said, "Stand up." He paused a moment, then followed with, "Please."

Clyde did as asked and Evan fumbled with the buckle on Clyde's jeans, then pulled them, along with his boxers, down to the floor. Clyde stepped out of his clothes and stood, naked and vulnerable, before Evan.

"Oh wow," Evan groaned, on his knees before Clyde. He looked up at him, seemingly soaking in every inch of Clyde's body. He ran his fingers up Clyde's legs. Past the thick, uncircumcised cock that stood up from his groin, stretched past his belly button and reached for the hard, rippled muscles of his belly, to Clyde's firm chest. Evan stared at the cock before him, the rubbery foreskin pulled back enough to give a glimpse of the moist head beneath. "It's big," Evan said with an echo of wonder in his voice, a fascinated, greedy joy.

Clyde took his words as something else though. He heard exasperation in the voice. Fear, that he couldn't accomplish what he felt Clyde wanted him to do. "You don't have to, if you don't want," Clyde said. After the random encounters in the picnic area, when he serviced men and didn't expect reciprocation because he might not get it, or deserve it, he could only expect the same from Evan. After all, Evan was stunningly handsome, in Clyde's opinion. How could he expect someone so attractive to sully himself, to dirty himself by sucking on Clyde's unworthy cock?

"Like hell I don't," Evan said and enthusiastically pulled Clyde into his mouth.

It was like a thousand mouths touching him everywhere at once. The soft lips, pulling him into the warm, wet mouth immediately softened the muscles in his legs and buttocks and he had all he could do to stay upright. Every nerve ending in his body seemed to erupt in vibrant, tingling sensations that ran up and down his spine and soared through each limb. The current reached the tips of his fingers and toes, then spun around and moved back to his shoulders and hips, only to do the same thing there and head back down his arms and legs again.

He could feel every ridge and bump of Evan's tongue as it squirmed over his cock. As it wormed in under the foreskin, then lie flat as Evan pulled in every inch of Clyde's rather oversized cock, until his lips meshed with Clyde's thatch of dark pubic hair.

Clyde could feel the back of Evan's mouth, then the tight throat muscles milking his cock head as he was pulled down into Evan's gullet. The warm, wet bath Evan was giving him was nearly too much. He could feel the orgasm building already.

Clyde nearly made him stop when Evan emitted a loud retch like he was about to vomit. He didn't want to hurt Evan and whatever pleasure Clyde was feeling, and there was a great deal of pleasure, was not worth making Evan uncomfortable. But then Clyde looked down and saw the joy on Evan's upturned face. The wide smile as their eyes met and Evan seductively lapped at the wet, glistening head, then plunged himself back down on his cock. He enjoyed giving Clyde this pleasure as much as Clyde enjoyed receiving it.

He was so close now, so damned close to coming he tried to think of something that would bring him back down again. Something that would hold off the inevitable for just a few more minutes. Nothing surfaced. "I'm going to come in your mouth, Evan. You better pull off me."

When he looked down, Evan didn't retreat as he expected him

to. Instead he worked more furiously on him. The smile wrapped around Clyde's girth was even more exuberant. Evan seemed to want to taste Clyde. He seemed to want his mouth to be filled with Clyde's seed. Evan wanted him.

That thought sent him over the edge. Evan wanted him!

The orgasm tore through Clyde like a firestorm. He felt everything in him ignite. Stars exploded in his head and he grabbed Evan by the shoulders to steady himself before he was pitched head first over him. His cock erupted and he felt Evan swallow and swallow as his mouth filled to overflowing.

Shudders rippled through Clyde's body as he collapsed backwards onto the couch. His cock slid from Evan's mouth with a slick *plop*. He panted, struggled to breathe as his heart slammed in his chest. He had had intense orgasms before, but never like this. Evan pulled trickles of sticky, semen from his chin with his forefinger, then slid the finger into his mouth with a satisfied sigh. "Yummy," he said.

The power of the orgasm as well as the realization that Evan wanted to touch him like this brought tears to Clyde's eyes.

"Jesus, I didn't think I was that good," Evan said as he wiped the tears running down Clyde's cheeks with his thumb.

"You're amazing," Clyde said. He scooted to the edge of the couch cushion as Evan rose to his feet. Evan's erection pointed at the ceiling. His balls had grown tight in the scrotum, like a small fist. Pre-come oozed from the head in a thick, syrupy river. Clyde lapped Evan dry, then pulled him into his mouth. He was back on familiar territory now, the giver of pleasure.

Evan could last no longer than Clyde had. After just a few moments of sucking on him, of pulling his sweet cock down into his throat, Clyde tasted the eruption of the sweet, bitter fluid. Evan grabbed Clyde's head, held him as he thrust himself further down Clyde's throat. He let out a strangled cry as his body quivered and shook. Clyde couldn't breathe, but he didn't care at that point. Evan tasted too good to worry about a minor thing such as breathing.

Finally Evan released Clyde and fell onto the couch next to him. Clyde leaned into Evan, pushed him until he was lying on the couch, then curled himself next to him. He kissed Evan's mouth, cheeks and throat. "What were the tears for?" Evan asked, his voice so low Clyde could barely hear him though he was only inches away.

"I don't know," Clyde lied. He knew perfectly well why he had cried after the orgasm. By allowing Evan to touch him like that, he was starting to reconnect with humanity. As though he was building a bridge with his own hands and heart. Setting the structural supports in place, planing the boards and hammering them in place. He only had to cross over to where the rest of the world waited for him. He was forcing a change in himself because if he didn't, this life of loneliness would be the only thing he would ever know. Clyde could not live like that anymore, but building this bridge meant change. Change, whether it leads to a better life or not, is almost always painful. "I guess you make me feel..." he paused a moment to consider what he was about to say. "You make me feel worthy."

"Worthy?"

"Yeah, like I have a right to feel as good as what you made me feel."

"You do have the right."

"Do I?" Clyde asked, not really sure he believed it.

"Yeah. You know what? You're going to feel that good again," Evan replied as he reached down between them, took Clyde's cock in his hand and slowly stroked him until his cock stood at its full height. He slid down the couch until he was between Clyde's legs. He opened his mouth and quickly pulled Clyde into him.

This time, thoughts of whether he deserved this or not never entered Clyde's head. He simply lay back and enjoyed it.

Chapter 10
Momma Goes Out

The trailer shook with a such a quick, booming quake, Clyde was nearly pitched from his bed. He jumped to his feet, his foggy mind still held firmly in sleep, wondering if the trailer's shudder had actually happened or was part of an elaborate dream. "Terrorists! The fucking Muslims are attacking!" he heard John yell from his bedroom and knew that the trailer had indeed been shaken. He ran out into the hall, nearly collided with John in the process. John, like Clyde, was in his underwear. He had an erection that tented the elastic band of his briefs so far from his belly that when Clyde glanced down, he could see the root of John's cock, nestled in the dark thatch of wiry hair. John's eyes were puffy with sleep and his hair stuck out of his scalp in nearly every direction, giving him the appearance, Clyde thought, of one of those Japanese Anime characters. He nearly let out a giggle until he remembered what had woken them.

"Mamma," they said in unison. They ran out to the living room and there she was, sprawled on the floor, the coffee table lying in pieces under her. She had fallen on it and all four of its legs had broken under her immense weight. The table was split down the middle. The television remote control, Mamma's bottle of lotion and all the other assorted junk that usually littered the table were strewn around the room. Mamma lay with her back against the couch, clutching her left shoulder. Her lips were purple.

"Oh... oh," she moaned.

John pushed past Clyde and dropped to the floor beside her. He took her hand in his. "Mamma, what happened?" he asked. Clyde suspected, with the purple lips, that it was her heart. He ran to the phone and dialed 9-1-1.

"It hurts," Mamma groaned, her right hand clutched madly. The flower print muumuu bunched in her fist, pulling up to reveal her red and bruised legs up to the knees.

"9-1-1, how may I assist you?" a pleasant, almost cheerful voice came through the cordless handpiece pressed to Clyde's ear.

"We think Mamma is having a heart attack. We need an ambulance," Clyde quickly blurted. He gave the operator their name and address. "Please, please send help now."

The 9-1-1 operator confirmed the address, then said, "The ambulance is on its way, sir. Do you have any aspirin? Give her some aspirin right now. It may prevent damage to the heart."

"John," Clyde said. "She wants us to give her some aspirin. I think there is some in the bathroom."

"Aspirin?" John screamed. "She ain't got a fucking headache, she's having a hah-t attack for Christ's sake!" But John jumped to his feet anyway, ran to the bathroom and returned a few seconds later with the bottle in his fist. He dumped a half dozen of the little white pills into his palm and dropped them into Mamma's mouth. "Chew these up," he said.

Mamma did as instructed. "Oh, they're bitt-ah," she complained. "Get me some soda to wash them down. They're horrible."

Clyde went to the refrigerator, the phone still at his ear. There was half a bottle of flat orange soda on the top shelf behind the gallon of milk. He pulled a dirty glass from the sink, rinsed it out, then filled it with the soda and handed it to John. John tipped the glass to Mamma's lips and she slurped some into her mouth. The soda dribbled out the corners of her mouth, down to the neck of her muumuu.

The operator said she would not hang up until they arrived. "How is she doing?" the operator asked. "Is she cold? Can she move, or stand?" When Clyde finally saw the flashing red lights moving up the trailer park road, he excitedly told the operator they had arrived, then thanked her and hit the END button on the phone, disconnecting the call.

John and Clyde were still in their underwear. John ran to his room, threw on the ratty pair of sweatpants with the hole in the leg that exposed his beautiful, muscled thighs and an equally tattered tee-shirt. Then Clyde dressed in the clothes he had on earlier in the night. The same jeans and tight tee-shirt Evan had so lovingly peeled from him before covering Clyde's chest with his hungry, kissing mouth.

Clyde flung open the trailer door and waved the EMTs inside. There were two of them, a husky man with thick, tattoo-covered forearms and a small, very pretty woman. She had long, blond hair pulled back in a ponytail that swayed from one shoulder to the other as she ran up the steps to the trailer door. John stood straighter when he saw her, sucked in the gut he did not have. The woman was carrying a large, plastic box that looked to Clyde like something one would carry their fishing tackle with. When she opened it though, it wasn't full of hooks and feathery lures, but syringes, cotton pads and small glass jars of clear liquids with names like Dipenhyrdramine and Epinephrine emblazoned across the labels.

"Mrs. Chute? My name is Sherilyn," the woman said, dropping to her knees beside Mamma. "I understand you are having chest pains. Is that right?"

"Yes. I think it's my hah-t. It hurts bad."

"Where does it hurt?"

"He-ah," Mamma replied, grabbing her ample left breast. "And down my left ah-m."

"Have you had this pain before?" Sherilyn opened the tackle box, pulled out a syringe and one of the the small medicine vials.

"No. I ain't never felt nothing like this before. What's that in the bottle? I just took some aspirin. My John gave it to me." Mamma looked over at John and Clyde. Clyde could see the fear in her eyes. They were wide, darting over John, himself and the male EMT, then flash briefly over the woman before starting back at John again.

"That's good," Sherilyn said in a smooth, calm voice. She wasn't panicked. The calmness of her voice suggested Mamma should not panic either. Clyde wondered if that voice was taught in EMT classes. "This is Streptokinase, it's to help break up any clots in your arteries, if you have any. This, along with the aspirin you took earlier, may prevent any damage to your heart, if you indeed have had a heart attack."

"You don't know if that's what it is?"

"No, ma'am. We are going to take you to the hospital and they will do tests there to find out exactly what happened. The Streptokinase is just a precaution." Sherilyn pushed the needled syringe into the rubber cap on the top of the bottle, tipped them upside down while pulling back on the syringe plunger, then slid the needle free. She held it in her mouth like a dog with his favorite bone as she wiped Mamma's arm with an alcohol wipe, then plunged the needle into her arm.

"Ooh," Mamma squealed at the quick stab.

The husky male EMT looked down at Mamma, then glanced back at the door they had come through. He pulled John aside and spoke to him in a whisper low enough so even Clyde, standing just six feet away, could not hear. John nodded his head at whatever the man was saying, then they walked out the door. The EMT went to the ambulance and John headed in the opposite direction, to the garage. Clyde watched through the window as the single bare bulb hanging from the garage ceiling came on and John pulled the tool box he kept under his weight bench, pulled a few items from it, turned the light out again and marched back up the short staircase to the front door. He opened the door and motioned for Clyde to join him outside. In his hand, bunched together like a bouquet of flowers, was a crowbar and an old wooden-handled hammer. He handed the crowbar to Clyde.

"We need to get the front door off," he said. "Mamma might not be able to fit even with the frame gone, but we need to try this before cutting a hole in the wall."

"Okay," Clyde said. This was going to devastate Mamma, he knew. She had been embarrassed about her weight and Clyde assumed she never went outside because she didn't want people in the park to see how big she had gotten. Or, at least he liked to think that's what the problem was. Deep down he knew, though, she hadn't gone outside in so long because she couldn't go outside. She had grown too large to fit through the door. He had not been oblivious to her size. But, like Mamma, had deluded himself into thinking it hadn't been a physical complication that kept her indoors, but a psychological one. The truth was she was just too fat to get through the door.

John hooked the claw end of the hammer into the thin vinyl strips of decorative molding surrounding the door and pulled them from the outside wall. They came away with a rumbling screech that reminded Clyde of fingernails on a chalkboard. He felt a cold shiver run up his spine. John opened the door, stepped inside and began working on the wooden molding inside the door. Mamma looked over at him, her head twisting as far around as it would move. The bulging folds of fat in her neck looking to Clyde like a pack of the cheap hot dogs they had by the dozens in the freezer. Sherilyn had the rubber-tipped ends of a stethoscope in her ears, the cold, round amplifier on Mamma's chest.

"What are you doing, John?" Mamma asked. John ignored her. He wouldn't answer because, Clyde was sure, this embarrassed John as much as it did Mamma. When he and Clyde began pulling the wood framing of the door from out of the wall, Mamma understood just what they were doing. "Oh," she muttered and there was a sob buried deep in that single word.

Mamma began to cry. A low, quiet sob she tried to shield from Clyde and John, but they noticed anyway and said nothing. They continued to work pulling the door and its frame from the front of the trailer. Clyde tossed the narrow wooden planks of framing onto the ground behind the steps railing, then he and John lifted the door and walked it over to the garage. They leaned it against the garage wall, then came back to the trailer and sat on the steps.

The tattooed EMT climbed from the ambulance, approached Clyde and John. The name badge sewn to his shirt said his name was Cody. It seemed a small, gentle name for such an imposing man, Clyde thought.

"I called in for a larger stretcher. I don't know if we will be able to get her out of there, but if we can, she won't fit on the bed we have," Cody said, keeping his voice to a low mumble. Lights had come on in some of the neighboring trailers and faces, puffy-eyed and curious, gazed out windows. Curtains held back with one hand while, in some of the very early risers, coffee mugs gripped in the other.

Clyde went into the trailer to start a pot of coffee and to check on Mamma. There would be no more sleep for anyone tonight. He glanced at the clock on the broken microwave oven. It was 3:15 in the morning. In another hour they would have been heading off to the woods to work. He wondered if Evan was awake yet. He and Dale would need to be told there would be no work for them today. Then as though John could hear his thoughts, he stepped into the kitchen, picked up the phone and dialed Dale's number. Clyde could hear Dale's voice erupt on the line. John quickly pulled the handset from his ear, then a loud beep echoed from the phone. The answering machine had picked up. John left him a message detailing the situation, that they would be at the hospital today but, no matter what, would come back to work tomorrow. He didn't say it, but Clyde knew John could not afford to take more than one day off. No matter how sick he was or whatever might be happening at home, he could not be out of work for more than a single day.

When he was done, John handed the cordless receiver to Clyde. "Call Evan," he said, then walked back outside to wait with Cody for the larger stretcher.

"Hello?" Evan asked, his voice cautious to be receiving a phone call at this time of the morning.

"Hey, Evan," Clyde said and felt his heart beat a little faster at hearing Evan's voice. Even with the situation going on around him, he felt a smile curling his lips, a flutter in his belly. He knew there was something between them beyond the sex they had shared just seven hours ago.

At least, he felt something more.

"Clyde? What are you doing calling? What time is it? Three? We are going to see each other in a few hours and..." he paused.

Clyde felt his belly drop. He sounded almost angry that Clyde had called him. It was early, but he had been awake already. He answered on the first ring. *What the fuck do you mean by calling me so soon?* Clyde read between the lines in his voice. *We fooled around, that's it. Jesus Christ, if I had of known you were so fucking needy I never would have...*

"Sorry. I'm still half asleep. Let me start over," Evan said, pushing the thoughts out of Clyde's head. "Clyde," he continued, "it's good to hear you voice again. This is the best wake-up call I've ever gotten."

Clyde started to reply, but his voice cracked in his throat. He wanted to tell Evan that it had only been a few hours since they were together on his couch, Clyde's fingers combing the thick fur on Evan's belly and he couldn't get the thought of him out of his head. He wanted to tell Evan how much he wanted to hold him again. To feel their bare bodies pressed against one another again. To taste him and not just his cock, though that was heavenly, but his whole being. He wanted to drink him as though he were a mountain spring, clean and pure. He wanted to... he wanted to love him.

"We're not going out to work today," he finally managed to say. "You have the day off."

"Really? Why?"

"Something happened to Mamma. The ambulance is here right now. They are taking her to the hospital."

"Oh Clyde, what happened? Is she alright?" Evan asked, real concern rippling his voice. A worried shiver. "Are you okay?"

"I'm alright. We think it's her heart. I think we are going to be at the hospital all day. But John wanted me to tell you that we *will* be working tomorrow."

"Okay. Should I call Dale, let him know?"

"No, John already talked to him," Clyde said and a quick question passed through him. Why had John told him to call Evan? Why hadn't he done it himself? John was the boss and he had made that very clear on more than one occasion. Informing Evan that there would be no work today was his responsibility that normally he would proudly have done. But he didn't. He wanted Clyde to do it. Was he still mad at Evan for the comments he had made that first day? They had apologized to one another so it didn't seem likely that...

Why had John apologized? He had only been honestly sorry once and that was for knocking out Clyde's front tooth. He threw sorrys to Darlene occasionally, but they were as light and fragile as popcorn. But there had seemed to be genuine regret in his voice when he apologized to Evan that day.

"Do you want me to meet you at the hospital?" Evan asked.

"No, you don't have to do that. Thank you though."

"You sure? I give great moral support."

"I'm sure you do," Clyde said and felt a laugh rush past his lips. "You don't have to come if you don't want to. We will probably have to work all day Saturday and Sunday to make up for today. This might be your only day off and you don't want to spend it in the hospital, do you?"

"I don't hear a no. I don't hear you telling me to stay away," Evan said and Clyde could hear the smile in his voice. He was not asking Evan to be with him at the hospital, but was not ordering him not to either.

"No, you don't hear that. You will never hear that from me. I would never ask you to leave me alone."

"Good. I'll see you there. I'll bring plenty of change for the vending machine."

Chapter 11
Like More Than Like

Clyde hated the hospital. He hated its cold sterility, the ultra clean stink of antiseptics and industrial cleaners. He hated its obsessive cleanliness, as though it were attempting to eradicate every trace of the people here, of the lives that began and ended here. He preferred the rich, earthy smells of the forest. The air cleaned by a summer rain, droplets pattering his shoulders as it fell from the branches above his head. He liked the feel of the soil beneath his feet. Crisp and dry in the summer, slick with melted snow in the spring. He was a man who lived outside in the natural world. The hospital was an indoor place where everything, even the temperature, was controlled. Everything but the fear he felt for his mother.

He sat in the waiting room, hands clasped, bent at the waist, staring at the perfect, freshly waxed floor tiles. John paced back and forth in front of him. Marching like a sentry, nervously stopping every few minutes to drop in the chair opposite Clyde, tap his boots against the floor until he could no longer tolerate staying seated and jump back up to pace some more. He was like a shark, moving constantly, swimming through the clean, quiet waiting area not looking for food, but some word that their mother was going to be all right.

"John, how is she?" Darlene walked into the waiting room and Clyde looked up, startled. She was carrying a cardboard tray with three coffees and a bag of pastries from the bakery in town.

"Hey, Darlene," John said. He took the food and drinks from

her, set them on a small table stacked with old magazines and wrapped his arms around her. "How did you find out?"

"Small town," she replied, then added, "Dale called me."

"I forgot how much you Pruitts love to gossip."

"So, was it her heart?"

"Yeah, she had a heart attack. Cardiac Infarction, I guess is what the rag-head doctor called it. Doesn't sound serious like that, does it? Infarction. Sounds like she has gas or that she shit herself. They're admitting her. We're just waiting for a room to open up, then we can see her."

Darlene looked over at Clyde. "How are you doing, Hon?"

"I'm fine. Thank you." Clyde smiled at her, then closed his eyes again. The exhausted fog had smothered his brain again, almost closing him off from the rest of the world. He needed sleep and lots of it.

"Poor baby is beat," John laughed. "He was out half the night again. Whoring around I bet."

"I wasn't whoring around," Clyde said, keeping his eyes closed as he spoke. "That's your job, John."

"Who's whoring around?"

Clyde's eyes snapped open like window shades in a cartoon. He could almost feel them spinning around and around a spring-loaded rod in his head. It was Evan's voice. He looked to the archway into the waiting room and saw him standing there. He had brought three coffees as well.

"John is. As usual," Darlene joked. "Hey, cousin."

"Hey," he said, then turned his attention to Clyde. "How is your mother doing?" His voice had dropped its humor and filled with sudden concern. Clyde not only heard the worry in his voice, but saw it in his eyes as well. Evan had never met Mamma though, so the concern must be for him. He hoped it was because he suspected if the roles were reversed and it was Evan's mother in the hospital, Clyde would be frantic with worry for him.

Evan noticed the coffee and bag of pastries Darlene had brought, set his own tray next to them on the table, then sat beside Clyde. "Is she doing okay, or..."

"She's fine. Well, she will be fine, they think."

"Good. And how are you?"

"I'm still conscious. Tired as hell, but still awake."

"Drink this." Evan stood, grabbed one of the cups of coffee he had brought and handed it to Clyde. "It'll perk you up."

Not as much as you do, Clyde thought, then thanked Evan out loud. He drank the coffee, but no amount of caffeine could shake the tired feeling from his bones. Nothing but sleep.

The day crew began to filter into the small hospital. Clyde watched as dozens of men and women in scrubs and rubber Crocs or clean, white nurse's shoes rushed past the waiting room. "Thank you for waiting here with me," Clyde said in a voice so low he hoped John, just eight feet away, could not hear. "You didn't have to do this, you know."

"Yes, I did," Evan said. The finality in his voice spoke volumes to Clyde. He not only had insisted on the phone earlier that he would be here with him, he needed to be here. Giving Clyde the support he needed at this time was as important to Evan as it was for Clyde in receiving it. He cared about Clyde.

"What are you girls whispering about over there?" John asked.

"I was just saying what a cute couple you two are. When are you going to make an honest man out of him, Darlene?" Evan replied.

Darlene let out a chuckle, but didn't reply. John rolled his eyes.

Finally, a nurse approached and informed them that Mamma would be going to the Intensive Care Unit in half an hour. They could visit for a few minutes once she was settled.

"Let's go for a walk while we wait," Evan said as he stood. Clyde followed him out of the waiting room and down the hall. They passed a few employees who nodded or smiled at them, then Evan ducked down a corridor that ended with a large metal door. A bright red biohazard sign blazed over the door, letting everyone know to keep out unless authorized. The hall was abandoned, it seemed to Clyde. Evan leaned against the wall, took Clyde's hand in his. Clyde nervously glanced over his shoulder, out at the busy, vibrant hospital. People passed by the entrance to the hall, but no one noticed them. No one really cared.

"I had a good time last night," Evan said.

"I did, too."

"You want to do it again? Soon? Maybe, you can stay the night next time."

"I'd like that. I think it would be nice, waking up next to you."

Clyde looked into Evan's eyes. The left eye had strayed slightly, but was more focused directly ahead than he had seen it before. It seemed like Evan was making a conscious effort to keep both eyes focused on him. "I... I like you, Clyde," Evan said.

"I like you, too."

"No, I..." Evan paused, struggled with his words a moment, then continued. "I really like you. We've only known each other, what... two days? Two days, and I can't stop thinking about you. When I bought that *Battlelines* game Monday night, I wasn't thinking how much fun it would be to play. I thought about how much fun it would be to play the game with you. When you came over last night, I never suspected that what happened between us would actually happen. I hoped it would and when you kissed me... I knew I would never have a happier moment in my life. Even if I lived to be a thousand years old, I would never feel as good, as special as that."

Clyde felt himself grow a little dizzy from what Evan was saying. Lightheaded. He made Evan feel special? How was that possible? How could he, a nobody, make someone as wonderful as Evan feel anything more than a casual interest? But he had. Clyde could feel a smile start to spread over his face. He felt the smile growing inside him as well.

"After you left though, I could still smell you on my clothes. I wanted you back there with me. I missed you just ten minutes after you were gone from my driveway. I lay in bed wide awake until just an hour before you called me this morning, with my shirt pressed against my face because I could smell you on it.

"My grandmother says that people our age are more... I don't know, susceptible to emotions than others. She told me once that we haven't grown cynical yet. We haven't grown that hard shell that older people have. Well, I don't want that shell. I like feeling this way, even though it's kind of... painful."

Painful? Clyde wondered if it was the same pain he felt just looking at Evan. A wonderful ache deep down in his insides that made his belly cramp and his heart beat like a maniac drumming his chest, but it felt so damned good as it tore him apart. Could it be that kind of pain?

"I don't know what I feel for you," Evan continued. "I think I love you, but I'm not really sure what love is. You read about it books and hear it in songs and being in love sounds so wonderful, like walking on the clouds. But, if love is what I'm feeling for you, it hurts. There is the cloud thing when we are together. When I can see you, touch you, I feel like a god. Like I can take on the world and nothing will hurt me as long as you are there beside me. But when you're not there? It hurts so fucking much I want to die."

Tears had formed in his eyes as he spoke. They ran down his cheeks and collected on his chin. Clyde reached out and wiped them away with his thumb, then leaned in and kissed him. A group of young nursing students walked by the entrance to the hall as Clyde and Evan kissed. The students let out a loud giggle, then moved on. Clyde heard them, but didn't care. He wasn't ashamed to be with Evan, he was proud. Evan wasn't the lucky one in this, he was.

"I like you, Clyde. I like you more than like."

"What does that mean?" Clyde said, his lips hovering just an inch or so from Evan's mouth.

"There are, um... four things a person can feel for another. Hate, dislike, like and love. I don't know if I love you. I probably do, but I've never been in love before so I don't really know. I know I more than like you though. So, maybe what I feel is somewhere between like and love. Extreme like, I guess."

Evan liked him more than like. It was an odd sentiment, but it fit what Clyde felt for Evan as well. Evan was correct about the other thing, as well. If this was love, then the songs had it all wrong. Love fucking hurt.

Clyde took Evan's face in his hands, then leaned in and licked the tears away. "Please don't cry anymore," he said. "I don't know why you like me. I really can't figure it out."

"Clyde, you..." Evan started. Clyde removed his hands from

his brother's cock down into his throat before John
. then angry? He would be angry too, Clyde knew
it be worth it?

n released him, rolled over onto his other side and
me more regular, steadier.

ted off to sleep, not thinking of John's hands that had
is lap, but Evan and his confession to him back at the
said he might be in love with Clyde. And Clyde thought
in love with Evan right back.

Evan's cheeks and set his left palm over Evan's mouth.

"Please," Clyde said, "let me say this."

Evan nodded his head that he would and twisted his fingers in front of the hand covering his mouth, as though he were turning a key in a lock over his lips.

Clyde continued, "I've never met anyone that makes me feel the way you make me feel. When I'm with you I feel like I'm going crazy. I want to touch you everywhere, every inch of your body at once. I want to press myself against you and feel your heart beat against my own. I want to enter you and see the world through your eyes. Maybe then, I might understand what you see in me. I want to know everything about you. I want to *know* you just like I know myself.

"Whatever I did to deserve you was the smartest thing I ever did. I can't stand *not* being with you. When I left your place last night, I wanted to turn around and go back to you even before I got off your road. Saying goodbye was so fucking hard, even though I knew it was only for a few hours. But, even a few minutes hurts like hell when I'm not with you.

"I feel crazy when I'm with you, but I feel like I'm dying when I'm not."

It was just after ten in the morning when Clyde and John arrived back at the trailer. They stumbled from the truck, John dragging his feet up to the trailer door, Clyde so exhausted everything in his peripheral vision was growing dark, like the sun was setting, but only for him. John forgot about the door and nearly pulled it on top of him. "Son of a bitch," he screamed and kicked it while still holding onto the doorknob. He left a large dent in the bottom corner.

Clyde stepped into the trailer and John followed him in, leaving the door leaning against the outside wall. "I'll get us something to eat," Clyde said, pulled a couple cans of ravioli from the cupboard, dumped them in a pan and spun the burner knob to low. John went to the garage, came back with a fistful of nails and began fixing the door. When he was done with that, the food was hot and they sat and ate.

"I hope that rag-head doctor knows what he is doing," John said, spoon dripping with tomato sauce hovering over his bowl.

"Actually I think he is Indian, not Middle Eastern."

"So?" John blurted, slamming his fist clutching the spoon onto the table. Tomato sauce sprayed across the room, nearly covering Clyde. "I don't give no fuck where he's from. He ain't American, that's all that matters."

"Alright. I'm sorry."

John looked at the mess he had made, grabbed the small towel hanging from the oven door and wiped the sauce from the table. "No, you ain't got nothing to be sorry for," he said, his voice surprisingly gentle. "I don't mean to yell at you. I'm just worried, that's all."

"I know. I am too, but you heard what he said. Mamma is going to be okay. We need to get rid of this shit food around here, though. Buy some fresh stuff."

They weren't really sure how to do that. The groceries John bought each month with Mamma's food stamps might be junk, but it was the only food he understood. The produce aisle was as foreign to him as Mamma's doctor.

After Dr. Sing made it clear to them what needed to change in their house for Mamma's well being, the hospital social worker made a visit to Mamma's hospital room. She explained to Mamma about the low-income charity program the hospital had for those without the money to pay for treatment.

MaineCare would pay for a great deal of the bill, but not all of it. The hospital program would try to take care of the rest.

John grumbled at first. He didn't like the idea of charity, no matter how needed it was. But when the social worker explained that their portion of the bill could easily be in the thousands of dollars, perhaps as much as five thousand, John relented and told her to go ahead with the paperwork.

Clyde finished eating, dumped the bowl in the sink without rinsing it, then went to his room. He pulled the curtains closed,

blocking out the sun and h
into bed. He didn't think l
second and was starting to
come into the room.

"I thought you might want s

"Sure. I'd love it," Clyde sa
wanted sleep more than anything
to him. He was scared about losin
well and he also knew that the fe
what John must be feeling. John had
their father when he died. He could r
it felt like to lose him. Mamma was t
least Clyde had John if things went b
have no one but Clyde, the brother he h

John was in his briefs, shining white
bed and turned on his side spooning Cl
John's chest and belly massaged Clyde
covering John felt like little fingers on his tir
in response to John's touch. It felt good. It fe
with his brother's body holding him, protec
himself back against him, felt John's body dig in

Clyde thought of Evan and wondered if he
pressed against his back. He thought he probabl
even like it better, he bet. John let out a little sn
the wet press of lips to his neck. A shiver ran up his

John was sleeping. Clyde could hear his stead
slow, regular pulse beating into his back. The steady
drew Clyde to the edge of sleep. He hovered there
edge of wakefulness. Then John's hand moved up ont
slid down over his belly and pressed into the rigid stan
erection. He hadn't even realized he was hard until John
That touch though, could not let him forget it. It thro
flexed, sending mad thoughts and desires into Clyde's
wondered, with John asleep, how far he could go with him b
woke. Could he get John out of his underwear? Could he pl
him until he was as hard as Clyde now was? Could he finally

taste of it, push
woke, confuse
this. But would
Finally, Jo
the snore bec
Clyde dri
just been in
hospital. He
he might be

Evan's cheeks and set his left palm over Evan's mouth.

"Please," Clyde said, "let me say this."

Evan nodded his head that he would and twisted his fingers in front of the hand covering his mouth, as though he were turning a key in a lock over his lips.

Clyde continued, "I've never met anyone that makes me feel the way you make me feel. When I'm with you I feel like I'm going crazy. I want to touch you everywhere, every inch of your body at once. I want to press myself against you and feel your heart beat against my own. I want to enter you and see the world through your eyes. Maybe then, I might understand what you see in me. I want to know everything about you. I want to *know* you just like I know myself.

"Whatever I did to deserve you was the smartest thing I ever did. I can't stand *not* being with you. When I left your place last night, I wanted to turn around and go back to you even before I got off your road. Saying goodbye was so fucking hard, even though I knew it was only for a few hours. But, even a few minutes hurts like hell when I'm not with you.

"I feel crazy when I'm with you, but I feel like I'm dying when I'm not."

It was just after ten in the morning when Clyde and John arrived back at the trailer. They stumbled from the truck, John dragging his feet up to the trailer door, Clyde so exhausted everything in his peripheral vision was growing dark, like the sun was setting, but only for him. John forgot about the door and nearly pulled it on top of him. "Son of a bitch," he screamed and kicked it while still holding onto the doorknob. He left a large dent in the bottom corner.

Clyde stepped into the trailer and John followed him in, leaving the door leaning against the outside wall. "I'll get us something to eat," Clyde said, pulled a couple cans of ravioli from the cupboard, dumped them in a pan and spun the burner knob to low. John went to the garage, came back with a fistful of nails and began fixing the door. When he was done with that, the food was hot and they sat and ate.

"I hope that rag-head doctor knows what he is doing," John said, spoon dripping with tomato sauce hovering over his bowl.

"Actually I think he is Indian, not Middle Eastern."

"So?" John blurted, slamming his fist clutching the spoon onto the table. Tomato sauce sprayed across the room, nearly covering Clyde. "I don't give no fuck where he's from. He ain't American, that's all that matters."

"Alright. I'm sorry."

John looked at the mess he had made, grabbed the small towel hanging from the oven door and wiped the sauce from the table. "No, you ain't got nothing to be sorry for," he said, his voice surprisingly gentle. "I don't mean to yell at you. I'm just worried, that's all."

"I know. I am too, but you heard what he said. Mamma is going to be okay. We need to get rid of this shit food around here, though. Buy some fresh stuff."

They weren't really sure how to do that. The groceries John bought each month with Mamma's food stamps might be junk, but it was the only food he understood. The produce aisle was as foreign to him as Mamma's doctor.

After Dr. Sing made it clear to them what needed to change in their house for Mamma's well being, the hospital social worker made a visit to Mamma's hospital room. She explained to Mamma about the low-income charity program the hospital had for those without the money to pay for treatment.

MaineCare would pay for a great deal of the bill, but not all of it. The hospital program would try to take care of the rest.

John grumbled at first. He didn't like the idea of charity, no matter how needed it was. But when the social worker explained that their portion of the bill could easily be in the thousands of dollars, perhaps as much as five thousand, John relented and told her to go ahead with the paperwork.

Clyde finished eating, dumped the bowl in the sink without rinsing it, then went to his room. He pulled the curtains closed, blocking out the sun and heat, stripped to his boxers and climbed into bed. He didn't think he could keep his eyes open another second and was starting to drift off to sleep when he heard John come into the room.

"I thought you might want some company," John said.

"Sure. I'd love it," Clyde said and pulled the covers back. He wanted sleep more than anything, but had hoped John would come to him. He was scared about losing Mamma. He knew John was as well and he also knew that the fear he felt was far different than what John must be feeling. John had been old enough to really know their father when he died. He could remember him vividly and what it felt like to lose him. Mamma was their only living parent, but at least Clyde had John if things went bad for Mamma. John would have no one but Clyde, the brother he had helped raise like a son.

John was in his briefs, shining white in the dark. He slid in the bed and turned on his side spooning Clyde. The hard muscles of John's chest and belly massaged Clyde and the thick dark hair covering John felt like little fingers on his tired body. Clyde moaned in response to John's touch. It felt good. It felt like he was safe here with his brother's body holding him, protecting him. He pushed himself back against him, felt John's body dig into him.

Clyde thought of Evan and wondered if he would feel this good pressed against his back. He thought he probably would. He would even like it better, he bet. John let out a little snore and Clyde felt the wet press of lips to his neck. A shiver ran up his spine.

John was sleeping. Clyde could hear his steady breathing. His slow, regular pulse beating into his back. The steady rhythm slowly drew Clyde to the edge of sleep. He hovered there, clung to the edge of wakefulness. Then John's hand moved up onto Clyde's hip, slid down over his belly and pressed into the rigid stand of Clyde's erection. He hadn't even realized he was hard until John touched it. That touch though, could not let him forget it. It throbbed and flexed, sending mad thoughts and desires into Clyde's head. He wondered, with John asleep, how far he could go with him before he woke. Could he get John out of his underwear? Could he play with him until he was as hard as Clyde now was? Could he finally get a taste of it, push his brother's cock down into his throat before John woke, confused. then angry? He would be angry too, Clyde knew this. But would it be worth it?

Finally, John released him, rolled over onto his other side and the snore became more regular, steadier.

Clyde drifted off to sleep, not thinking of John's hands that had just been in his lap, but Evan and his confession to him back at the hospital. He said he might be in love with Clyde. And Clyde thought he might be in love with Evan right back.

Chapter 12
Who Do You Want to Be?

Clyde woke with a scream struggling to claw its way from his throat. Sweat dampened his body. His armpits, chest and back were slick with the salty moisture that trickled down into his boxers, making the thin cotton material cling to him like plastic wrap. His eyes snapped open.

Where am I? his mind nearly screamed aloud. He saw the sunlight coming in through the thin curtains over his head. He saw the bedside table with the electric alarm clock and the lamp with the ripped shade. He was in his room. He was safe and in his own bed. The quick thumping of his heart still beat-beat-beat, but was beginning to slow. Clyde could feel himself begin to calm. His breathing was becoming more regular. The quick, burpy pants, the furious intakes and exhales slowed to a more regular rhythm.

John lay under him. Clyde's head was on his brother's belly and John's slow, steady breathing nearly lulled him back to sleep. Then he remembered what woke him. He remembered the dream.

He had been in the section of woods where he, John, Evan and Dale had been working all week. His dream self could smell the comforting rush of sawdust, old leaves and his own sweat. He loved the smells. The aroma of nature and hard work. He could feel the early morning dew rising up from the forest floor to dampen his boots and pant legs. Felt the moisture on his face as it dropped from the branches over his head.

He stepped into a clearing and saw someone lying on the forest floor. He saw the long expanses of flesh, and knew the person was nude. Excitement fluttered inside him. He stepped closer. The person lying on a bed of pine needles was a man. Clyde could see the cock, draped over the thin hip. The man was hairy, very hairy. Pine needles and decomposing leaves weaved in and out of the hair on the man's chest and belly as though they had been carefully placed there. Like they had been meticulously woven into the hairy carpet.

Clyde took another step closer to the man. There was something familiar about him. The look of his body, the beautiful circumcised cock lying there waiting to be toyed with. Then Clyde realized who it was. It was Evan.

What is Evan doing lying naked on the ground? Clyde thought. *Is he...* but he wouldn't finish the thought. He couldn't allow himself to even think the word. Dead. He stepped even closer, hoping to see Evan's chest rise and fall with his breaths. *He has to be breathing. He has to be okay.* A mud handprint covered Evan's left shoulder. The hair flowing up from his chest, clumped with the filth. It was a large hand that had touched him there, that had gripped his shoulder. It was the same size as John's hand.

He saw Evan's chest move with his breathing and Clyde let out a long, steady exhale. He hadn't realized he had been holding his breath.

John appeared then. He, like Evan, was nude as well. His hard, muscular body shimmered with sweat as he knelt between Evan's legs and lifted them, exposing the furry, muscled slabs of Evan's butt. John was erect, the thick foreskin of his cock pulled back revealing the fat mushroom head. He grabbed his cock at the base and pushed it into Evan. Evan moaned a deep pleasured grunt as John pushed himself inside him. John shoved himself balls deep in the first thrust, tearing into Evan with his long, fat cock.

Evan turned his head towards Clyde. A laugh poured out of him. A happy, joyful laugh as John pounded harder, deeper into him.

"Who do you want to be?" Evan had asked, his voice echoing through the pines. Reverberating against the trees. "Who do you want to be, Clyde?"

That's when Clyde had woken up, his head on John's belly. Now he studied the thick trail of hair tracing down John's abdomen into the confines of his white—*well, mostly white*—briefs stretched out before Clyde like a highway. The mound of his crotch, like one of the great hills surrounding Devon, hovered there in Clyde's line of sight. It beckoned to him. *"Climb me,"* it said.

Clyde wondered if he was still dreaming as the mound began to move. It shifted and rumbled as a fast quake rippled through it. He could see the outline of John's cock begin to slither under the cotton material, like a snake moving through tall grass. It slowly pushed its way out from under the elastic band, facing Clyde. The foreskin sealed over the head in a thin, flat line, looking like a pair of lips wearing a grimace. Then they separated, exhaling a breath of vinegary, unwashed cock. Clyde inhaled the hot, musky smell and felt his own cock growing hard even with the weird, surreal situation.

The foreskin lips spoke. "Touch me," they muttered. "Taste me."

He wanted to touch it. He wanted to taste it. He had wanted this for as long as he could remember. Clyde moved in closer so his own lips brushed the foreskin lips. He slid his tongue from his mouth and reached for his brother's cock with it. It made contact, but when he looked down, saw that a small, thin tongue had flickered out from John's cock and that was what his tongue was touching. The foreskin tongue was split, like a snake's. He was French kissing John's cock.

Clyde woke, really woke this time. He was in his bedroom, in his bed. John was lying under him. Clyde's head on John's belly. The cotton mound of John's crotch hovering there before Clyde's eyes just like in his dream. It didn't move, though. A snake cock did not slide out and flick a forked tongue at him. He was back in the real world, bathed in sweat, his heart hammering in his chest like a jackhammer.

The dream began to fade, to drift away like a morning mist rising from a cool lake. He tried to catch it, but it slipped through his fingers. Evan was in it, wasn't he? There was something about a handprint. A mud handprint and John in the woods and... and it was gone, leaving only a weak feeling of unease and six little words.

"Who do you want to be?" Who had said it? Was it Evan? John?

Clyde looked ahead, down John's thick pleasure trail to the white mountain ahead of him. The mound of gorgeous cock and balls wrapped in cotton. John's cock and balls. There was no dream anymore. The point of his decade-long obsession drew every ounce of his attention. His head rose and fell with John's breath. John's belly moving like waves on the ocean, Clyde's head, the ship that carried him towards the snow-capped mountain of John's crotch in the horizon.

Clyde lifted his hand and slowly, so slowly as to not wake John, set it on the mound. He could feel the fat orbs of John's testicles, held tight by the briefs, but loose in the wrinkled, furry sack. He traced his fingers up to the cock, traced the length of it. Felt it pulse and flex in response to his touch. It began to grow, to stretch along John's hip, inflate with the warm blood pouring into it.

Clyde could smell the sex coming from it. The hot stink of sweat and musk. And when the thick head pushed its way out from under the elastic band, the acidic vinegar stench of his dirty cock swam into Clyde's face, stinging his eyes and making his mouth water. The head was pointed directly at him, the foreskin rolled back enough for the glistening moisture trickling from the piss-slit to reflect the dim light of the room.

He wanted to taste it. Feel it grow rigid in his mouth. He wanted to impale himself on his brother's long, fat pole. To feel it thrust down his throat. To push down into him further than any had ever been. He wanted to choke on it, feel it split him like an ax blade through a chunk of pine. Feel it tear him apart, then afterwards, John would reassemble him. Like piecing together a jigsaw puzzle.

The only way to do all this was to free his brother's penis from the stained underwear. Release it from its cotton prison. Clyde slid his fingers under the elastic band, his thumb briefly making contact with the head peeking out at him, like a watchful eye. It rose involuntarily at the touch, hovered over the thatch of pubic hair, the underwear band stretching, then dropped back down again. He pulled on the cloth, lifting it two, three, four inches into the air. It was all there in front of him now, down in the dark underwear cave. Everything he wanted since he turned twelve and discovered that his penis was for more than just peeing.

He hooked his thumb into the elastic band and pulled the briefs back. Hooked them under John's scrotum, leaving John's beautiful, magnificent, glorious genitals naked and exposed for him to worship.

"You having fun down there?" John's voice broke the quiet of the room.

Clyde's balls shriveled up to his chest. Fear made his head swim drunkenly and his stomach tightened to a hard knot. He felt sweat suddenly dampen his forehead and armpits.

"What?" Clyde moaned, feigning sleep, as though John's sudden voice had just woken him. He inhaled a quick catch of John's sex smell, then lifted his head from John's belly. He rubbed his eyes, squinted them to continue the illusion he had woken only seconds ago instead of minutes and gave his brother an innocent smile. "Good morning," he said, even though he knew perfectly well, it was the late afternoon.

John pulled his underwear back up, covering himself and rose from the bed. He glared at Clyde, as if gauging the honesty of his act. He opened his mouth to say something, but no sound came from him. He clamped his mouth shut again and stalked out of the room. "Go make some coffee," he ordered, his heavy footsteps stomping towards the bathroom.

Clyde crawled from the bed, his erection blaring out through the hole in his boxers. He stuffed it back inside, then walked out to the kitchen to make the coffee John had demanded.

When the kitchen filled with the rich scent of fresh coffee John appeared in the doorway. He sat at the table, still wearing just his underwear. He stared at Clyde as Clyde rinsed two mugs from the pile of dirty dishes in the sink, set them on the counter and pulled the powdered creamer and sugar bowl from the cupboard.

"What were you doing in there?" John asked.

"Where?" Clyde replied, not looking at John. He couldn't make eye contact with him. John would see the fear in his eyes and whatever lies he would have to come up with to cover-up what he had just done would be moot. John would know the truth if he saw the terror in Clyde's eyes.

"You know what the fuck I'm talking about. Don't fucking play games with me, Clyde." John rose from the table, took a step towards him, John's fists flexing and releasing again and again. The thick, blue veins running up his arms bulged under the skin.

Clyde backed into the counter. He could feel the heat of the drip coffee maker at his back as the decanter filled with the hot brew. "I was dreaming, John. I was just having a dream. I didn't know what I was doing," he whined, fear quivering his voice. John was going to hit him. He could feel the rage building in his brother as John stepped closer. John was furious and he might not stop at one punch, he might let it go on to two, ten, twenty. He might not stop until Clyde was bloody, broken, barely alive. That is, if John stopped even then. "Please, John," he begged.

"You want this, don't you?" John said, grabbing his own crotch, the thick fistful of cock and balls straining against the piss-stained underwear. "You've always wanted this. Ever since you was a kid, you tried to sneak a peek at this, haven't you? I seen you staring at me, wanting me. I let you see it a few times, too. Yeah, nothing more fun than teasing a little pussy-boy like you. I let you see what you couldn't have. It made you crazy, didn't it? Made you want me even more. You're just like those bitches at Sparky's. Sniffing around, wanting all this man inside them. Is that what you want? You want this cock in your little asshole? You want me to stretch you out like an old, worn cunt?"

Clyde felt his chin begin to quiver. Tears filled his eyes, but he couldn't, wouldn't let them fall. He was more scared now than he had ever been. Scared of John, scared of himself for what he had almost done in the bedroom. John stepped closer to him. Clyde could smell his breath in his face, feel the heat of his body as John's naked chest touched his own. He felt John's cock, now stiffened to the point it strained against the underwear, press against Clyde's own flaccid crotch.

"It's time you got what you wanted for so long. You deserve it. It's time you knew what it feels like to have my cock tear into you." John grabbed Clyde by the throat, spun him around and threw him into one of the kitchen chairs around the cheap Formica table. He stepped in front of him, yanked down his underwear and thrust his cock in Clyde's face.

Clyde stared at it. The engorged, fat, purple head hovered before his eyes. The raw sex stink flowed from it, filled his sinuses and, much to Clyde's disgust, made his mouth water. He glanced up at John's face. There was hot rage in his eyes. A violent anger that forced his pupils down to tiny specks in a hazel sea. Clyde kept his mouth firmly shut, refusing John to enter him.

"Suck it!" John bellowed.

Clyde wouldn't. He backed from it, pushed back into the chair as deeply as he could.

Who do you want to be, he heard Evan from his dream say.

"You wanted this, now take it," John said. He was right, Clyde had wanted it. When he was younger, he had wanted John so badly it hurt. Now though—with the object of years of sexual desire just inches from his face—Clyde realized he didn't want John and never really had. John was his brother, but also a man who raised him as a father would. He was his closest friend for most of his life. All of his life actually. Until Clyde met Evan.

Who do you want to be?

He didn't want to be the Evan in his dream, getting fucked by John. He didn't want to be the sort of man who had sex with his own brother. He didn't want to be that sort of man who *wanted* sex with his own brother.

He wanted to be a man whose love was returned the same way he gave it. A man who would feel no shame in who he fucked and was fucked by. A man who was proud of the man he wanted. Like the pride he felt earlier at the hospital, when the nursing students had seen him and Evan kissing in the hallway.

Who did he want to be?

He wanted to be the man he already was. A man who was loved by and in love with Evan.

"You fucking faggot, suck my cock!" John grabbed Clyde's face with one hand and tried to pry his mouth open. The other hand wrapped around Clyde's neck and John tried to pull him into his cock. "You wanted it. Now do it!"

Clyde brought his hands up and pushed John's hands away. "Enough!" he screamed.

John came at him again. He grabbed him by the neck again and dug his fingers between Clyde's lips, finally forcing his mouth open. "You're gonna take this cock. If I have to..."

But John couldn't finish the sentence because Clyde *really* had enough. He knocked John's hands away from him, jumped from the chair and pushed John back into the counter. John's elbow struck the coffee maker, pushing it into the wall behind it. The decanter slipped from the heated base enough to teeter on the lip of the machine, then it dropped onto the counter. It didn't shatter, but coffee poured over the counter and splashed against John's bare back. He let out a loud yelp and jumped away from the wall. "Motherfucker!" he screamed.

"Enough," Clyde said again, softer this time. He set the glass pot back in its base, the plunger that stopped the flow of coffee into the decanter opened and started filling it again. He grabbed a handful of paper towels from the rack under the cupboard, wet them and touched the paper cloth to John's back. John tried to pull away, but Clyde held onto his shoulder.

"Stop squirming. Let me see how bad this is," Clyde said and John did as told. There was a red patch of skin on John's lower back, where the coffee had splashed him. A minor burn, nothing to worry about. "You'll live," he said and tossed the soggy paper in the trash.

Clyde looked into John's eyes. The rage was gone. John quickly turned from him. His cock was still hanging out of his underwear. The flash of pain from the coffee had deflated his anger as well as his dick. He pulled the briefs back up where they belonged. "I... I'm so... I don't know what came over me," John said, his back still turned to him.

Clyde could hear a waver in John's voice, as though he were fighting tears, or had already lost the battle. He had gone too far, and he knew it. But, so had Clyde. He had been doing just what John thought he had been in that bed. He had been attempting to, at the very least, molest John in his sleep. At the most, rape him.

How far would he have gotten if John hadn't woken and stopped him? "I'm sorry, John," he said.

"I... I..." John stammered, never turning to look at him. "We have to get dressed to go see Mamma." John walked out of the kitchen and down the hall to his room.

Chapter 13
Working for the Weekend

John and Clyde went to the hospital and stayed with Mamma until visiting hours ended. The ride to the hospital and back home again were mostly silent ones, broken only by the occasional slurp of coffee from their travel mugs or John pointing out someone he knew from Sparky's. "There's Janice," he would announce, then give the horn a quick beep. "Marla!" Another quick honk, this one followed by a wave as he drove past.

When they arrived home again John turned on the television, settled onto the couch. Clyde went to his room, dug the last of his pot from the small metal can in his dresser and shared it with John. They smoked, watched the reality show with the big breasted porn star, then John said he was going to bed. Very few words had passed between them after the incident in the kitchen earlier.

John had scared Clyde badly, but not as much as Clyde had scared himself. Clyde had attempted to have sex with John while he slept. He had attempted to—*no, please don't say it, don't say the word*—rape his brother. He hadn't, but only because John woke and stopped him. Of course, he had the opportunity to have John immediately after and he had turned it down, but still...

Could I have stopped myself if John hadn't woken? Would I have gone through with it? Would I have crossed that line and become a person that would do something like that?

He hoped he wouldn't, but he couldn't say that with any surety. He would never again have the opportunity to prove to himself that he could resist the temptation. Not that he really wanted the opportunity.

Once John went to bed, Clyde called Evan. He needed to hear his voice again, needed to hear the... what? Love? Admiration? Whatever it was he needed to know he was not a monster. He needed to hear that he was worthy of whatever it was Evan felt for him.

"How is your mother doing?" Evan asked.

"She's doing all right. She has to change her diet when she comes home. No more junk food in the house. No more fatty meats. Just lean chicken and vegetables."

"Oh, that kind of sucks. Well, if you want pizza or a bag of chips, you can always get some here."

"Is that an invite?"

"That's an open invitation," Evan said. "You can come over any time you want. You want to come over now? I'm going to bed right now, but I'll leave the door unlocked for you. You can just climb into bed with me."

"I'd love to, but..."

He wanted to tell him about what had happened between him and John. He wanted to hear Evan say that he understood. That he was still a good person, no matter what he might have done, or almost done. But, he couldn't. He couldn't tell him and probably wouldn't tell him. Not now at least. Maybe, some day in the far off future he might bring it up, but even then...

"I'd love to," he repeated, "but I'm beat. I'm going to go to bed, too. I'll see you in the morning."

"Okay. I'll see you out there in the pines."

Clyde started to hang the phone back on the wall when he heard Evan speak again. "Oh, and Clyde?"

"Yeah."

"I like you more than like."

Clyde grinned into the phone. "Yeah, I like you more than like, too." Then he hung up the phone and went to bed.

When they had their first break of the day at nine in the morning, John used Dale's cell phone to call the hospital to check on Mamma. She told him she was being discharged later in the afternoon. So, at three John left work to pick her up and take her home. "Can you give Clyde a ride home?" he asked Dale.

"Of course," Dale quickly replied.

"Thank you." John turned to Clyde. "You're in charge. I'll see you back at home."

"What?" Clyde said, astounded at what John had just said. He was in charge? John never let him have any authority in the business. "I'm in charge?"

John said, quietly so Evan and Dale could not hear, "You are a man now. You proved that to me yesterday. You stood up to me, fought me. I respect that. It's time you had some responsibility."

Clyde opened his mouth to reply, then snapped it shut again. What could he say? How could he react to this new respect John had for him without gushing or sounding like a fool? "Well, I appreciate it, John. Thank you," he finally said.

"Maybe you might help me expand the business a little. Get a bigger contract with the paper mill. If we do, maybe we could hire these guys permanently. I can't do it alone, Clyde. I thought I could, but I need your smah-ts to make a better life for us."

"Sure. I'll do what I can to help you."

"No, you won't be helping me. It'll be for us. We will be pahtners. Equals."

They worked through the rest of the afternoon until the usual quitting time at six, then they piled into Dale's truck and headed home. The trailer park was on the east side of town, Dale and Evan lived on the west so Dale took Clyde home first. When they pulled in the driveway, John and Mamma had not arrived back yet. "You want to stay here with me for a while? I'll give you a ride home after Mamma and John get back," Clyde asked, his fingers secretly rubbing the small of Evan's back.

"Yeah, that will be cool."

They slid from the truck, Clyde thanked Dale for the lift, then they went into the trailer. Clyde immediately slipped his arms around Evan once the door was closed behind them. "I've been wanting to do this all day," he said and pulled at the buckles holding the overalls onto Evan's shoulders. The overalls dropped to the floor, Evan stepped out of them, then Clyde dropped his own pair to the floor. They moved into Clyde's bedroom, kissing, touching one another as they traversed the narrow hallway.

In the bedroom Clyde pushed Evan onto the bed, straddled him and began tugging his clothes free until Evan lie naked, so beautifully naked, beneath him. Clyde stripped and they tangled themselves into one another. Arms, legs, whole bodies became one. They were both still hot and sweaty. Clumps of dirt clung to their bodies and a day's worth of hard work had matted the ample hair on Evan's body. They both smelled of old sweat and pine sap.

Clyde liked the smell. It was a manly smell. Raw and primal. He took Evan deep into his mouth, sucking on him until Evan began to squirm under him.

"Do you have any lube?" Evan asked.

"No. I think we have some vegetable oil, but..."

"That'll work. Go get it," Evan said.

"What for?"

"Just do it. Please." Clyde dutifully followed his request, ran out to the kitchen, his erection swaying from one hip to the other. He opened the cupboard, grabbed the oil and hurried back to the bedroom. Evan stood. "Lie down," he said.

Clyde settled on the bed, Evan pushed him down onto his back and straddled his hips. "What are you doing?" Clyde asked. His mouth had gone bone dry. He knew what Evan had in mind and the thought terrified him.

Evan was about to settle himself down onto Clyde's cock, an act that Clyde could see no physical pleasure in for Evan. This, he thought, was for Clyde's pleasure and Clyde's pleasure only. It would hurt Evan, just like the one time Clyde had slid an index finger in his own butt while masturbating. It had burned, like he was on fire down there, and that was just a finger. Clyde's cock was nearly as big around as his wrist. He is going to rip Evan.

"Are you sure you want to do this?" Clyde asked, hoping Evan would back out of it. He didn't want to hurt him, but he didn't want to deny Evan what he wanted.

"I'm sure," Evan replied and filled his palm with a pool of the oil. He coated Clyde's cock, then reached back and slid his slick fingers between his buttocks. He set the bottle on the table next to the electric alarm clock, then held Clyde's cock as he slowly pushed himself down on it.

As the head broke through the tight opening, Clyde nearly lost control. It was so incredibly warm and wet and the way Evan's body hugged him was... was... he didn't want to come yet. He wanted this to go on and on. Clyde turned his mind away from what was happening between them right then. He tried to think of anything to prevent himself from going over the edge already. He thought of Mamma's ugly, bruised legs. He remembered seeing the man stabbed to death at Sparky's last year. They had no effect. He was so close already he didn't think it was possible to reel it back in.

Then, he looked up and saw a clamp-toothed painful grimace on Evan's face. "Stop," Clyde said just as Evan had pushed himself all the way down on him. His entire cock was now engulfed in Evan's heat. "I don't want to do this if it hurts you."

"It hurts, but it feels good too," Evan said as he pulled himself up a bit, releasing Clyde's cock, then pushed back down, swallowing him again.

"Oh," Clyde moaned. "Are you sure?"

"Very," Evan said.

Clyde lifted his hips and pushed himself deeper into Evan. They began to work in tandem, Clyde pushing up as Evan forced himself down, their thrusts building in ferocity.

He watched the look of ecstasy on Evan's face. Eyes shut,

bottom lip firmly clamped under his teeth. His hard cock slapped Clyde's belly with each downward thrust. Evan was in control of this. He was on top, riding Clyde. But now Clyde wanted the driver's seat. He wrapped his arms around Evan, pushed himself to his knees, never letting his cock pop from the hot, tight hole. Evan wrapped his arms around Clyde's neck and held on as Clyde turned and laid him on his back. He pulled Evan's legs up onto his shoulders and pushed himself all the way into Evan. His balls, low and heavy in the warm room, slapped against Evan's ass.

Evan squirmed beneath him, moaned, lifted his hips and pushed back against him. "Oh, it feels so good, Clyde. Fuck me."

Clyde pulled nearly all the way out of Evan, then slammed back into him again. The headboard banged against the wall. He watched the pleasure on Evan's face, heard the grunts and happy exclamations flowing from his panting mouth. The small twin bed squeaked and screamed as Evan lifted his hips and fucked Clyde back with the same force Clyde gave him.

He couldn't take much more. He was so close to coming now that nothing would prevent it. He could think of dead puppies and it still wouldn't hold off the inevitable. But he wanted Evan to come first. He reached between them and grabbed Evan's cock. The head was sticky with pre-come. He ran his oil slick thumb from the balls up to the head and felt it throb under his touch. He felt a response in the tight channel he was buried in, up to the balls, as it tightened even more around him. It felt like his cock was being strangled.

He couldn't stop the orgasm from coming now. He pressed his mouth against Evan's, their tongues mashed against one another as the explosive release rippled through him. Evan wrapped his arms around Clyde's back, pulled himself to form a seal between them. Clyde felt the hot wetness on his belly as Evan came with him. They screamed into one another's mouths as they came, not wanting to break the kiss even to catch their breaths.

As the waves of orgasm slowly subsided, Clyde slid from Evan. His cock, slick with vegetable oil and semen, plopped out from between Evan's hairy buttocks. Evan winced as it left him.

Clyde stood, pulled a dirty sock from under his bed and cleaned the come from Evan's belly, then wiped himself clean. He dropped the sock on the floor and climbed back on the bed. He slid his right arm under Evan and held him. He could feel the whispered beginnings of hair along Evan's shoulder blades. *By the time Evan is thirty*, Clyde thought, *his entire back will be covered in the same thick, dark hair that fills in his chest.* He hoped they would still be together when that happened.

Clyde settled in, set his head on Evan's chest. "Jesus, that was amazing." Evan said, running his fingers through Clyde's hair. Evan's voice was a hollow booming over the quick heartbeat that was beginning to slow as his body relaxed. "You fuck like a maniac, you know that?"

"I didn't hurt you, did I? I don't ever want to hurt you," Clyde said. It was true, he never wanted to hurt Evan. He knew that for many men their age, relationships generally didn't last too many years. But right at the moment, Clyde vowed to himself, he would do everything in his power to make sure that never happened to them.

Clyde vowed he would constantly try to improve his relationship with Evan. Even when it seemed perfect, he would try to make it better. Would try to keep Evan happy and, if possible, make him even happier. He lifted his head and looked into Evan's eyes. Clyde saw passion there, staring back at him. Sated passion for what they had just done, perhaps, but there was an emotional zeal there as well. Evan liked him more than like, and Clyde knew, Evan would do everything in his power to keep their hold to one another fresh as well.

"You didn't hurt me. It felt great," Evan said. "I never want to hurt you either. Never."

Clyde realized then that he hadn't worn a condom. Everything he had been taught in school and read on his own told him that the unprotected sex they had just experienced with each other was very dangerous. He was confident he had no STD's to pass on to Evan, but wondered if Evan could claim the same thing. He sat up, looked Evan in the eyes. "Are we safe?" he asked.

"What do you mean?" Evan replied.

"We didn't use a condom. I'm pretty sure I'm okay, but..."

"You're right. We should have used something. I've only done that with one other guy, though. We were each other's first. But, just so we both feel safe, we can go to Lewiston to the free clinic and get ourselves tested. It might take a week or two to get the results but, we can get some condoms and use them from now on. Okay?"

"Okay," Clyde said and began to set his head back on Evan's chest when they heard the sudden rumble of John's truck pulling into the driveway. They leapt from the bed, quickly tossed on their clothes and Clyde hurried the bottle of cooking oil back into the kitchen cupboard. He opened the front door and went to the truck to help Mamma into the house. Her skin was pale, a light sweat had risen on her brow from the effort of leaning over her walker, taking one precarious step after another. But, otherwise she looked good considering what she had been through in the last twenty-four hours.

Mamma had lost thirty pounds in the hospital. It wasn't thirty pounds of fat, but fluid. Her heart had been strained with her excessive weight and lack of exercise for years and because it had not been running at full capacity, fluid had built up around her heart and dumped into her extremities. With injections of a diuretic every eight hours, the doctors were able to push the excess fluid from her. Now Mamma could actually fit (just barely) through the door without having to remove it from the frame.

Clyde introduced Evan to Mamma once she was settled into her chair. "Oh. Is this the boy you told me about, John?" she asked.

"Yeah, that's him, Mamma."

"Well, I'm glad you and Clyde hit it off so well. He's a good boy and he needs a good friend like you."

"Thank you, ma'am. Clyde's a great guy. I needed a good friend too. I'm glad we found each other."

"You can thank John. That's the reason he hired you." Mamma pulled her walker closer to her chair, used it to lift herself to her feet. Clyde moved in to help her, but she shushed him away. "I'm fine. Thank you anyway. Mamma's gotta go pee. That damn Lasix they got me on is gonna keep me strapped to the toilet for a while. I'm gonna run a trench in the floor between my chair and the bathroom taking these damned pills."

She started down the hall, then stopped. "Oh, John picked up a few groceries on the way home. They're in the truck. Why don't you bring them in, Clyde. When I come out I'll start cooking. We got chicken, poe-tay-tahs and a nice squash. You staying for sup-pah, Evan?"

"Oh, thank you, Mrs. Chute. but I'm pretty beat. It's been a long week. These guys been running me ragged out in the woods. Can I take a rain check?"

"Dear, you are a friend of Clyde's. You are welcome here anytime you want to come."

"Thank you, ma'am."

"Just call me Mamma. That's what my boys call me and I think, looking at you and Clyde together, you gonna be another son to me. Ayuh, you gonna be together a long time."

Chapter 14
Crossing the Bridge

"Why didn't you want to stay for dinner?" Clyde asked once they were back in Evan's driveway. They were in the Escort, windows rolled down, dust settling on the hood. The car was idling, heat waves rising off the hot metal of the car.

"I wanted to. I want to spend as much time with you as I can. Your mother just came home. She's tired, and I think you need to spend time with your family tonight.

"But you are mine this weekend," Evan continued. "I want you to spend the night with me Saturday. No, actually, I want you to spend the entire weekend with me. I don't care if John needs us to work Sunday. I'll happily work like a dog Sunday because I will have woken next to you that morning. Stay with me Saturday. Stay with me Friday, too. Shit, stay with me every night."

"I think we are going to have a good weekend," Clyde said. He kissed Evan, their lips parted and he pressed his forehead to Evan's. "Oh man, Evan. I don't think I like you more than like, anymore. I think what I'm feeling is off the chart. You make me feel so fucking..." he paused, searched for the right word. "So fucking special. No one has made me feel like you do.

"I am proud with you at my side." Clyde's voice dropped to a whisper as his lips moved closer to Evan's ear. "I'm proud that you want to be with me. I'm proud of myself when I am with you. You make me feel like I am a good man. I must be, to have someone as wonderful as you, want to be with me. But, I want to be a better man for you, because you deserve the best.

"I'm not going to say the L-word though. It's not a bad word like the N-word. In fact, it's a beautiful word. But, I'm not going to say it until I can prove to you that I mean it. I could say it right now and I would know it's true, but that is meaningless unless you know it." Clyde kissed him again, long and slow. Taking the time to feel every curve and groove in Evan's lips with his own. He sighed, heavily. He didn't want today to end. He didn't want to leave, but knew he had to. They would see each other again in less than twelve hours, which was a comfort. But saying good-bye was the hardest thing he ever had to do.

Finally Clyde muttered, "I'll see you in the morning."

Evan slipped from the car. His eyes were wet. "I can hardly wait until the weekend," he said and walked into his home.

"I can hardly wait until tomorrow," Clyde said to himself, then pulled out of the driveway and headed back to John and Mamma.

"So, you get your little boyfriend home alright?" John asked when Clyde stepped back into the trailer. Mamma was in the kitchen, leaning over her walker, mashing potatoes in a large kettle. The trailer smelled of cooked chicken and buttery squash. It made Clyde's mouth water and reminded him of Thanksgiving dinner Mamma cooked each year when his father was still alive. He almost expected to see the Macy's Parade running on the television.

"Yeah, I did. What of it?" Clyde replied. He felt a sudden rush of anger rise up in him. He looked down and noticed his fists flexing and releasing just as John's did when he is mad.

John smiled. "I'm just joking, bud, no need to get defensive."

"I'm not defensive," he said and released his fists. "And I'm not joking either. Evan is my boyfriend."

John froze, a flush of red rose up his neck and turned his face the hot red of arterial blood. "What did you just say?" Clyde had seen that look before. It was the same look on his face as yesterday afternoon when they had their scuffle in the kitchen. It scared him now as much as it did then. But, this was important to him. He needed to tell John the truth. This, like the revelation Clyde discovered about himself yesterday, that Evan was more important to him than that stupid sexual obsession he had for his brother, needed to be brought out into the open air. They needed to talk about this.

"I said, Evan is my boyfriend. I'm gay, John."

John stepped up to him, his face inches from Clyde's. His breath warming Clyde's face. His mouth set in a thin line. John's nostrils flared, like an enraged bull. He was furious, but Clyde didn't care. This was not about John, this was about him. "This is who I am John. This is who I have always been, and always will be. I am gay."

John took a step back. He closed his eyes, counted to three. *One-one thousand, two-one thousand, three-one thousand,* then he opened his eyes and smiled at Clyde. "I know. I've always kind of known."

"No you didn't," Clyde said incredulously.

"Yeah. I did. I knew you were lonely too. I saw it on your face all the time. You were always so sad. That's why I always wanted you to go to Sparky's with me. I figured you might find a nice girl or something. But you never did. So that was why I hired Evan."

"You were playing matchmaker?"

"Yeah. Darlene told me a few weeks ago her cousin had just moved into town and was looking for a job. He was about your age and she thought he might be... ah, well, you know. Like you."

"Gay. It's okay to say it, John," Clyde said, even though the word felt foreign on his own lips as well.

"Yeah, whatever. Anyway, I figured, what the hell? Let's give this a try. You are both guys that like other guys. One dick is just like another so you will probably get together. Maybe that will stop you from moping around here all the time."

"One dick is not like another. Just like one man is not like another. They are all different shapes, sizes."

"Okay, gross," John said. "Look, I'm not going to pretend I understand or like it, but you are my brother. You are a decent guy and if you want to get rammed in the ass, then... well, who really cares?" He bent in closer and whispered so Mamma wouldn't hear from the kitchen, "What I did the other day... well, I'm sorry about that. I'm so sorry. I was mad and I hoped... shit, I hoped it would get you to do this. To come out. A real man lives honestly, and now you are a real man. You are my brother and nothing could make me stop loving you.

"Also," he continued, a light sparkle in his eyes, "I know all you fancy boys want me and I was just fucking with you."

"I guess I proved you wrong," Clyde said. "I didn't touch you so I guess not all us *fancy boys* want you."

"No, you still want me, you just want Evan more. And that's fine by me."

Clyde nodded his head toward the kitchen. "Does Mama know?" he asked.

"Probably. You didn't really hide it all that well. We all saw you mincing around the house."

"I never minced a day in my life."

"Maybe not. Maybe you never sprouted butterfly wings and fluttered around the trailer, but even someone as dim as me knew you were a cock-gobbler from way back."

"You're a jerk," Clyde said and smiled at his brother.

"I know. That's why you love me." He pulled Clyde into his arms and hugged him. "I love you so much, Clyde. You're my favorite brother. I just hope you're happy."

"I am happy. Evan makes me really happy." Clyde realized it was true. For the first time in more than a decade, Clyde could honestly say, he was truly happy.

The cool, clean sheets felt good against Clyde's skin. He looked over Evan, lying in the curl of his arm, head on Clyde's chest. His slow, steady breath ruffled the thin spattering of hair around Clyde's nipples and the patch between. Evan was asleep.

Clyde pulled him closer, hugging Evan to his side a little tighter. He kissed the top of Evan's head, the curly black mop tickling his nose and smelled that strawberry shampoo again. Clyde's hair smelled the same. They had come to Evan's after work, showered together and fell into bed where they finished what was started in the shower.

It was Saturday night and they had just made love. Yes, made love, that is what it was for Clyde. It wasn't fucking or even just sex. There was too much involved to be just sex. It was an intimate, emotional connection that just happened to involve an orgasm.

They hadn't said THE word to each other yet, the L-word. Clyde felt it for Evan and he knew the sentiment was returned, but neither man dared say it. Not yet at least. It had become somewhat of a competition between them. Who would say it first.

John had decided to give everyone Sunday off after all. Before he told Dale and Evan that they did not have to come in Sunday, he consulted with Clyde to make sure it was okay with him. Clyde was now, officially, a decision maker in the business. He quickly agreed, thinking of tonight, of sleeping with Evan in his bed all night. Of holding him in his arms all night.

He was holding Evan, and not just physically. He was also protecting Evan, making sure he had a job with them for as long as he wanted it. Yesterday Clyde called Mr. Wentworth, the man in charge of hiring contracted employees for the mill. He requested a meeting with him. It was set for one day next week. Clyde would inform Wentworth they are expanding the company, had hired two temporary men, but wanted to make them permanent. He planned to request a contract for a larger section of the forest.

If the meeting went well, they could possibly hire even more men, build themselves to level of financial stability neither he or John had ever really known.

And he could still work with Evan every day.

He was taking care of Evan. He was doing what a man did, protect the ones he loved.

Of course Evan was helping Clyde as well. Just by being with him Clyde's confidence was improved. He still wondered if he was worthy of Evan's attentions, in bed and out, but he was working on it. They were working on it together.

Clyde kissed the top of Evan's head again. "I love you," he

whispered, sure that Evan was asleep and wouldn't hear him. The competition for the L-word could continue.

Evan's eyes snapped open. "I win," he said, smiling that smile that excited Clyde so.

"You caught me. I said it first though, so I win," Clyde said.

"No. You love me. I'm the winner," Evan said. He kissed Clyde's chest, worked his mouth down over the hard, muscled belly. It still bothered Clyde to be touched like this. He still felt undeserving of the attention. But, Evan enjoyed doing this for him and Clyde liked to see Evan happy. He was beginning to appreciate the sensations of being touched, of lying back and letting Evan explore. It made him want to touch Evan that much more. Evan continued to descend until he was completely under the sheets. "You win too, Clyde. Because, I love you as well."

Then Evan opened his mouth, drew Clyde in and proved it.

Clyde leaned back and let him.

About the Author

P.L. Ripley (1968-2017) was a born storyteller weaving worlds since he could first express what he saw in his head. Fascinated with human sexuality, erotic fiction was a natural place for him to explore the connection between sexual excitement and our emotional responses to it. He lived near Bangor, Maine with his partner of twenty-four years. Writing was a very important part of Ripley's life, and he was as delighted to publish his works with us as we were to work with him.

About the Publisher

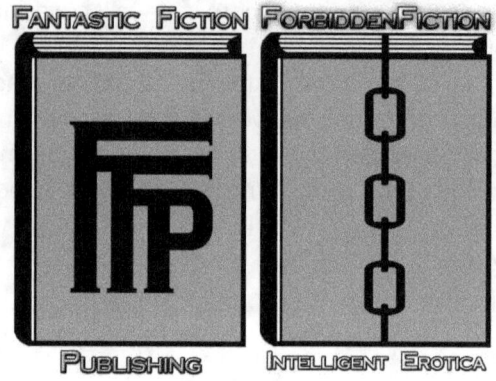

ForbiddenFiction.com is a publisher devoted to writing that breaks the boundaries of original erotic fiction. Our stories combine intense sexuality with quality writing. Stories at ForbiddenFiction.com not only arouse readers through sensations, but also engage them emotionally and mentally through storytelling as well-crafted as the sex is hot.

ForbiddenFiction.com is also designed to be a social reading environment. You'll have fun even if just reading the latest post each day, yet you will have the chance for so much more. Readers and authors can be part of ongoing discussions of specific works and individual authors as well as more general topics. Sign up for a FREE Membership today at ForbiddenFiction.com.

www.ingramcontent.com/pod-product-compliance
Lightning Source LLC
Chambersburg PA
CBHW070449260626
47161CB00004B/1248
* 9 7 8 1 6 2 2 3 4 3 3 8 6 *